OF SWORD & SILVER
A CONQUEROR'S KINGDOM

JANUARY BELL

OF SWORD & SILVER

Published by January Bell

www.januarybellromance.com

Copyright © 2024 January Bell

This is a work of fiction. Unless otherwise indicated, all the names, characters, businesses, places, events and incidents in this book are either the product of the author's imagination or used in a fictitious manner. Any resemblance to actual persons, living or dead, or actual events is purely coincidental.

Ebook & Paperback Cover by Alison Milsap
www.ozarkwitchcoverdesign.com

Illustration by Julio Porta Rocha
https://www.julioport.com/

Hardover design by Book Brander
www.romancepremades.com

Edited by Happy Ever Author

All rights reserved. No portion of this book may be reproduced in any form without permission from the publisher, except as permitted by U.S. copyright law. For permissions contact: admin@januarybellromance.com

For sub-rights inquiries, please contact Jessica Watterson at Sandra Djikstra Literary Agency.

❀ Created with Vellum

EVERY GOD HAS TWO *faces*

PRAY

You Get The One You

WANT

And Not The One You

NEED

FRAINOS

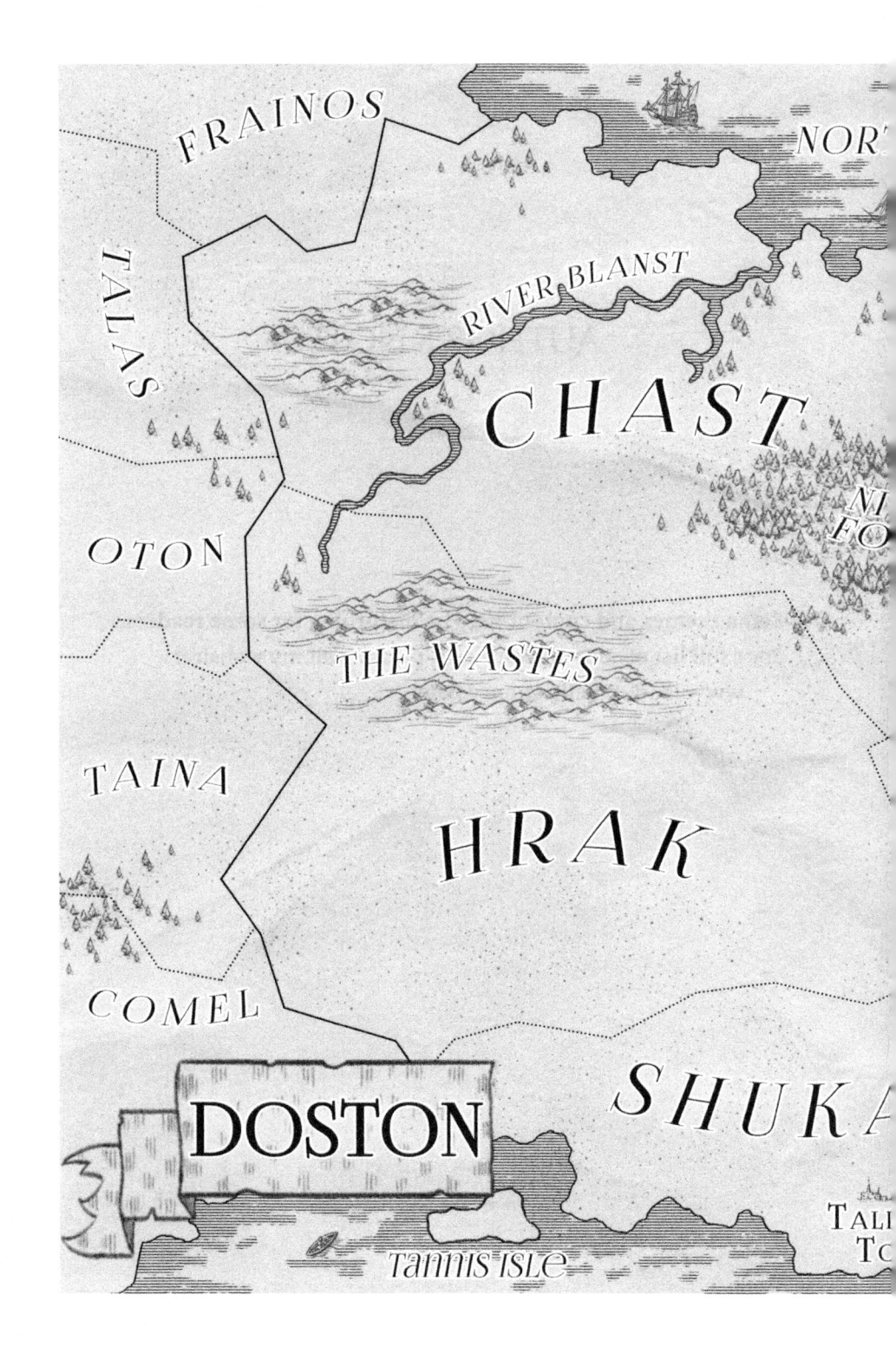

NOR

TALAS

RIVER BLANST

CHAST

OTON

N
FO

THE WASTES

TAINA

HRAK

COMEL

DOSTON

SHUKA

TALI
To

Tannis Isle

HESKA
RN SEA
COTTLESIDE
HIIREK MOUNTAINS
EFFINGWICH
YZBERN
LEINIA
TEMISBURY
SYLSIP
VRYDAK STEPPES
SILVER RIVER
SKANI
ROVINE MOUNTAINS
SYNV SEA

"A year. If you're lucky."

"Fuck." It comes out on a gust of breath, and I stand up so fast my wooden chair falls to the floor behind me. My chest heaves as I try to calm myself. I'm scared shitless, but I try to hide it, pretending that I meant to turn over the chair.

"Sorry. I thought I saw a big spider."

Lara gives me a long look, and I can tell she sees right through the terrible lie.

"Fine, I am freaking out." I crinkle my nose. Well, that cat's out of the bag.

Shouldn't put cats in bags, anyways.

"You said there might be a way out of it? To break the curse?" I pick up the chair and clear my throat.

Her lip curls to the side and she tilts her head at me, pushing her curtain of long, dark hair behind her shoulders.

"It won't be simple. Maybe you can just enjoy the rest of the year, take some time off, you know, live like it's your—"

"Like it's my last year? No. Thank you, Lara, but no. Tell me how to break it." My voice shakes.

I have too much to do. I have people depending on me, damn it. I have a fucking score to settle.

"I am not just going to give up." There's enough menace in my tone that she raises her eyebrows.

"We-ell." She sighs, drawing a pattern on the soft velvet tablecloth. Some of the tattered rune cards scatter slightly, as if pushed by an invisible wind.

The hair stands up on the back of my neck.

Magic might be a pretty normal part of life for Lara, and sure, there's magic in my silver tongue, but I don't try to use it, not like she does.

"You're not going to like it."

"I don't like the idea of dying, either." Pulling the dagger from the sheath at my hip, I use it to pick at my ragged nails. No, I'm not ready to die.

Besides, I can't stand the thought of spending the afterlife in the presence of the goddess who's made my life a living hell with her so-called gifts and her so-called disciples. I cough again, like the sound will cover up my blasphemous thoughts. As far as I know, though, my goddess isn't a mind reader. I hope.

"The Sword," Lara intones, staring at me with hooded eyes.

"A sword? What sword?" I blink, nonplussed.

"Not a sword, *the* sword."

"Listen, I know being all mysterious is part of your gig, but can you just be a little more clear for me? Your oldest friend?" The enchanted request rolls off my tongue and Lara stiffens, her eyes dilating as the whiff of my power hits her.

Ugh. I hate when it happens on accident.

"The Sword. Hrakan's right hand, the disciple of Death. He's imprisoned for murdering hundreds of Sola's followers. He despises her, and all who've pledge themselves in her service. He is the only one who can help you break your curse."

"Fuck me." I pinch the bridge of my nose.

Of course it would be the death god's disciple, and of course he hates all of Sola's followers.

We're going to get along swimmingly.

"Well," I trill, smiling at her. "It sounds like he and I have a lot in common."

Lara gives me an apologetic grimace. I sink back into the chair, gathering my thoughts and confidence around me like armor.

My attention skips to the pantheon of six, their facial features uncarved, their likenesses never committed to any artistic medium.

Maybe I should just enjoy my last year of life without bothering with a jail break for some sullen Death's disciple who's more likely to kill me than to help me. His god, Hrakan, the god of death and time, and my goddess, Sola, the goddess of chaos and lies, despise each other. According to the Heskan common book of prayers, the two gods warred before the age of man, using the long-extinct Fae and other legendary creatures to fight their battles for them.

Even now, their followers mix like tinder and spark.

Well, maybe I can make his life a living hell until I break the curse or die.

Could be fun.

I brighten slightly.

"What prison?" I ask, already sure of her answer. Mass murderers, especially of the disciple variety, all end up in one place.

"Cottleside." Lara raises both eyebrows, shuffling the rune cards back into order.

"Of course it is Cottleside." The most heavily guarded prison in all of Heska, located in the province of Lojad, the god of order and war. The followers of Lojad are a bunch of self-righteous warriors with sticks up their asses and rocks for brains. Unfortunately, they're renowned for their fighting ability.

Still, I'd rather be there than in Sola's city-state, Chast.

A plan starts to form in my mind, a plan for breaking out the Sword... goddess, do I really have to call him that? Now that I'm thinking about it, I might actually remember hearing about this man. What kind of an asshole goes by just "the Sword"? My nose wrinkles in disgust.

"Do you know his real name?" I ask. "I'm not calling him that."

Lara looks at me like I've lost my mind. Fair enough. I don't know that I've ever truly been in full possession of my wits.

He throws his head in clear agreement, and I make a mental note to give him a treat at my first opportunity.

"Let's go steal a Sword," I say, then snort at my own joke.

By the gods. I roll my eyes, watching the stars twinkle in the night sky high above.

Only I would have to steal a man named Sword to beat Death at his own game.

2

THE SWORD

Frigid wind whips through the barred window of my cell.

It's cold. It's always fucking cold.

Iron manacles bite at my wrists and ankles, chains clinking against the rings where they're attached to the ceiling and then the wall. I ignore them, used to the raw pain there. It's been over ten years, and there are some things about this gods-damned prison that I've become inured to.

The cold is not one of them.

It seeps in from Heska's Northern Sea, so frigid and wet it settles in my very bones.

I grit my teeth, continuing training like my thoughts aren't blacker than night. As though I have made my peace with this forsaken cell. As if I am repentant for the vengeance I meted out.

I am not.

Those bastards deserved to have their miserable lives cut short.

I don't mourn them, or my choices.

I mourn the ones they took from me.

My fingers grip the rusting iron tightly and I lift myself up again, crunching my knees to my chest. Flecks of blood-colored rust rain down on my face, my arms screaming with overuse.

I should have been there when it happened. When Sola's disciples invaded the secret village, when the few Fae that remained were slaughtered.

My bare feet meet the floor and I grunt, curling up again, slowly, so slowly, savoring the pain.

The cries that echo in my memories are so much worse than anything I can inflict on my body.

I was too late. Humid late spring air misted above their broken bodies. I was too late to save any of them. Sola's followers hunted them down one by one. Their laughter filled the evening when they slaughtered my people, as they bled into the Heskan soil. They hoped it would be enough to incense me, that it would be enough to draw me out. And it did.

Sola's desire to punish me for wreaking my vengeance on her followers is nothing compared to what I want from her.

So I wait.

And I punish myself, here in my prison cell, the only way I know how, with pain. With training. I keep my body primed and my mind agile, ready for the moment all my planning comes to fruition.

The beam running across the ceiling of my cell creaks under my weight, the screws that anchor the rings straining under the pressure. I press on, up and down, up and down.

These walls have held up Cottleside Prison for centuries. Lojad, god of war and order, would hardly approve of it otherwise. I won't bring it down, either, especially considering I'm no longer as healthy as I was when I entered ten years ago.

A boom sounds, close enough to catch my attention.

My chains clink as I drop back to the ground.

Outside the slit that passes for a window in my cell, the moon spills over the quiet town of Cottleside, just visible across the river, chimneys puffing smoke into the frigid night air. It's so clear and cloudless that I can make out the sluggish ice dotting the River Blanst, the water slower during the colder months, and usually enough to drown out most sounds.

Another loud crack sounds, one that triggers a memory of long ago, of another centuries-old building, and my full attention goes to the world inside the prison.

Faint sounds of shouting filter through the thick stone walls, only audible thanks to my superior hearing. Normal Fae are better at most things, stronger, faster, all of our senses more in tune with our surroundings than any human—and I'm no normal Fae.

My gaze drops to the manacles on my wrists and feet, then rises to the length of chain that keeps me from moving very far... or is supposed to.

The guards don't believe they'd be able to keep me here without them. The corner of my mouth twitches, a smile threatening, but it dies before it has the chance to form.

I don't remember the last time I smiled.

I don't know if I even can. I certainly don't deserve to.

Not anymore.

The sound of steel on stone rings out, unmistakable. Footsteps, accompanied by more shouting, additional cries going up as more blasts reverberate through the prison walls.

The voices fade in the distance, and a glance outside my window shows smoke curling from the northwest wing of the prison, along with green-tinged flames.

Perfect. I don't say that out loud, though. No reason to tip my hand. *Let her think she needs me more than I need to get out.*

I watch her lazily, letting the seconds stretch between us.

"We don't have long." She leans against the stone wall, then belatedly notices how foul it is and straightens instead. "Make up your mind before I leave you here with whatever slop they feed you and the terrible view."

"What do I get in return?"

"What do you want?" She steps closer. Within reach of my chains. "Sex?" She has the audacity to wink.

I stare at her, and she smirks.

"You're not my usual type." A long, elegant finger coils around a loose lock of hair, and she grins at me. "I suppose I could make an exception..." her voice trails off.

I could throw a chain around her elegant neck and be done with this farce right now. *But I need her. If she's here... then it's time.*

"Vengeance." It's not a lie.

"Charming," she says on a sigh, then smiles, showing even white teeth. "Against whom?"

"Against those who have wronged me. Against *your* goddess."

Her green eyes narrow.

I grunt, set on ignoring her again.

"My goddess?" she asks, and there's a hint of disgust in the way she says it. Fascinating.

"Silver tongues only gravitate towards one Heskan deity." I jerk my head at the green-tinged smoke now curling through the slit in the wall. "This... *display*—it screams chaos. That's Sola's specialty."

"Fair enough." She considers me for half a beat, a muscle in her temple jumping. "You help me break my curse, and I will help you with your revenge issues."

"Swear it," I growl, stepping closer, so close I can feel the heat rolling off her body.

So warm.

So different than the many, many nights I've spent alone in this cell.

"I swear it." She shrugs a shoulder.

"Swear it the old way, Silver Tongue."

"Why?" she asks.

"I have my reasons. Now swear."

"Tell me your name," she counters, raising a reddish-brown eyebrow. This close, I can see amber flecks in her eyes, the color of honey mead.

"My name is irrelevant." I turn back, leaning against the furthest wall, one foot propped behind me.

She puts her hands on her hips, clearly miffed. "You expect me to just call you the Sword? Or Sword? I'm *not* doing it."

"Then leave me here." I turn from her, watching the chaos unfold outside as best I can. She set most of the damned prison on fire just to get to me. She's desperate.

I don't have to wait long before she breaks.

"Fucking hells," she snarls, temper flaring. "I swear it on Heska's hearth, from Dryda's Silver River to the wastes of Death himself. I swear it on Nakush's unknowable power, on Sola's whims, and Lojad's laws. I swear I will do all in my power to help you claim vengeance, Sword." Her eyes grow wide as the bond between us begins to form, and I swallow in surprise.

It's no small thing.

"Then I swear it too, that I will help you break your blood curse to the best of my abilities, Silver Tongue. I swear it on Heska's hearth, from Dryda's Silver River to the wastes of Death himself. I swear it on Nakush's unknowable power, on Sola's whims, and Lojad's rules." The oath between us draws tight, and the magic of it allows me a glimpse at the deep well of the woman's power.

Very interesting. Especially for a *human*. Especially for one of Sola's followers, one with a curse of Hrakan.

"Wonderful," she says briskly, though her face has gone pale at whatever the magic is making her feel. It shouldn't make me feel gleeful to see her stumble slightly, not when she's sworn to help me, but I can't deny my amusement. "Now, let's get out of here and get on with it."

She produces a leather roll full of lock picks, and I look her up and down then let out a great sigh of annoyance.

I don't move.

"Oh, please, yes, please be less excited about getting free of here. It simply thrills me to see what a wonderful companion you're going to be." With a roll of her eyes, she motions for me to hold my wrists out, and despite thinking vicious thoughts at the redhead, I comply.

Working with this woman is going to be a trial.

Unfortunately, it seems I'm out of better options—for now.

The locks around my wrists click open in a surprisingly short time and I grunt again, impressed in spite of myself. The cold air bites at the ruined skin around my wrists, and the woman crouches down, unlocking the manacles from my ankles.

Gods, it feels blissful to have the weight of the chains off me, and I stand there for a moment reveling in it.

Until the silver tongue ruins it again by opening her charmed mouth. "Don't bother thanking me. I simply love breaking giant men out of prison. Do it every so often, just for fun."

I'm glaring at her when a sudden flurry of movement catches my eye. I have just enough forewarning to shove her out of the way, my red-headed ticket to the next stage of my plan, and I throw the loosed chains around the guard's neck.

The woman's dagger slices through his neck, sending a thick spray of blood across the walls.

I give her a long look, silently commending the guard's soul to Hrakan. "That wasn't necessary."

"You were taking too long," she says.

"He didn't need to die."

She blinks. "A Death worshipper who's worried about killing people? A *murderer* who is worried about killing people? Little late for that."

"This man was innocent," I snarl. The guard stares lifelessly at the ceiling. Crimson puddles on the grime-coated stone beneath him and I narrow my eyes at the silver-tongued woman, barely holding my contempt in.

"Lojad, forgive us," I say, hoping the god of order and war is slumbering, as he has for a long time.

She sneers at the words.

Just like all of Sola's followers, she lacks regard for anyone but herself.

Still, I need her. *It will be worth it, in the end.*

She crouches next to the guard, rummaging through his pockets. Disgust rises in me and she finally turns, triumphant, clutching a ring of keys and a small clanking bag of coins.

"Just what we needed." She deposits the coin bag into a leather satchel at her waist. "Take his sword."

I grunt. I am not going to loot this corpse. Instead, I pull the chain tight, yanking it from the bolt in the wall with several heavy tugs.

"Why didn't you just do that when you got here?"

"I deserved my time here." I coil the chain around my forearm. "I was waiting for the right moment."

"Waiting for the stars to align," she drawls, clearly amused.

"Yes," he rumbles.

"You should know I just rolled my eyes so hard I'm surprised I can't hear them rattling around, too. I'm surprised my eye roll hasn't brought down the entire host of Cottleside guards onto our heads. That's how hard I rolled them."

He grunts. No snort of amusement, no witty retort. Nothing. Just *grunts*.

I grit my teeth and keep forging ahead. It just had to be *this* male that could save me. This hulking dude whose otherworldly good looks are completely wasted on his nonexistent personality. I've had second-hand leather trousers with more personality.

Now I'm forced to travel goddess-only-knows how long with him, forced to trust him to find this cure for me when he can't even manage a polite chuckle at a joke... it's going to be torture.

At least he's nice to look at. Not that it matters.

"There," I say in a low voice, pointing to a seam in the floor. "That's the best route out."

I don't bother telling him that it's—

"The only route?" he asks in a dry voice.

Footsteps sound and we both freeze. He draws his sword, and something about him... shifts. Gone is the reluctant prisoner escaping, and in his place is a warrior.

I swallow hard.

A guard appears, running up the hallway, and at first, I think he's missed us completely. I'm standing stock still, letting the shadows fold around me. He runs by us, glancing over us like we're not even there.

I don't dare breathe.

The guard looks back.

His eyes widen, and we both step towards him, me with my dagger and Sword with his... well, his sword. Ugh.

Before either of us can move to quiet the yell that's no doubt coming, the unthinkable happens.

The guard goes still, like a marionette drawn up by invisible hands. Smoke, black and viscous, curls from the corners of his eyes, a sick simulacrum of tears.

It drips for a moment, running down his cheeks, into his nostrils and open mouth. No sound comes from him, just the unmistakable sheen of terror in his eyes at his obvious inability to move.

He slumps to the floor, that same wicked smoke spiraling from his body until it dissipates completely.

"What the fuck was that?" I whisper. My stomach's in knots. "Was that you?"

"It wasn't you?" he asks, nudging the body with his foot.

"No. What was it?"

"A sign," my companion says brusquely.

"I don't like the way that sounds." My voice is hollow.

"You shouldn't." He spears me with a glance, his expression inscrutable as always. "The gods have taken interest in our mission."

"Then we better not waste the opportunity," I say thickly. Sheathing my dagger, I go to my hands and knees, half expecting him to make a lewd joke as I press my hands against the trap door the prison architect hid here... just in case he ever fell on the wrong side of the law.

I push the stones just right, using all my strength.

"Too heavy for you?" He sounds amused. What a dick.

The latch clicks a moment later, and the trapdoor creaks as it lifts slightly. I pull it the rest of the way up, at least, I think I do, until I realize the Sword's holding the stone door over my head like it weighs nothing at all. Like this, we're almost touching, our hands side by side and his breath gusting over my cheek.

For a split second, I stare at him, off kilter.

"After you," he says in that gravelly voice.

My eyes narrow. I don't trust him, but I don't like the idea of him closing the door after me even more. The possibility of getting caught here, in Cottleside prison after helping him escape... it wouldn't be great.

Without wasting any more time, I slip inside the pitch-black tunnel that should lead us to safety.

I look back, just to make sure my prize Sword is following behind me.

Instead, my gaze slips over the fallen guard, his open eyes as dark as the tunnel I'm about to climb through.

I don't know what kind of a sign from the gods this is supposed to be, but it doesn't feel like a good one.

4

THE SWORD

The woman is quiet as we make our way through the tunnels under Cottleside.

Thank fuck.

I do not wish to make small talk with any of Sola's followers, least of all this silver tongue.

The sewage stench gets heavier and the air warmer with every step we take, which means the tunnel from the prison will soon take us to the sewage system beneath Cottleside, the so-called city of order. No matter how much the worshippers of Lojad might think otherwise, their shit smells as bad as everyone else's.

"Good thing it's freezing," the woman says conversationally. "Would be much worse in summer."

She stops, and I have to rock back on my heels to avoid running into her. "Here," she says in a low voice, "for the worst of it."

She holds out a black strip of fabric, and I watch her face

Foolishness. I must be starved for a crumb of kindness after my decade in Cottleside.

Every horrible moment within those walls was well-deserved in preparation of this moment.

The great game has begun anew.

I pull my bitterness and anger close to me like a cloak, ice-cold flames that will fuel me until I'm done with the woman steadily picking her way through the sewers and leading me to freedom.

5

KYRIE

Fresh air blows across my face, whipping my hair from its braid in a relentless icy blast. Northern Heska summers are cold, but to come up to Cottleside on the cusp of winter?

Frigid doesn't begin to describe it.

"A bit brisk," I say as the Sword finishes climbing out of the tunnel behind me. I eye his bare feet, which are filthy with the grime and dirt of the sewers.

His silence is oppressive, but he closes his eyes, lifting his chin. The wind seems to pick up at his attention, sending his white-grey hair blowing in tendrils around his face. It's an absurdly masculine face, too, his jaw so strong and cheekbones so sharp I half wonder if they'd cut to touch.

There's something youthful and ancient about him all at once, a compelling juxtaposition of opposites. I tug my cloak around me, grateful for its warmth.

Sleeping Cottleside stretches out below and behind us, and

I shiver at the dark, turbulent waters of the North Sea beyond it, white-capped waves only visible when the oil lamp of the lighthouse catches them in its gaze. Within the city, a few windows are lit from within, glowing like tiny beacons under the cloud-cloaked night sky. A bit further north, smoke drifts from the prison walls, and my lips twitch in a grin at the absolute havoc I wreaked.

No doubt no one there is sleeping.

Ha.

My skin prickles, and my attention jerks back to the prisoner I freed from its walls.

He's watching me, an impenetrable expression on his face. I know enough about people to see he trusts me about as far as I could throw him.

And since there's no way I could throw him, I should probably watch for a knife in my back.

"I am glad I had you swear an oath to me as well," I grumble.

He doesn't respond to that, either.

"Anyone ever tell you what great company you are?" I squint at him.

"No," he says, dark eyebrows lifting slightly.

"Shocking." I wait, hoping he'll at least rise to the bait.

He doesn't.

Ugh.

"My supplies are way up there." I jerk my thumb behind me at the purple-blue stain on the skyline. "The Hiirek Mountains. I figure we need to get as far as we can from Cottleside as fast as we can, just in case the guards decide their god of order needs you back in a cell."

I pause, waiting for input, but he's looking past me at the Hiirek Mountains jutting into the night.

"The night should help hide us," I continue, but the

Sword's already moving, his long legs eating up ground as he heads in the direction I pointed.

"Right." No point in talking.

The ground's uneven, rocks frozen to the dirt, and I'm annoyed at how fast the Sword's able to make his way across it.

"I don't know what I expected," I grumble to myself, keeping one eye on the uneven ground and another on the Sword's broad back. "A thank you? Gratitude? Oh, Kyrie, thank you so much for saving me," I tell myself in a rough approximation of his rumbly bass. "I am in your debt. Together we will find a cure."

Carefully, I step over a rotting log, one I nearly slipped on earlier on my trek down the mountain. "I am with you, Kyrie, sworn to help, and it's the least I can do for getting me out of Cottleside."

I keep up a steady stream of mumbling, mostly because I hate being quiet when I don't have to be, and secondly because from the way his stomping becomes exponentially more aggravated, I can tell I'm getting under his skin.

I grin.

"It really was good of you to break me out," I continue in his voice. "Oh, don't even mention it," I reply to myself. "Not a big deal at all. I think we're going to be the best of friends."

He stops, his shoulders heaving.

"Do you ever *shut up*?" He rounds on me, something dark moving through those blue eyes. Power rolls from him in a wave, and I grit my teeth, more annoyed than scared. Well, both, really, but I am not about to let him know that.

And when *I'm* annoyed, I make *everyone* annoyed. It has nothing to do with being a silver tongue, but it's just as much a part of me.

"Now I'm not going to." I raise my eyebrows in a challenge. "Ever."

heavy and already muffling the normal night noises of the forest clawing up the face of the Hiirek Mountains.

"I should leave you here, disciple of Sola, and let you die a slow, agonizing death from the curse you no doubt deserve."

"You will not leave me, disciple of Hrakan." The words fly from my mouth, shot through with the toxic power of my silver tongue. I should regret it, using my so-called gifts without meaning to, but I don't. Not at all, not when he's being an asshole to me for no reason after I helped him, and not when my life is on the line.

"You swore an oath to me." I almost make him swear to laugh at my jokes, too, just to be a bitch, but I think that would probably get on my nerves, too.

Besides, I like to earn my laughter. Most of the time.

"Tell me thank you for saving you," I say, my voice thick with my power, my tongue numb with the amount of it I'm funneling out of me.

A cold sweat breaks on my forehead and lower back, a sign I'm pushing my gift further than I should.

The man standing in front of me shivers, and for a second I think I have him. I've done it.

"I will not thank you for something I could have done myself, disciple of Sola."

I wince at the last words: disciple of Sola. Nameless, worthless even, without the goddess who plucked me from the streets as a child and raised me in her temples.

Not that I had a choice.

Never a choice, not with Sola.

"Then why didn't you do it yourself?"

"Because I didn't want to," he snarls.

I push my power further, knowing it's going to exhaust me, but too pissed off to care. "Why didn't you want to?"

The magic of our bond—the oaths we've sworn to each

other—stretches taut as I pour my so-called gift into it. It's like nothing I've felt before, eldritch and thick with power, nearly tangible where it tugs at my stomach.

The Sword staggers slightly.

So, it affects him too. He feels it too.

My eyes go wide at the magic coursing between us.

He finally turns back around, staring at me with a new light in his eyes, a light that's more terrifying than anything he's said thus far to me.

"How, exactly, did you receive your curse?" There's a strange gravity to each syllable that seems to force the snow to blow sideways.

I shift my weight, shrugging my shoulders.

"It's not important. Freezing to death before curing it would be a problem, though. I suggest we get to where my supplies are and make camp before this storm gets worse."

I don't add that it seems to be getting worse only now, after the bond between us flared.

A bond I created because I wasn't sure he wouldn't slit my throat while I slept.

My fingers absentmindedly go to my neck. His gaze follows the gesture, something like sorrow in it, before his face shutters. He nods once, then continues heading silently up the mountain slope.

At this point, silence is fine by me.

I don't feel like talking anymore.

6

THE SWORD

I am not surprised she's already used her goddess-given power on me. I am surprised by the strength of the oath we swore to each other, its presence tickling between my shoulder blades like she's attached to a lead there. I can sense where she is behind me, thanks to that oath.

An oath that snapped this bond between us tight, clarifying and confusing everything.

It shouldn't affect me like this.

The trail of broken twigs and crushed vegetation the woman carelessly left finally ends, and I glance around in grudging admiration.

The thicket of mountain vegetation gives way to a clearing, just the right size for a camp. It's far enough up the mountainside that I doubt we'll have company anytime soon, especially given the increasing ferocity of the winter storm.

The wind's quieter here, the boughs above us creaking as the trees are caught in its frigid embrace.

The woman doesn't spare a glance at me, heading towards a pile of rocks on the far side of the clearing, which she quickly moves, unearthing several thick leather and wax-coated satchels.

She might be a thief and a liar, but she seems, at the very least, intelligent and prepared.

Of course the one with this... *particular* curse is as obnoxious as they get.

Sighing heavily, my lips thin and I force myself to help her move some of the larger rocks.

Her green cloak slips from her head, the red of her hair bright as fire even in the darkness. I swallow thickly.

"I would not have killed you." I wince at my own unexpected words. Better to stay silent around her.

"I don't believe you," she says, matter of fact.

She sifts another bag from the rocks, then pulls out a weathered measure of waxed canvas. "Especially when you find out I only have one of these, and we're sharing it if you don't want to die of cold." Her green gaze drops to my feet. "I didn't think to bring you shoes, either."

I grunt, taking the waxed cloth and the heavy stakes she produces. "I will take care of that."

She eyes me speculatively, then shrugs, deciding against more questions.

I shouldn't have threatened her to shut up, but I know better than anyone the past can't be undone, and I can't unsay that.

It's better this way, anyway, with her disliking and distrusting me.

She should.

"If you put the tent up, I'll start the fire and some food. Unless you like cooking."

"Fine by me," I say, striding over to where it's clear the

tent's been pitched before, a series of indentations across the relatively level ground.

Loose strands of vibrant hair whip around her face as she watches me through narrowed eyes. The tip of her nose is red from the cold, color high in her cheeks, setting off those spring green eyes and lush lips.

"I could make you tell me your name," she finally says, pulling canvas-wrapped logs from the rock-covered pile.

"I know," I answer. If she wanted to, she already would have tried. I wouldn't tell her. As hard as her compulsion is to resist, and the fact we're inextricably bonded now in ways she doesn't even realize makes her gifts even more difficult to shrug off, I cannot give that part of me away.

Not when so much depends on our entwined fate.

I shrug it off though, shaking my head, disgusted with myself, and focus on driving the thick wooden stakes into the soft forest floor.

How long did she camp up here, waiting for the right moment to strike Cottleside? Waiting to break me out, to save her own skin?

"I'm Kyrie."

I glance over my shoulder at her, but she's not paying me much attention, stacking logs expertly. "I presumed."

"I knew you could hear me." A quick smile illuminates her face, gone just as fast. "Kyrie Ilinus, sworn to the goddess, well, you know her name. I was a foundling."

A foundling. I stretch one sheet of canvas out across the ground, then pull the other waxed sheet over the stakes.

"I'm sorry to hear that," I finally tell her. I am, too. Sola's disciples are known for... creating foundlings. Killing their parents, ensuring the best and brightest and most likely to serve the goddess will fall into their care, calling it destiny.

A truly evil practice, and therefore perfectly in Sola's wheelhouse.

I want to ask how old she was when her caretakers murdered her parents, but I don't.

It doesn't matter.

"This is the part where you tell me your name, with your own free will." Her voice is lilting. Cajoling.

I grunt, ignoring the invitation. There's no need to get to know her better. In fact, it will only make it harder for both of us in the end.

Better to keep as much of a distance as possible.

The tent stands complete in front of me, and my irritation increases. Keeping my distance from her is going to be a physical impossibility.

Is it part of her plan? To keep me off balance? My frown deepens, and I force myself to test the stability of the structure despite my misgivings.

Snow drifts down steadily from cracks in the fir trees, beginning to blanket the world in white and otherworldly quiet. My feet are numb from the cold, and sleeping anywhere but by her side in the tent is out of the question. I am used to cold, used to discomfort, thanks to my time in Cottleside, but I am not enough of a fool to think I should test my own fortitude by sleeping outside.

"Should be ready soon," Kyrie announces, wiping her hands on her pants. "Killed the hare myself this morning, and I've been saving the carrots and potatoes."

I glance in the fire and am slightly surprised to find a soup pot nestled in the flames.

"Now that the carrots are safe..." she trails off, then closes one eye, staring into the thicket of fat-trunked trees. "Here, Mushroom, here, Mushroom," she calls out, her voice a perfect soprano.

I roll my eyes and sit next to the fire, warming my feet. The woman must be half out of her mind. No matter how strong her silver tongue abilities are, no disciple of Sola can sing a mushroom into a stew pot.

If she is out of her wits, it's going to make my work much easier. So will hating her.

I content myself with that thought as I rub my tingling feet, pain from cold and heat shooting up through me.

I need clothes, I need to clean myself, and I need food to regain my strength so I will be able to enact my own plan where Kyrie is concerned. Discomfort makes me shift, but it's not from the pain in my freezing feet.

It's from the knowledge of what part she will play in the little theater of the gods she's stumbled into with her... death curse.

I will do as I always have, though—what I must.

Something large crashes through the underbrush, and I'm standing again a half-second later, ready to fight.

"There's my Mushroom," Kyrie says in a sing-song voice, and I blink in disbelief.

A grey-brown horse... no, not a horse, a mule, emerges from the underbrush, shaking snow from its hide. Long ears twitch towards me, its brown liquid gaze trusting and sweet.

"Mushroom," I repeat, realization dawning. She was calling the mule. "Why would you let prey roam these woods alone?"

"I couldn't exactly leave him in the city. I was rescuing a death knight, remember?" She gestures above her head. "About this tall, unfriendly, his handsomeness wasted on his shitty personality?" She beams at me. "Maybe you know him?"

I don't give her the satisfaction of reacting to her remark.

She called me handsome.

The ground seems colder beneath me as I sit back down,

trying to shake off the unexpected compliment couched in insults. A true compliment, no matter how backhanded, from the goddess of liars' chosen.

Will wonders ever cease?

The woman—*Kyrie*, I mentally correct myself—is unpredictable. I would do well to keep that at the forefront of my mind, despite whatever tricks she has up her sleeve. Despite how different from Sola's followers she pretends to be, the only reason Kyrie broke me out of Cottleside was to save her own hide.

That is the only truth that matters, and no matter what happens, that's the fact I must cling to. I blink, swallowing heavily as I stare into the flames.

Kyrie's securing the mule to a nearby tree, throwing a blanket over the beast and tending to it, cooing over its feet as she checks it for injuries and even sneaking the mule a long orange carrot.

Another memory assaults me, and my knuckles whiten as my hands clench into tight fists. A memory that hasn't faded, not across dozens of human lifetimes, not across decades of service to Hrakan. Cruel, high-pitched laughter, dissonant against the sound of screams, the cracking of timbers and the scent of charred flesh and greasy smoke. My throat tightens, my pulse pounding, and I squeeze my eyes shut, blocking out the fire in front of me.

It does nothing to dull the memory of fire in my mind.

"We need to get you clothes," Kyrie's voice cuts through the noise of the past, clear as a bell. "A weapon, and some boots for sure. I don't know why I didn't think of that," she muses. "I guess I was in too much of a hurry."

I open my eyes, annoyed at the gratitude I feel towards her for interrupting my thoughts, her inanity cutting through the memories of that night, the night that changed everything.

"Your kind aren't known for thinking of more than their own skin," I finally say.

"Don't hold back," she says brightly, crouching before the flames, fanning her fingers out. "Wouldn't want to be confused about how you really feel about me. That would be a tragedy."

My irritation transforms into something violent and poisonous, rooting deep in me, finding all too willing anchors in my very bones.

"The tragedy is what your goddess has done to Heska. What she did to you and all the foundlings whose families were murdered, and what she did to—" I make myself close my mouth, staunching the flow of words.

It doesn't staunch the wound, though.

Nothing ever will.

"On that delightful note," Kyrie says, her green eyes flashing, her lush lips a thin pink slash across her face. "The food is ready. That is, if you're done with your rant?" The question is sweet and light, but I hear the censure in it, the hard edge.

She sets the steaming pot on the snowy ground, producing a set of spoons. I raise an eyebrow, then decide merely asking her where she got them isn't worth the effort of conversation. No doubt they're from one of the satchels she pulled from her stash in the rocks.

No doubt all of it is stolen from some poor family who could hardly afford it.

I make myself eat anyway.

The first spoonful is scalding hot, searing the top of my tongue, but I don't care. It's the best thing I've eaten in years. The food at Cottleside was... enough to keep me alive.

I'm nearly through the thick rabbit stew before I realize she's barely eating, letting me take most of the food.

Shame fills me, and I drop the spoon in the pot.

I ate nearly all her food.

A glance over at her reminds me of who she is, though. Of who she *will* be to me, as well, and the shame's incinerated, fury replacing it easily.

"You should eat," I say gruffly.

"You need it more than I do," Kyrie says simply, lacing her hands over her knees. "Besides, I lost my appetite in the sewer."

I grunt, then shake my head. It doesn't matter if I need it more. I'm not eating it. I'm not going to fall for her manipulations. All her kindness is feigned.

A lie, just as the disciples of her goddess taught her to do.

I stand quickly.

"Soap?" The thought of being clean and being able to sleep lying down, with a full stomach, is nearly more than I can bare.

She rummages through a leather pack, snow landing in her long, light brown lashes and hair. The flakes stand out like diamonds on the blood-red of her braid.

"Here," she says. Her warm fingers brush mine, and a tingling awareness of her power, of her physical body, sings through me, a siren song.

My body tenses, immediately wary. It's been... years since I was last with a woman, a decade since I was able to do more than relieve myself in the rare occasions I was unrestrained in my cell.

My fingers close around the wax paper and twine-wrapped cake of soap, and I rip my hand away from hers.

Best not to think of anything but the inevitable outcome of the oath we've sworn to each other.

back in a few minutes, I'm coming looking for you." Silence is my only answer. I grit my teeth. *Infuriating.*

"I don't care how shriveled your tiny dick is from your snowbath," I yell out. "I will drag you back here by it, and Mushroom will help."

Mushroom tosses his head in agreement.

A shadow appears on the edge of the clearing, and my throat grows dry. White hair, dark eyes, features cut from a cloth that is anything but human.

"I'm here, woman," he growls, stalking across the clearing. "Any louder and you'll bring whatever predators roam these mountains down on our heads, and that curse of yours will be the least of your problems."

"Oh, now you can talk." It comes out breathless and I cough, trying to play off the fact that I'm breathless… because of him.

He's not wearing clothes.

I mean, his dirty shirt's wrapped around his waist as a small nod to modesty, but otherwise, he's…

I swallow hard.

He's stunning. Too thin by a mile, but there's no mistaking the elegant lines of his body, the powerful musculature that once was, that will be again.

I close my eyes and turn around, then berate myself silently because I might as well shout to him that despite my brain knowing better, my body is clearly responding to his.

Ugh.

"Good, glad I don't have to send out a search party," I say woodenly, all but running towards the tent.

"Right. You and the mule. Quite the party." His low voice rasps over my skin, and despite the fact I'm fully dressed, it feels too intimate.

Tent. Tent. Tent.

I throw open the flap and toss the satchels inside, collapsing onto the waxed canvas that smells distinctly like horseflesh and dirt.

I've smelt worse.

Then he's there, the Sword, crowding into the tent, too large and too naked and altogether too much. It's dark in the tent, especially with the clouds full of snow blotting out the stars and the fire slowly dying outside.

I staunchly avoid looking at him, just in case.

And I definitely do not notice he does, in fact, smell much, much better. I sniff at my own armpit surreptitiously because now I wonder if I smell terrible.

Better to smell terrible, though. Safety in stink, or something.

I clear my throat as I pull off my boots, unfastening my cloak so I can use it as a blanket. Using my sock-covered toes, I push the packs into the middle of the tent, safely between the two of us. Not that we need the physical separation.

There's no way in the hells either one of us wants to get any closer to the other than we have to. He's made that abundantly clear.

Disgust curls my lip. He might be nice to look at, but I've never in my life met anyone who looked at me with so much undisguised malice. He'd rather stab me in the back than try to cop a feel in the middle of the night, I'm sure of it.

Plus, I smell bad. So *there*.

I start to unstrap my dagger belt from my hips, but stop at the last minute.

"Don't touch me," I tell him suddenly. "Keep your hands to yourself tonight, and every night." My words are as sharp as the blades askew at my waist.

He grunts in assent. "Don't flatter yourself."

For some reason, his blunt asshole of an answer helps, and some of the tension melts from my muscles.

With that, I unbuckle the belt of daggers and lay it out flat next to me before curling up under my cloak, tucking one arm under my head.

In the darkness, the sound of the Sword lying down feels disproportionately loud, and I squeeze my eyes shut—only to be accosted by imagining what he's wearing.

"You better be wearing pants," I hiss into the darkness.

He just laughs, low and mellifluous. The sound sends a shiver up my spine. Only because it's shocking. I haven't heard him laugh yet—or seen him smile, even.

It's the last thing I hear before I fall asleep, exhaustion tugging me under.

❄

I SIT UP SUDDENLY, awake in an instant. It's full dark, the once-crackling fire silent as the grave. My fingers close over my daggers, and even though I don't know what's dragged me from sleep, my heart's pounding, my nerves on high alert.

Then I hear it.

An odd coughing sound. Snow crunching beneath something heavy.

I start to stand, ready to cut whatever is out there to shreds, when strong arms bracket my shoulders, a clean warm palm across my mouth. My eyes go even wider and I struggle for a second.

Lips press against the shell of my ear and I go completely still, my knuckle cracking as I grip a dagger too tight.

"It's alright. It won't hurt us. Or the mule. Most likely," he whispers into my ear. "If you scream, or attack it, though?

You'll regret it." One hand strokes easily up and down my back, like he's trying to comfort me.

Which is absurd. Completely, absolutely absurd. Ridiculous. Maybe I'm dreaming.

The sound of footsteps crunching on snow draws closer still, and the Sword tightens his huge hand over my mouth, not violently, just enough to muffle any sound I might make, should I decide not to listen to him.

He must not understand how much I value my own skin.

Whatever is out there is big, and the fabric of the tent shudders as the creature moves around it. A drift of snow sloughs off the roof of the structure, but the Sword's hand keeps running up and down my spine.

It's warm and snug in the tent and I blink, slowly, slower still, and I'm tired enough to relax back into his huge, hot body in spite of myself.

He's not holding me because he wants to, I rationalize.

He's just trying to keep me from doing something that will keep us both killed. Probably thanks to the oath we swore.

Might as well take advantage of his body heat... and the feeling of safety. From the oath, of course. He won't hurt me; he can't.

It's with a sense of surprise that I doze off again.

※

A RUSH of wings outside wakes me up and I shift, the blanket heavy and stifling hot all around me.

Heavy. My eyes fly open and I stiffen... only to realize I'm not the only stiff thing in the tent.

It's not a blanket. It's not even my cape, which, based on the tangle around my feet, I kicked off sometime in the night... and replaced with the Sword.

He's curled around me, his breathing deep and even, and if it weren't for the fact his cock is well aware of me in his arms, I might even be able to trick myself into falling back asleep.

Because he's warm and comfortable.

That's the only reason.

But his cock is very much awake, and the odds of me falling back asleep with it prodding my spine are absolutely zero. I try to roll away, to wriggle free, but he grunts in his sleep, his arms tightening around me. My eyes widen as he throws a well-muscled leg over mine, effectively trapping me next to him.

Traitorous heat floods through me, and I grit my teeth against it.

No way am I attracted to *him*. He goes by the Sword, for goddess's sake! He could not be more obnoxious or high-handed and so what if he's objectively beautiful?

He clearly despises me, and seeing as how I am my own favorite person, that dynamic would never work.

A bird trills outside the tent, its shadow rippling across the waxed canvas exterior.

I need to get him off me, and I need to do it quickly—the more obnoxiously the better. An evil grin kicks the corners of my mouth into a smile, and instead of rolling away from him, I snuggle closer, rubbing my ass against him before turning to face him.

For the first time in my life, I hope my breath is absolutely horrible when waking up next to handsome man.

"Good morning. I see now why they call you the Sword." I sing the words because that seemed to irritate him the most yesterday.

His eyes open slowly, his dark lashes standing out against the white of his hair. In waking, his face seems younger, less angry. His silvery-white hair slips as his head moves, revealing those pointed, not-human ears.

How old is he?

My eyes drift from his ears back to his now wide-awake gaze, his brow furrowed as he regards me.

I swallow, slightly less confident in the way I'm playing this.

"I thought you hated me." The words surprise me, and I regret them as soon as they slip out of my mouth on a whisper. I make myself smile again, and this time it's jagged as broken glass.

"The only way I could get any sleep was to stop your teeth from chattering in the night."

He rolls off of me in one elegant, fluid motion, and embarrassment burns across my cheeks and chest.

"I do hate being sworn to you. Immensely. Maybe more than you will ever understand."

"Oh? Is that why your sword was so hot and hard against my back?" I flutter my eyelashes, even though I'm slightly ashamed of how easy it is for me to resort to goading him. Not enough to stop, though. "Is that how you earned your name? The Sword? Because I have to admit, it's much bigger than I thought it would be, considering how—"

"They call me the Sword because that's the last thing my enemies feel." A chill emanates from his words, and I hug my arms around myself, feeling the truth of it hit me. I am a consummate liar, thanks to my abilities—but my talent works both ways. He's not lying. "I am a slaughterer. A warrior and a murderer."

I roll my eyes because, my goddess, what an ego. "Oh please, great and terrible Sword, I cower at your feet."

He scowls at me, tugging on his ragged shirt. My mouth goes dry as it hits me: we weren't just cuddled up. He was holding me to his naked body.

An inferno rages over my face and I turn away, too quickly to be able to pass it off as playing it cool.

"You need better clothes," I force myself to say. "I can slip down to Cottleside and steal you some—"

"No."

"No?" I repeat, fastening my cloak around my neck. Highly annoyed, I shake my braid out and rake my fingers through the tangled mess of my waves, staring him down. "What do you mean, no? Would you prefer to have frostbitten toes? Oh, Sword who hangs heavy and low, we tremble before you, toeless one." I genuflect before him, and when I glance back up, I swear I see a hint of a smile before it's replaced with that same gloomy scowl.

"I do not need you to steal for me, thief. I have my own ways of finding what I need."

"I don't have time to take care of you when your feet freeze off. Don't be a stubborn ass."

"It's infantile to call names. Though I suppose... it fits." His gaze runs up and down my body, the sneer of his lip making me want to punch his very punchable and too-good-looking face.

Goddess, couldn't it have been anyone else to help me find a cure for this stupid curse? It had to be this asshole?

"And how old are you, exactly? I suppose when you were born a thousand years ago, everyone else seems infantile to you. You know, maybe I should call you Grandfather instead of Sword. Grandpapa. Ancient, rusty, derelict Sword, the mighty relic of Death himself."

His eyes flash with pure anger and I grin at him, delighted to have finally annoyed him enough to get that reaction.

"Come on, Grandpapa," I sing out. "You're not all there anymore, are you? But if you insist on walking barefoot through the snow, I can't stop you. Have to respect my elders and all that, right?" I wink up at him, thrilled to have the upper hand.

He moves closer, filling my vision—my awareness—with him.

Maybe I overplayed my hand.

Wouldn't be the first time.

"You'll pay your respects to me in good time, on your knees," he growls.

Fury wipes away any remaining enjoyment of needling him. I tug on my boots aggressively, thankful for the rich fur lining on the interior. Without the asshole warrior wrapped around me, it's freezing cold. Or it should be—but I'm steaming hot from his remark.

I don't give him the satisfaction of responding, simply throwing open the tent flap and letting him think he got the last word.

It's to my shame that I am bothered by it. The thought of being on my knees before him. The thought of doing exactly what he insinuated, even though he said it just to piss me off.

My own fault for bothering to acknowledge his anatomy this morning.

I stomp onto the snow, then pull up short, looking around in fear.

"What's wrong?" the Sword asks, somehow right behind me. He follows my gaze.

"I wasn't sure if I dreamed it," I say. Did the Sword really... hold me tight and stroke my back until I fell asleep again?

Half of me doesn't believe it, especially considering the animosity between us, but here's the evidence that I did not, in fact, dream what woke me in the middle of the night.

Massive footprints in the snow. I crouch down, inspecting them, spreading my fingers and placing my own hand in the divots left by a huge creature. There's room to spare.

"I'll be damned," he swears.

"No argument from me," I say sweetly.

He doesn't respond, though, simply walks around the tracks, pausing to tie back his shoulder-length hair, carefully tugging it over his pointed ears.

Not that I'm watching him.

"Direcat."

"No way," I stand up, brushing my hands off on my pants.

"Better check if your mule was a meal last night."

Panic grips me, my eyes going wide. "Mushroom?" I call out, racing to the side of the clearing where I tied him last night.

Mushroom whickers, walking sleepily towards me, long ears flicking all around.

Oh goddess. I close my eyes and tilt my face skyward, sucking in a huge breath of relief.

"You're fine. It's fine." I pat his neck, and when I turn, I find the Sword staring at me with a calculating expression, his pretty eyes narrowed.

"Not meat after all," I say, like I could care less. I don't need him to know how much I love the stupid beast. I don't need him to hold it against me, the way the Sisters of Sola would.

My chest tightens, and I toss my hair. "You've got enough meat for everyone, I think." I wink outrageously at him again and am rewarded with a dark look.

"I thought direcats were extinct." I'm still stroking Mushroom's neck lovingly, and I make myself give him one more pat before turning away.

"They are of the goddess Dyrda," he says in a low voice, his attention fully back on the huge tracks peppered throughout the campsite. "I do not think many exist still, considering the wars."

"The wars?" I frown, completely thrown off. "You mean

Doston trying to take over Heska?" Doston, our southern neighbor, has no regard for Heskan religion and magic, and their incursions have been more in earnest the past few years.

Chaos is good for business though, so I haven't given them too much thought, except to avoid most jobs in the southern parts of Heska.

"No," he says firmly, which doesn't shed any light on anything.

Right. So there's some kind of war that I haven't heard hide or hair of, or good old Sword is a bit behind the times after his stint in the pokey.

"How are your toesies, old man?"

"Ready to get the hells on with it," he growls. "Don't call me that."

"Old?" I ask. "An antiquity like you shouldn't be concerned with something as petty as age."

"A man," he corrects, turning away.

Right. A man. Wouldn't want to be associated with us lowly humans. I stare at his back for a moment, at the way the ragged shirt lines up with white scars across his back, some pinker and newer than others.

What the hells is he? Elves have pointed ears like that, or at least, the stories say they do, but he is too large to be an elf, too broad. They're supposed to be slender, willowy. Nothing about the Sword is slender or willowy. My eyes narrow as I watch him move. Elegant, precise, efficient—he moves with a grace and light-footedness that belies his size.

My lips twist to the side. He must have some kind of Fae blood—though the Fae are also supposed to be all but extinct. They did it to themselves, factions warring between themselves on behalf of the gods until the age of the Fae ended and became a tale humans told each other in warning.

Maybe he *is* a thousand years old.

Alarm colors the thought.

Banishing it, I turn towards the snow-covered utensils from our meal last night, packing everything up neatly. Humming to myself as I work, I try to remember what little I learned about the Fae war. My mother used to hold me close on her lap, smelling of baked bread and lavender, whispering tales about long-dead Fae warriors as the fire crackled in the hearth in front of us. If I close my eyes, I can hear her voice, feel her fingers as she combed and braided my hair.

All I can remember, though, is what she told me every night before I closed my eyes.

"I want you to fly, little bird. I want you to soar."

I wish I could remember her face.

I wish I could see her again.

A lump forms in my throat, and I hold on to the feel of her warm fingers in my hair for a moment longer before it vanishes as quickly as it came.

Heaving a sigh, I continue working. She would want me to fight this curse. She would want me to live.

Determination stiffens my shoulders.

The Sword makes quick work of the tent, and between the two of us, the camp empties, Mushroom whickering as I load him down with packs full of my ill-gotten goods.

The Sword might look down on my particular skillset, but he certainly isn't averse to making use of everything I've stolen.

I file that fact away for later, ready to shove it under his nose at just the right moment.

A gleeful grin spreads across my face at the heartening thought, and I even manage to sing a little under my breath as I finish strapping everything onto my trusty mule.

"The sparrow flits from tree to tree,
sorrow in her song.

For her babes were taken cruelly,
winter's latest wrong."

I stop singing, leaning my forehead against Mushroom's warm neck. Poor bird.

Snow covers my fur-lined boots as I pivot, my heart oddly heavy. Snow—fresh and white and pure, sparkling in the weak winter sunlight—blankets everything, drifts of it weighing down every branch.

Was I ever like that? Fresh? Pure?

Maybe it's not worth it—this quest to find a cure, the time I'll spend with another who so clearly despises me. Maybe I deserve it—the curse and his hatred both. Maybe I should give up, take up drinking in earnest, and wallow until the curse is well and truly set.

"I want you to fly, little bird."

My mother wouldn't want me to give up. My family would have wanted me to live.

"Second thoughts?"

I startle as I realize the Sword's watching me carefully, his muscled arms bulging as he crosses them over his chest.

Strange how the question knocks me right out of my dismal reverie.

"If I don't take care of myself, no one else will." It's not a real answer, and it makes me feel indescribably small to say it out loud. *No one else will.*

I might be sworn to the goddess of chaos and lies, but it's the largest truth of my existence.

For a long time, I've been the only one who's really cared about me. I'm too stubborn to give up now.

I suck in a breath of freezing air, so cold it bites at my lungs, my shoulders heaving.

The Sword raises one dark eyebrow, severe compared to the

silver-white of his hair. He doesn't comment on that, doesn't even manage one of his grunts in reply.

Probably because he knows it's true. I bet he thinks I deserve it, too.

"Thank you for breaking down the tent," I make myself say. The words feel thick in my throat, with an emotion I don't want to put a name to.

"We should go. You're right, I need clothes if I'm going to blend in."

He hands me the carefully, expertly folded and wrapped tent canvas, and I am halfway through packing it on Mushroom's back when the meaning of his words sinks in.

He needs clothes if he's going to blend in.

With humans.

He doesn't need them because he's freezing. He needs them because he's not human.

I swallow hard, my chest tight with real fear for the first time since I met him, like this— his acknowledging it, his true nature—portends real danger.

I must be a fool, too, because even with my fear, it gives me hope. Hope that Lara was right, that her god did not steer us both wrong, and that having this... Fae on my side will be what I need to live.

Who better to have on my side than someone who scares even me?

The dark clouds of my thoughts scatter slightly, letting hope shine through.

"Where to, Sword?" I ask.

"Higher. There's something I need up there."

Why won't he tell me what we're after? Sighing, I blow out a breath. Patience has never been one of my virtues. As a thief, that trait either comes in incredibly handy or can result in having your hands in the stocks or a rope around your neck, depending on the way luck blows.

"Higher it is," I belatedly answer.

I sneak a glance at him, but he's not paying me any attention. A muscle in his temple twitches, and he stares through the snow-cloaked trees like he can see something I can't.

The thought makes me shiver again, and I pull my cloak around me tight. Mushroom's lead is half frozen, and I tug it gently to get him moving.

Together, we follow the Sword through the wild Hiirek Mountains. My stomach grumbles, and I'm sure Mushroom is hungry too, but the Sword seems unbothered by such human problems. The snow muffles the normal noise of the forest, or maybe it's just that most animals are smart enough to be hunkered down in their cozy dens after last night's storm.

I rub my stomach, then take a moment to root through the food pack for a length of peppered jerky for me and a bruised apple for Mushroom. Chewing thoughtfully, I study the Sword's back as he leads us through the snow-dappled trees.

There's no disguising the fact he's not human, and I don't know why I didn't see it before.

Any question of it in my mind is completely erased by the sight of him in the daylight, the sun reflected on the pockets of snow between the thick evergreens. He's too beautiful, too perfect. Even the ropes of scars across his back add to the effect instead of diminishing or marring it.

He's powerfully built, which... is odd. He should be leaner than he is after a decade in a cell. Should be weaker, too, but he doesn't seem to struggle at all as the air grows thinner and colder. I'm not about to complain, but I huddle as close to Mushroom's huge warm body as I can, and the mule seems to enjoy nudging me off balance as part of his fun for the day.

The Sword never seems off balance.

In fact, he seems to not only be going further up the summit of the Hiirek range, he also seems to know *exactly* where he is going.

My brow furrows as I watch him through the icy cloud of my own breath.

If I really, wholly trusted him, I would be elated to have someone so sure of himself at my side.

Problem is, I don't trust him.

There's no way he trusts me either. In fact, he's made it clear he despises me and the other Sisters of Sola. He made it clear by murdering them by the dozens.

Fair enough.

Can't really hold that against him. If I were braver, or if I had a death wish, I might have done the same.

I tick it off on my fingers. This male, this death knight, he knows where he's going, he isn't human, and he hates me. My fingers go limp, and I pet Mushroom for good measure. He's sworn to me now, though... I cringe. And I'm sworn to him.

What could possibly go wrong?

My cheeks puff up as I take in a breath and hold it, trying to warm it up so it doesn't send spikes of pain through my lungs.

"What's the plan?" I ask, half sure he won't answer because he seems to hate talking. Or maybe it's just me he hates.

I shrug at Mushroom. "Doesn't matter if he likes me, as long as he helps me find a cure for this stupid curse."

I say it low enough that I jump when the Sword responds.

"Tell me something, Silver Tongue."

"Sure," I answer blandly.

"How did the draught from the chalice taste?"

His voice is so low, so melodious and lovely, that answering seems the most natural thing in the world.

"It wanted me to drink it," I say slowly, the memory sluggish and strange. "It smelled... like springtime. Like fresh flowers and melting ice. It tasted like... life." My nose scrunches and I shake my head, then narrow my eyes at his back.

Except... it's not his back. He stopped at some point, turning to fully face me, to watch me as I answered.

"It tasted like life, but it was death instead," I finish with false cheer. "How clever. What a fun trick."

Time spins slower, the odd flake falling from the needles above in slow motion as our gazes meet. There's an odd look to his eyes, like he's seeing me, truly seeing me, for the first time, and he doesn't quite know what to do with me.

"I have the same reaction when I look in a mirror," I tell him, and the moment shatters, time back to normal.

He grunts. The snow races down again on its quest to reach the forest floor and transform to water and ice.

I want to ask him why.

Why, of all the things he could have asked me, is that what he wants to know? If he's such a terrible warrior, a dark knight of death, why should he care what death tastes like?

He's dealt it enough.

We continue walking. I continue chewing the smoked jerky, and I continue trying to catch my breath in the thinning air. Snow crunches under my feet and I hum occasionally, dreaming of fireplaces and warmth and a hot drink.

Minutes pass. Hours.

"Here," he finally says.

I stop, leaning my back against Mushroom, mentally sending thanks to Lara for the cloak that's now fully responsible for the fact I'm not frozen completely.

Something crashes through the trees, too close for comfort. I still, Mushroom tossing his head, prancing on the snow. The rope lead falls to the ground, my daggers against my palms in the next instant.

The Sword stands his ground, his stance wide and easy, but the sharp alertness to his eyes makes me warier than ever.

If he's assessed that whatever lurks out there is a potential problem, then I definitely won't like it.

My attention jerks left, caught by movement between the trees.

"Hold the mule," the Sword demands.

I curl my fingers around his halter. Mushroom attempts to rear back, making a panicked scream of a noise.

"It's probably birds—" I stop speaking nearly immediately. It's not birds, not at all.

8

THE SWORD

Luminous emerald eyes focus solely on Kyrie, who watches the beast right back. It's nearly the size of the mule, with black tufted ears and a thick grey-brown pelt and paws the size of the prints around our tent last night.

A direcat.

"Do not move," I hiss out.

The woman hates to listen to me as much as I hate to hear her, but I hope for both our sakes' she does as I say this once. It would be a tragedy to get this close to my goals only to have a direcat snuff her out.

The direcat continues stalking towards us, long whiskers twitching as it tests our scents.

Kyrie remains blessedly still, and the direcat doesn't stop, one paw in front of the other, the ringed tail flicking backing and forth.

My breath catches, an emotion I haven't felt in a very, very long time sending a single shiver down my back: awe.

The direcat regards me with one baleful look, mouth half open and showing off three-inch-long incisors.

Unpredictable creatures.

Beautiful, magnificent even, but entirely too fickle for my tastes. It makes perfect sense that the beast is drawn to Kyrie, though.

I frown.

It's thin, too thin, its ribs showing as though it's been months since it had a good meal, and for the first time since I met the woman, fear stakes through my heart on her behalf. My shoulders tense, my body ready to protect her even if my mind grapples with the idea.

The cat is nearly soundless on the snow, and it's that, more than anything else, that sets my mind at ease.

If it were truly intent on eating her, it would be silent.

We wouldn't have heard it moments before it appeared.

"Don't hurt it." Kyrie's eyes are glassy, and she sheathes her daggers. "It's not going to attack us."

I tilt my head. I knew that, of course. I haven't spent a lifetime around the Fae gods' playthings only to fail at understanding them now.

The question is, how did she surmise that?

The great direcat sniffs at her head, then knocks the hood from it with a push of its nose. Kyrie's stock still, and the whites of the mule's eyes show as it likewise freezes in place in pure fear.

Neither move as the direcat continues to scent her, then nearly pushes her over as it rubs its cheek across her shoulder.

Marking her.

If there were any doubt left in my mind about Kyrie's fate, it vanishes now, and I'm sick with the knowledge of it.

She is the chalice's chosen. The direcat's mark, a sign of the wild goddess Dyrda's approval, puts that beyond a doubt.

I suspected it. Dreaded it.

Tested it, with my questioning—which she answered truthfully, unthinking, naïve.

But the direcat's presence, its fascination with her... it means there are more gods at play than I originally thought. My heart hammers against my chest.

"We need to move more quickly."

The sands of time are slipping faster and faster now.

Kyrie reaches up, and the cat's eyes close as she strokes her fingers through its fur.

I grit my teeth, an uncomfortable feeling prickling through me.

A rumbling begins, and Kyrie glances over at me with a wide-eyed expression of wonder.

"It's purring."

"We don't have time for this," I growl, and the rumbling breaks off as the cat stares me down, its long striped tail lashing back and forth in irritation. "Dyrda knows it as well as I do, direcat."

The beast blinks slowly, then stands, stalking towards me.

And nearly knocks me onto my ass when it rubs its huge head against me, marking me, too.

I roll my eyes at the impudence. "I am not yours, nor Dyrda's, cat."

It chuffs, watching me with insolent intelligence I recognize all too well.

"We'll need more than the three of us in the end, I fear," I tell it quietly, then turn, continuing towards the cave entrance I remember from years and years ago.

Kyrie and the animals follow, and I try to block out the way she speaks to them both in the same soothing, sing-song tone.

She could talk them into their own deaths if she wished. That is the power of the silver tongue, *that* is the power of Sola and chaos. I need to keep that fact at the forefront of my thoughts.

The memory of those the last silver tongue murdered in just such a way has never receded, and it won't now. I know all too well what Kyrie is capable of.

The snow recedes the closer we get to the cave, turning to slick ice across the rock and gravel terrain. The cat keeps pace with Kyrie, and though she seems oddly at ease with the monstrous feline, I am anything but.

The gods are watching.

Dyrda has sent aid. My lip curls as I glance back at the too-thin direcat. Aid, such as it is, that we will accept. My smile dies as quickly as it started.

The turmoil between the gods is coming to a head.

Heska's fate is at hand.

"What's in there?" Kyrie calls out. The pack mule eyes the direcat warily. "Don't eat Mushroom, big kitty. He's poisonous. He will definitely make you sick."

The cat chuffs again, then plops to the ground, licking one massive paw.

"The direcat won't bother him," I tell her.

She lifts her gaze from the direcat and meets mine.

A bolt of recognition goes through me, striking me to the core.

I shift my weight, uneasy with the weight of what must be done, with the knowledge of what destiny has in store for us.

So much responsibility, so much heartache.

She will regret the chalice, she will regret her oath to me, and there is nothing I can do to stop it.

For her, either way, the outcome is inevitable.

"I didn't know you cared," she finally says. Her fingers dance along the dagger belt slung around her hips, like she's daring me to start a fight.

The uncanny sensation that she's read my thoughts fills me until I realize she means about her clearly beloved mule.

"I don't. But the cat's smart enough not to kill the animal hauling our supplies."

She barks out a laugh. "Right. Sure. Is it your Fae senses telling you that?"

"You can feel it as well as I can." I'm too old to play these games, too old for her, too old for the entire world. "I saw it in your eyes. You said yourself not to hurt the creature." My eyes narrow as I regard her. "Dyrda sent the beast."

"Dyrda? The goddess of nature? Since when do gods care enough to do anything but harm us humans?" She laughs again, but it's humorless, and it soon lapses into silence.

Another moment ticks by, and I watch her carefully.

She is faithless.

That is very much to my advantage.

I turn my attention back to the more pressing problem, scrutinizing the cave entrance. It's been a very long time since I was here last, and my memory is fuzzy on how to get through the wards. My imprisonment likely further dulled my memories, my magic even, worsened by the chaos breaking Heska, and the proliferation of the faithless, just like Kyrie.

I am not what I once was.

I resist the urge to look over my shoulder at the red-haired thief, but the thought hits me just the same as if I had.

She might make me whole again.

9

KYRIE

The direcat should be terrifying. It was last night, when I didn't know what it was. But now, in the early afternoon light, it seems every bit a large—okay, enormous—house cat.

It's dozing in a patch of sun-soaked snow, paws flexing and curling as it dreams.

Mushroom is less enthusiastic about our new friend, and I do my best to comfort him with what little oats we have left. I'm tired. More tired than I should be, even though that was a challenging, and overly long, hike. A muscle in my chest twitches, and I wince.

The curse, a little voice in my head tells me.

I glower.

I'm about sick of that little voice's input.

The Sword sits on a flat black rock, staring at the mouth of the cave like it's a puzzle to be solved.

I've asked him ten times now what the hells it is we're

doing up here, but he just gives me a pitying look that annoys me more than anything.

I busy myself with making a small fire, heating up snow in a pot for Mushroom to drink, and then refilling our own water pouches.

Doesn't mean I'm not itching to keep annoying the Sword. Better to do it hydrated, though. I take a long drink, wiping my mouth across my sleeve.

"Is sitting on your ass part of your solution to saving me? Or are you just going to run out the clock, or even better, hope the direcat eats me before the curse takes me out? Maybe you're thinking hypothermia?"

"Could you be quiet and let me think?" he asks through gritted teeth.

"Thinking doesn't seem to be your strong suit," I tell him sadly.

He glares at me. I grin.

"You know, if you told me what your plan was, maybe I could help?"

"Oh, do you know how to get past a warded entrance? Are you suddenly a master of spell craft? You don't even know *why* I brought you here."

I raise my hands in disgust, rolling my eyes. "Correct. Because you haven't told me, and I'm not a mind-reader, you asshole. But if you did tell me, I might come up with a plan because unlike someone here, I'm not the muscles of the operation. I have to rely on other things."

He stands up and I tense because gods damn it, I wasn't lying. He is the muscle, and I probably shouldn't needle him because he's fucking huge.

My hands are on my dagger handles in a flash, but he's even faster, moving before I realize it, before I can react.

Quick as thought.

Not human.

His hand raises and I flinch, thinking he's going to hit me—but the direcat's there first. One huge paw slams down on the Sword's shoulder, sending him sprawling back towards the matte black rock. Blood trickles from his arm where the cat must have caught him with a claw, and he lies there for a moment, watching it puddle onto the surface.

I exhale. Was he going to hit me?

Did the cat just keep him from doing it?

No. He wouldn't have hit me—he swore an oath, the oldest of vows, not to hurt me.

Heat crawls up my chest.

He was going to touch me, though. I know that as surely as I can see the crimson blood pooling on the surface of the stone in front of the cave.

Why was he going to touch me?

Why does the thought of him touching me make me hot all over?

Probably because he's the worst.

I toss my braid over my shoulder, scowling down at him. "Good kitty," I croon at the direcat.

"Good cat, indeed," the Sword echoes. "Look."

The entrance of the cave shimmers slightly, like a heat wave on the hottest day of summer. Which makes no sense, considering it's freezing. My throat tightens, the magic spilling over me as the shimmer disappears.

He stands, wiping the blood with his ragged shirt, which really, I can't see the point of, but who am I to help him at this point? "Blood ward. I forgot..."

"Training your mind is as important as training your muscles, Sword," I say blithely. "Are you going to tell me now why we're going in this warded cave? Or did you want me to make you bleed more, just to make sure the spells are happy with what you've offered?"

He regards me for a long moment because, apparently, that's his whole annoying schtick.

"To commune with the dead." He pronounces it with the air of someone who thinks they've just let me in on the secrets of the world.

I bark a laugh. "Oh, great. Excited for this. What's not to love? Someone with the personality of a corpse talking to their counterparts." I rub my hands together. "Are you going to share secret recipes? Gossip from beyond the veil? Find a way to break your vows to me?"

He blows out a low, long breath, and I suspect I've finally truly gotten on his nerves by being unimpressed. Wonderful.

"By the end of this, you'll wish it was the latter, Silver Tongue, but I'm not an oath-breaker."

"For someone who acts like they're above it all, you really do enjoy shoving my rare talent down my throat as often as possible. I have a *name*, you know."

"I think you like having things shoved down your throat."

I let out a shocked laugh because—"Did you just make a sex joke? There's hope for you yet, oh terrifying Sword of Death."

It's obvious from the color rising on his cheeks that he didn't, in fact, mean to make a sex joke, but his embarrassment just makes it that much funnier.

"Stop. Talking," he grits out, and I laugh again, beyond pleased with myself that I've gotten under his skin.

"*Absolutely* not. No. You opened the door on sex jokes, turnabout's fair play." I wink at him outrageously, and his lip curls as he growls—growls—low in his chest.

"Is that the noise you make when you shove your sword down someone's throat? Or is that the noise you use to commune with the dead?" I pitch my voice lower in an excellent mockery of his voice, if I do say so myself. And I do.

His eyes flash, and a hot awareness blazes low down my spine.

"Is there a reason, Silver Tongue, that you are bent on thinking about sex with me? It seems to occupy your thoughts." He raises one dark eyebrow, and of all the tracks I thought he might take during this conversation, that was not one of them.

But if he thinks I'm going to back down, he is sorely mistaken.

I lick my lips, making my face and body go soft. Inviting.

"Yes," I say. "I told you as soon as we met that I was breaking you out of prison for sex. You're the one playing coy."

I'm playing with fire, and it makes me gleeful. His hand raises, and this time, the cat's simply watching from the ground, without a care in the world.

He brushes a lock of my hair from my forehead, and I fight not to close my eyes at the sheer pleasure of his touch. Which is stupid. The Sword is annoying, a cocky idiot, not at all my type and not at all enticing.

But one touch from his calloused hand nearly has me panting.

Either that, or the altitude is messing with me. It must be the altitude. I don't pant over sex. Sex is easy and cheap.

How outrageous.

I stare up at him. "Are you going to let me sheathe that sword?" I bite my cheeks to keep from laughing at my own horrible joke.

Really, though, he shouldn't go by that name. Makes it too easy.

He brushes his thumb against my cheek, all pretense gone,

until it's just his skin against mine, his rough hand gentle on my face.

What would it be like with him? Would he be a selfish lover, or would he be as single-minded and efficient in bed as he seems to be in everything else?

"You aren't ready for me, Silver Tongue."

My jaw drops, but he's already abandoned me, heading through the entrance of the cave. The cat stands, stretching long, then gives me a look as if to say, *you're an idiot.*

I am. I definitely am.

Because now I can't stop thinking about sex with him.

And we need to go commune with the dead.

Whatever that means.

10

THE SWORD

The woman constantly has me off balance. Which makes perfect sense, considering she is an agent of pure chaos.

And makes me incandescent with rage.

This entire situation is absurd, and as with all ridiculous scenarios, I know it will end in utter tragedy.

It always does around me. It always will.

Tragedy is the whetstone of Death's blade.

I stalk through the cave, my feet remembering the way, even if my mind does not. Kyrie's light feet barely make a sound as she enters behind me, the cat with her. The mule remains in the entrance of the cavern, safer for him to wait there for our return.

She might think it's fun to play these games with me, but she will be the one who loses in the end.

My stomach twists at the thought.

Still.

Still, I have a vow to fulfill, and what's more, a destiny to pursue. Fate's wheel does not slow for anyone, not even me. Not for Kyrie, either, and she's caught in its spokes.

All the more reason for me to keep myself in check around her.

The cave winds deeper, the path narrow and steeper the further we go. Kyrie murmurs something in low tones to the direcat, and I realize with a twinge of guilt she's likely using the beast to guide her.

Humans can't see in this kind of light.

"I have to say," she calls out loudly, further ruining the stillness of the cave, "I am not typically the type of woman to blindly follow a man into a dark cave. Unless he's the mark and I'm going to hold a knife against his throat."

"You did not have to come down here." She did, though. In fact, she is necessary to accomplish what I must here.

"You must think I am really stupid if you thought I was going to let you out of my sight when you're supposed to be the key to saving me, Sword."

"Stupid? No." I shake my head, even though she won't see it. "I do not think you stupid."

A harsh laugh bounces off the walls. "Careful. That's almost a compliment, coming from you."

The direcat makes that odd coughing sound again, and I wonder just how intelligent Dyrda's chosen animal truly is. It wouldn't surprise me at all if it understood everything being said.

Discomfort me, though? Perhaps.

"It's a sad truth of how few compliments a woman like you has been paid if you're seeking them out in that statement."

She goes silent, and I know I've gone too far—I know as well as any how the Sisters of Sola dole out their praise.

"Do you get a prize from your god for being cruel to me?

Some reward in the afterlife for tormenting Sola's favorite silver tongue?"

"Some fate she allowed for her so-called favorite," I retort, then immediately regret it.

It's remarkable how far and close she is to the truth all at once.

Even her renewed silence seems hurt, because we both know the truth about the goddess of liars.

She does not care one whit about Kyrie or any of the rest of her followers, nor does she care about any of the beings in her territories—only what little entertainment they can bring her. Unfortunately for Heska, the entertainment Sola prefers is anything but kind.

"You know, since we're on the topic of fates and gods, why is it you think Hrakan left you to rot in that cell in Cottleside?"

The name Hrakan sends a bolt of shame through me, as it has for years now, and I nearly stumble over a rough patch on the cave floor.

"I think we need light," I mutter.

"Here," Kyrie says, and a moment later, her cold fingers brush against my hip. "Sorry. Can't see. Flint."

I take the rocks from her, slightly bemused because I need them to make fire as much as I need the light to see.

Which is, of course, not at all.

Better to pretend, though. Pretend I'm no more than the male she found filthy and tethered by chains in that cell in Cottleside.

Sola herself would approve, I'm sure.

The thought makes my stomach twist, and I can't bring myself to use the human's rocks.

"I have a better way," I say, my voice abnormally quiet, so low I doubt she's even heard me. "An easier way."

I speak the word the cave wants, a word that makes the

flesh behind my eyes spike with pain to use it, as weakened as I've become.

My palm slams against the wall and I grit my teeth, dipping into my power, my true self, for the first time in years.

"What in the hells are you doing?" Kyrie's voice is harsh in my ears.

The word, the cave needs more. I should know.

I designed it to be this way.

I dip my fingers into the scratch the direcat gifted me until they're warm and wet with blood, and I speak the word again, letting the power swell as I smear the fresh blood against the rock wall.

Pain shreds through me, and that, more than anything, concerns me about how long we have. It shouldn't cost this much to use this spell.

We. Kyrie. Me.

Finally, light blazes down the length of the tunnel because that's what this is. That's where we are.

It is no mere cave in the Hiirek Mountains, no mere warded entrance.

"Oh, fucking hells," Kyrie swears. Her fingers dig into my wrist, as though she's drawing strength from my presence here. A strange thought.

The flickering blue light illuminates what was hidden, and guilt, unbidden and unusual, slides through me at the sheer terror on her face.

"You could have told me you wanted to go in a gods-damned barrow, Sword." Her brow furrows, anger pulling her lips into a thin slash across her face. Blue wode light makes her pale skin appear ethereal, her red hair nearly purple, her pink lips now ripe as summer berries. "You thought I wouldn't figure it out?" She gestures to the line of human skulls with rictus grins smiling down at us from their eternal perches on the walls.

"Why? Would you have decided to stay on the mountainside?" I raise an eyebrow.

"No, but you could have warned me where we were going." She huffs and crosses her arms over her chest.

So very human.

"Then you expect too much from one like me." I watch her carefully, but the warning doesn't seem to register.

There's nothing I can do to block the machinations of fate, no matter if I would prefer a different ending.

My whims and desires have never been taken into account. Why would they be now, after all this time?

Her hand tightens on my arm, forcing me to shelve my thoughts and look away from the blue-lit tunnel ahead.

"Next time, let me know what the plan is, that way I can prepare myself." There's a firm edge to Kyrie's voice and I wait for the pulse magic that will make it an order, that I'm sure will follow—but it doesn't. "That way I can help. I know you despise me, you've made that clear, but until we fulfill the vows we stupidly made to each other, we are partners in this. I can tell you haven't worked alongside many, and I won't lie, I prefer to work alone, too. But our success depends on both of us now, and I would very much like to stay alive. That's the whole point, isn't it?"

I blink, taking in the desperation in her voice, and the fact her very mortal, very soft skin is still up against mine, warmer than the icy thin air of the barrow.

Staying alive. Is that the point?

I don't answer her question, because I don't think I have it. Not anymore.

"We'll find your cure," I say instead, harshly, shaking her off my arm and moving forward.

Unlike Kyrie, I speak the truth.

She pads along behind me, quiet yet again save for the quick sound of her feet on the tunnel floor.

"Listen, okay, I'm sorry I touched you. And I am sure you have good reason to hate Sola's followers and, er, trust me, murdering loads of us has crossed my mind more than once too. But we have to work together. That means telling me when you plan to go through a fucking Hiirek barrow. That means telling me you know how to light a fucking wode fire and that you have some kind of insane Fae magic. What else are you hiding?" Her anger grows more palpable with every sentence, and I round on her, suddenly furious with her judgment and her prying.

"Everything," I tell her curtly. "I am hiding everything, and it is not for you to question."

For a moment, the furious fire in her eyes banks at the reprimand. She's so very, very young. She lifts her chin and her mouth opens, and I know she's preparing to argue more for working together, for a fresh start between us, or some other foolish nonsense.

I step closer and she steps back, thudding into the moss-dusted stone walls of the barrow. I advance once more, and she raises her eyes to meet mine, still undeterred.

"I am hiding everything," I repeat, slowly this time, willing the words to sink into her fragile flesh, "because at the end of this quest for your life, to find the cure for a curse you willingly drank, willingly stole, I will continue to be who fate has ordained me to be, and you will continue to play the role fate gave you." Another warning. As much a riddle as anything else.

"Fine," she says slowly, her gaze darting between my eyes. "Lovely. Let's just make everything harder on ourselves. Why not? What could go wrong?"

The question she should be asking is what happens should it all go right.

"Why do you think you felt compelled to drink from it—from the chalice?"

"What do you mean?" Her face scrunches up adorably in confusion, her delicate features highlighted in the wode light. "Of course I felt compelled to drink from it. It smelled delicious, like everything I ever needed. Who wouldn't have?"

"Who wouldn't have?" A harsh laugh sputters from my throat. "The disciple that owned the chalice, and the one before him, and anyone else who had it in their possession before you came along, I presume." I stare at her, trying to get her to see the truth of it, to look beyond.

She tosses that long red infuriating braid, and I grind my teeth. "They knew it was cursed. Obviously they wouldn't have drank it."

Frustrated, I pound the tunnel wall above her head with my fist, guilt flitting through me as she flinches. "Would you still have drank it if you knew what would happen? That you'd have to free me? Work with someone like me?"

For a second, it seems as though she might answer truthfully, like she might piece together the heart of the matter.

"Of course not," she lies easily, the way one trained by the Sisters of Sola does, without a second thought, without a hint of deceit. I see past it only because I witnessed the aftermath of another silver tongue, during the last Fae war.

She tilts her chin up, her pulse thrumming in her neck. "But I did, so here we are, and the least we can do is respect one another."

"Respect is the least of my worries." I push off the wall, too aware of her scent, of the smell of her red hair and the lie in her green eyes, of the way her constellation of freckles reminds me of stars I haven't seen in over a decade.

"Staying alive is the most of mine, so if you can at least clue me in on what the hells we're doing here, I would be so honored." The word drips with sarcasm.

"The dead are nothing to be feared," I tell her. Something I've always known, and true, though not the answer I think she wants.

"No shit, they're dead. I'm more worried about whatever nasty thing's taken up residence amongst their corpses, you asshole."

Irritation rankles me, not for the first time since the incorrigible woman freed me, and certainly not for the last. "Did you forget who it is you're with?"

"The great and terrible Sword, who is so great and terrible that he refuses to tell me his own name," she says in a mocking voice. "So great and terrible that he doesn't even have a sword besides the one swinging between his legs, likely doing all the thinking for him as well—"

My irritation erupts.

"Maybe if you spent as much time thinking about why we're here as you have about my cock you wouldn't annoy me with your petulant questions."

"You wish I was thinking about your cock, *Sword*," she retorts.

My fists clench at my sides.

The problem is, I do wish that. It would make things much easier if she were pliant and amenable to me.

But she's not, nor am I to her, so I banish the thought, and hope to never suffer it again.

II

KYRIE

It's just so easy to needle him. Really, it's too much fun.

I've said I like to work alone, and mostly, I do, but there is something very satisfying about being able to annoy the Sword whenever I get bored. Especially when he's such an easy target.

He's silent after my latest barb, predictably about his sword again, and I can't help grinning to myself.

The direcat bumps my back, bringing up the rear of our ridiculous little trio.

The wode light he conjured is strange, the blue fire lining the walls burning cool and preternaturally, but I'm not naive enough to be afraid of it, or afraid of the corpses buried here with them.

It is concerning, though, that the Sword has enough power to summon a spell like that so easily.

The wode light, if I remember correctly, is made from Fae

spells... or is it considered a godly gift? I shake my head, because it doesn't matter. The Fae are long gone, and if there are any still around, they certainly don't concern themselves with the matters of Heska.

The gods are another matter.

Still.

It's strange. Odd.

So is his aggravating preoccupation with the chalice. My nose scrunches and I kick at a bit of bluish-green moss on the tunnel floor, still annoyed with myself for drinking out of it.

Would I have done any differently had I known?

I bite my lip, because that's the real thing that has me out of sorts.

I never even considered not drinking it.

I never even truly regretted tasting it. The mere memory of the sip sends a pleasurable shiver down my spine. Sure, I was furious with myself once I figured out it had done something to me, but then I went to Lara, and now I have the Sword, and we're going to figure out a solution.

It's all going to be fine. My breath hitches. For the first time, true concern tightens my chest, making it hard to draw breath.

It is going to be fine, right?

Or have I been lying to the most important person of all... myself? My fingers scrabble across my blouse, and I try to loosen the ties at my throat, too hot.

What if it's not all fine? I'm in a barrow, with a... male of unknown descent, who hates me. What if my time has run out?

What if I'm going to die, right here in this blue-lit barrow, with the direcat and the fucking Sword as my only companions? Not even Mushroom with me.

Will the direcat eat me if I drop dead right here?

A harsh laugh bounces around the wode-lit tunnel, and too late, it hits me that it's mine.

"Steady," the Sword says slowly.

We've both stopped our downward progress. My hands shake, and I stare at them in dismay.

"Breathe, woman."

His hands are on my shoulders. When did his hands get on my shoulders?

"Breathe, Kyrie. I won't let you die here. I told you already: I am no vow-breaker."

I can't. I can't breathe. I shake my head, and the direcat pushes against my shoulder with his whiskered face.

"Breathe, Kyrie. Breathe," the Sword commands, patiently, yes, but there's an obscene undertone of ordering me around that grates on me just enough to help stem the rising panic.

"Good," he nods, like he managed to calm me with the bare-bones directive to inhale.

I stare at a skull above his head. Bare bones. Heh.

The direcat's purring up a storm, and I half expect the walls to shake with the force of it. I scowl at the Sword, but he's already turned around, all broad shoulders and swaggering walk.

Ugh.

"Since you asked so nicely," the Sword says, and I blink. I didn't ask anything, nicely or otherwise. "I left certain... items here that I knew I would want when I finally left Cottleside."

Oh. He's answering my question.

"Left?" I attempt to scoff, but it comes out high-pitched and shaky. I cough. "I freed you. You didn't just waltz out of there."

The slight stiffening of his shoulders tells me he's irritated by my comment, and I don't expect him to respond... but he does.

"Yes. You freed me before... I didn't expect to be freed."

My eyes widen, and I glance behind me at the direcat, who's bringing up the rear like this entire expedition is the most normal thing in the world.

Maybe it is. I don't know what direcats get up to.

I make a mental note to do some asking around on direcats at the next town we hit.

"I told you before, I deserved to pay penance for my crime against... your sisters."

He drags the last word out, like it's foul on his tongue but he can't quite get the taste off.

"I've never understood that," I interrupt. "The Sisters of Sola. The Sisterhood." My mouth twitches to the side. I wanted him to talk to me, and now I'm the one cutting him off. Typical silver tongue bullshit. I shrug one shoulder because I might as well say my heretical piece. I doubt that bitch goddess Sola is listening anyway.

Maybe we're too far down the barrow for her to hear.

"They were never sisters to me," I continue, babbling now, sudden nerves getting the best of me. "Or brothers. Never family. They made me watch—" My throat gets thick, but there's something about the blue wode light that keeps me talking. Or maybe it's simply having Sword as a captive audience. Maybe it's simply feeling like I need to finally say it out loud. "They made me watch, you know? When they killed my family. Told me: *'Look, little girl. See how they can't help you now. We're the only ones who can help you now, Silver Tongue. They'd be your servants and slaves, they would hate you, but we'll teach you control.'*"

I draw in a long breath, trying to comfort myself, trying to ground myself in this moment, because I don't talk about that. What the hells has gotten into me? I don't get nervous and just drop that memory.

I'm off kilter, out of sorts... and I wonder if the curse is to blame.

"Fucking Sola," the Sword rumbles.

His curse surprises me. Not the hatred in it, because that's never been in question, nor the disgust, because he's made that clear as well.

But the pity in the two words—for me.

"Why? Why did you swear to her? Serve her?"

"I chose to live," I answer simply, without a second thought. "I could have let them kill me too, any number of times. And it's selfish, and I know that, but I chose to live. I chose me, and I'm going to keep choosing me." I swallow, the fear in my mother's eyes—green eyes, like mine—still haunting me after all these years in forced service to Sola.

The last word she mouthed at me, her voice silenced by the knife wound in her throat.

"Live. Kyrie, live."

The sisters called it a favor to me. Made me work for them to pay my debt to them, my debt for freeing my family from my... peculiar Sola-gifted magic.

I wipe the back of my hand over my cheek, unsurprised to find it wet. Tears are a weakness, the sisters said. Tears are punished.

"And still you weep for them," the Sword says, face curious.

It's not until then that it dawns on me: I must have spoken the last bit out loud, too.

"Your tears are not wasted on the dead. Your compassion is not wasted on the living," he says softly.

I want to make a joke, to reclaim some of that hard shell that's mysteriously failed me, but I don't. I'm too empty, like the memory's hollowed me out and scraped me to the bone.

It must be the curse at work.

"Here," he says abruptly, and the blood-soaked memories disappear back into the past where they belong. "We're here."

My eyes go wide, because holy pantheon of Heskan gods, this is the sort of treasure room I would have staked my life on to access.

I move forward, clocking precious artefacts and relics draped over stone tombs and dangling from overloaded wooden chests, crumbling in the damp dark. Rubies glint purple in the wode light, and I crouch next to a jewel-crusted pendant with the likeness of some long-dead Fae etched onto its gilded surface. I frown at it, mesmerized by the pointed ears, the graceful cheekbone and sweep of the jaw.

"I need the chalice," the Sword says, unmoved by the riches all around us.

Must be nice.

"The chalice?" I repeat.

"You," he answers.

I squint at him. "What?"

"The chalice. You are now the chalice."

"Are you feeling well? Did you hit your head?"

"You drank the contents. You hold the contents still."

"Stop talking in riddles and tell me what the hells you want." I feign a yawn, and it turns into the real thing.

He blinks, waiting.

I raise my eyebrows.

"Your blood," he finally answers.

"You can't be serious."

"Serious as the grave." He knocks on one of the stone tombs.

My jaw drops, and I huff a laugh. "Did you just make a joke? My gods, there might be hope for you yet."

He knocks on the stone tomb again, ignoring me, and I roll

my eyes. Clearly, he wouldn't know a joke if it grabbed his sword in the middle of the night and called it hard.

With a mighty shove and an annoyingly masculine grunt, the stone top of the tomb slides off and the Sword wipes his palms together, dust clouding the air in front of him.

"Your blood," he repeats, one dark eyebrow raised in challenge.

"Your blood," I counter. "Why does it have to be mine? I'm attached to it."

He snorts, and that stops me in my tracks. He might not have been making a joke earlier, but he did just laugh at mine.

I purse my lips. "You must really want my blood."

"I don't want it." He jerks his head at the inside of the tomb. "He will, though."

I can't help myself. I stand, walking towards the open stone coffin. Curiosity really should kill this cat, but I just keep on living. My mouth scrunches to the side as I reflect on that. Living… for now.

"There better be something really great in there," I tell him. "Something I can sell."

I climb up the two-step dais to where the Sword stands, reaching out to brace myself against the stone structure for balance.

The Sword grabs my hand, quick as a flash, before I have time to react, pinning my wrist against the lip of the coffin.

It should be impossible for anyone to move that fast.

"Give your permission," he all but snarls at me.

"For you to take my blood?" I ask sweetly, unnerved but not nearly enough to give him the satisfaction of seeing it. Blue light turns his features even less human.

"For the blood to give us answers." He stares into my eyes, and dread curls in my belly. There is something… so inhuman in them. Unfathomable. Dark.

"You have my permission," I say on an exhale, unable to stand the pressure of his gaze.

Instead, I look into the coffin, where something very dead is staring up at me.

And it blinks.

12

THE SWORD

The sooner Kyrie understands that I am not like her, not at all, the better. The sooner she falls into line and understands her role in this age-old dance of gods, the easier it will be. For both of us.

So I let it slip into my face.

What I am. Who I am.

And she looks right back at me, without the terror or tears that most mortals would show. Instead, she gives permission, and it infuriates me even more.

She should be afraid. A weak, short-lived creature such as she should be quailing, and yet, she persists.

Admiration and respect take root in spite of myself.

I should keep hating her.

It will be easier in the end if I can dig out those feelings before they bloom into something more, no matter what fate expects. It will be easier for both of us.

Kyrie glances back up at me expectantly, though her face is

even paler, her freckles standing out like morning stars against her skin.

"Well? Are we doing this or what?" she snaps out, all fire, though even my dulled senses can scent her fear at what I'm about to do.

The direcat paces on the dust-covered stone behind us, a low growl in its throat.

It takes me by complete surprise: the urge to comfort her, to tell her she is going to be alright, that she has nothing to fear from the dead in this crypt.

And I know in the same heartbeat that no matter how hard I push her away, how solidly I construct a wall of malice between us, it's too late.

She's already under my skin.

Anger rises at the immutability of fate, of what I'll have to do to this... *mortal* who's already crawled her way into my life and made herself at home.

She hasn't pulled away from my grip, just waits patiently, a lamb to the slaughter.

I take her wrist, raise it to my mouth. Kyrie doesn't falter, doesn't pull away, barely flinches as I press my teeth to the thin skin there and rip at it, the warm salt of her blood flooding my mouth.

Flooding my being—with her power. Opposite of mine, full of life, the song of the chalice mingling with her own magic in a heady flow. My body trembles, and though the moment lasts less than a split second, it feels like a lifetime.

I regain enough of my senses to push her bleeding arm away from me, then fit her body into mine, her back rigid with tension as I lean her over the stone crypt, letting the hot trickle of her potent blood dribble into the mouth of the dead.

"Power from mortal willingly given," I chant, the words as familiar as the day I wrote the spell. "Pact with the dead unwillingly made. Order and chaos together unriven. Death is ordered to give aid."

Power surges between Kyrie and me, but a soft gasp is the only sign she gives that she feels it.

I close my eyes briefly, as though that can block out the soft way her body melts against mine.

Focus.

If this doesn't make her turn away from me in utter disgust, if this doesn't see her running from me, then nothing will.

She'll run. Mortals can't stand to be in the presence of death.

The corpse twitches. Its eyes, which should be long rotted away, are cloudy orbs in too-large sockets, and its eyelids blink slowly as the spell takes hold.

"Who calls me?" His voice is raspy, and the sound echoes more in the cavern of my own skull than in any real capacity.

Kyrie cringes against me, but I hold her tight, keeping her wound positioned over the corpse's mouth. More crimson blood drops from her wound, and the corpse blinks again, the spirit held in this barrow coming more into focus.

Recognition dawns in my old servant's eyes, and I realize I've made a significant error.

"It does not matter who we are." The words boom out of me, an order and a plea.

"Of course it does," the spirit answers. "But I died to serve."

I wince at that.

Kyrie's breaths are ragged and fast, and still, she doesn't fight, but submits to the current of power running through us both, fueling the magic.

She is braver than I gave her credit for. Much braver than any of Sola's chosen I've been unfortunate enough to meet.

"We have need of the knowledge you keep," I say thickly,

because one wrong answer, one wrongly worded question, and this servant of Death could make things much, much harder.

"Speak your need," he grates, the spirit gaining energy from Kyrie and me, the face of the corpse more animated now. "I died to serve."

I glare at the spirit's eyes from over Kyrie's trembling shoulder.

He grins, the skin splitting along his lips. He knows exactly what he's doing.

"We seek the cure," I say simply. "There is an instrument I need."

"Which?" the corpse interrupts, then wheezes a laugh. "You have grown even more obtuse in your old age."

"Glad to see I'm not the only one annoyed by you," Kyrie mutters.

I tighten my grip on her waist and she stills. Pleasure, unbidden, crawls up my spine. Not from the task at hand, at using my dark powers to locate the artefact hidden from my sight or from bidding the dead, but from Kyrie herself.

From the warm heat of her body, the scent of her hair, the smell of her life's blood.

"Chaos and order, lies and truth, death and desire, gods and gold, Sword and Silver Tongue," the corpse laughs again, and Kyrie shivers.

I am well and truly fucked.

"I need Sola's Crown. To save the woman. I've sworn an oath to render her aid. Where is it?"

"Do your eyes not see? Have you changed so much since we last spoke?" The corpse inhales, desiccated tongue flickering from his mouth.

Kyrie gags, but she doesn't pull away.

"You have changed. I feel it now." His death grin splits the mockery of flesh clinging to his bones.

"Where is the Crown of Sola? You are sworn in death to serve," I say, nearly adding the words that will give it all away.

Give me away.

"The crown is in the spired city. It no longer rests in vaunted halls of yore. Many-eyed Sola watches while you scurry. To deceive the King of Diamonds, you'll need four more."

"Fucking riddles," I swear, and the corpse wheezes again, clearly amused. "Say what you mean."

The corpse sits up, eyes flashing, clearing, dust clouding around him.

Belatedly, I realize we've fed him too much power.

Between the chalice and Kyrie and even my dwindling magic, he's taking advantage of the link.

"You died to serve," I thunder, rage building, rage at my own impotence, my fall from grace—

And then Kyrie is in motion, slashing with daggers, sawing at the dried tendons.

"Fuck this," she snaps, then simply vaults into the crypt, smashing the corpse's head in with the heel of her boot in a sickening crunch.

I blink.

Her chest heaves as she stares at me, holding her bloody wrist to her stomach.

She's going to truly hate me now. This is always what makes the mortals turn on me, this dark power, the gift of parting the veil between worlds.

"That was sick," she says, tilting her head. "Wicked magic trick, though. You'd be a real asset to a thief, you know? Maybe we should discuss extending our partnership once we find a cure."

"I..." I don't know what to say to that.

"No, seriously, that was fantastic. I wish I knew how to do

that. It would make my life so much easier." Her voice drops a few octaves. "Tell me where the treasure is. You died to serve," she booms in an enthusiastic, if overwrought, imitation of me.

"He didn't tell us anything useful," I say, frowning. "He was no help at all."

Kyrie furrows her brow at me before jumping out of the coffin and back onto the floor. "Ew," she says, her lip curling in disgust as she scrapes the sole of her heel along the stone step. A slimy substance oozes from it. "That's seriously so disgusting. Great work."

"How was that great?" I raise my hands, frustrated with her taunting and with myself, with the clear evidence that I'm fading as quickly as the silver tongue's curse continues to spread.

"What are you talking about? He told us exactly where to go to find the Crown of," her voice drops, "well, of you know. Her." She cringes, and I realize she doesn't want to say Sola's name.

She's afraid of her own goddess.

I study her for a moment longer, the way she holds herself and stares defiantly at me.

No, it's more than fear. Kyrie isn't without faith. Kyrie believes—it's simply that she despises Sola.

My throat constricts.

The more I learn about this mortal—about Kyrie—the clearer it becomes that fate will be impossible to defy.

13

KYRIE

I run my hands through the direcat's soft fur, trying to center myself, trying to regain some semblance of calm.

That was... I've seen a lot of things, but I've never seen a dead body talk, much less sit up.

I've never pounded a skull in with my foot, either, and I would very much like to shower off whatever other remnants cling to me as soon as possible.

I clear my throat instead.

The Sword is into some dark shit. That was a whole other level of magic. I certainly could make use of it... if I manage to live.

Narrowing my eyes, I loosen my grip on the direcat, who's purring thunderously at all my attention.

"You didn't understand what our favorite new friend said?"

The Sword is pacing back and forth on the highest step next to the stone crypt.

I suppress a shudder. Our favorite new friend was a nasty piece of work.

His gaze swings to me, unknowable, then away again. "How could I know what any of that means? The King of Diamonds? The spired city? It's nonsense. Gibberish."

My face scrunches up in confusion. "Are you being serious? It's completely obvious."

"Oh, of course it is," he huffs, amused by me.

Except I'm not joking. This time, anyway. My foot taps against the floor, and I cringe when it sticks slightly.

Nasty piece of work, indeed. And now that nastiness is all over my favorite pair of winter boots. Also known as my only pair of winter boots.

"How long were you in Cottleside again?" I ask, confused by his confusion.

"Too long, too long I was away from the world," he shakes his head, something odd in his tone.

"Ri-ight." I stretch out the word. "Well, the King of Diamonds is worse than that fucker I just stepped on," I jerk my thumb at the tomb behind the Sword. "The spired city is where he lives and runs his stupid little cohort of mercenaries and thieves."

"Thieves?" He glances at me again, then his attention slides away just as quickly.

I look down at myself, wondering what it is he finds so suddenly offensive about my appearance. Maybe it's the wound he bit open.

"Did you have to bite me?" I poke at the jagged tear in my wrist. I'll have to put a poultice on that. Goddess only knows where that male's mouth has been.

The sound of his footsteps stops.

"Yes," he grinds out. "I did."

"Charming ritual. I could have used my daggers—"

"I just said I had to bite you. Your daggers wouldn't have worked."

"Sure." I lean against the direcat, grinning up at him. He's clearly annoyed and frustrated, and I'd be even more of a liar if I said I wasn't enjoying seeing him out of sorts. "Or maybe you just wanted to put your mouth on me."

His attention jerks to my face, then slides down to the wrist I'm still cradling against me.

"I mean," I drawl lazily, "I don't know what kind of weird sexual stuff you're into, but I'd prefer if you didn't bite me until I bleed next time. A little love bite is fine, you know? A little rough, sure, but not that rough."

His cheeks pinken, and my jaw nearly drops in shock.

Got him.

I just... didn't expect his embarrassment would be so... cute.

"It did not give me pleasure to hurt you," he says in a low voice, then pivots away from me, continuing his pacing.

The direcat shoots me a mischievous look, like it understands, and I swear, this animal is way more intelligent than it should be.

"Whatever you need to tell yourself," I say seriously, knowing it will bug him even more.

"Where is the spired city?" he demands.

If he thinks I'm not going to press my advantage, he's wrong. I nearly laugh.

"Please," I say instead.

"What?" He stops pacing, staring me down.

"Ask nicely," I tell him mildly.

"Do you forget that we are doing this to end your curse?" His face is furious.

I sigh, rolling my eyes. "Of course not. But is it a life worth living if I can't have fun making the dark death knight who hates me even more annoyed?"

He opens his mouth, and I hold up a finger. "Don't answer that."

His eyes flash, and I can't hold in my laughter anymore.

"Fine, fine, the spired city is Nyzbern. Obviously." I drag out the word, enjoying his discomfort very much. "The King of Diamonds won't be happy to see me, though." My lips twist to the side as I think back to what the dead person said. "Was that possession? It wasn't really talking, whatever that was."

"Something like that," he mutters testily. "Need four more."

"Ugh, yeah." Four more. "Maybe we can bring Lara."

"Another thief?"

"No, more than one thief's a crowd," I tell him. "You can't trust thieves."

"My thoughts exactly," he interrupts darkly.

"You can't trust thieves other than me." I blow out a breath. "We swore an oath, or did you already forget? No, no more thieves. Lara's a mage. Precognition, a seer, all that Nakush magic woo-woo." I wiggle my fingers. "She's the one who told me to find you."

"A mage helped you?" He gawks at me, which is a new expression for him, and I would laugh at him if his disbelief weren't so rude.

"Lara is my friend." I pull the leather cord off the end of my braid, shaking out my hair and running my fingers through it. I can't quite rid myself of the crawling sensation on my scalp.

"A mage... is your friend?"

"At least I have friends." I smile up at him. "Ones that are alive, at least." He scowls.

Heh.

"And why, exactly, won't the King of Diamonds be happy to see you?"

I blow out a breath, then put my hands on my hips, ignoring the twinge of pain in my wrist.

"Well, because he wanted to marry me, and you see, I might have, ah, left in the middle of the night with the engagement ring." I wink outrageously, and to my surprise, the Sword does not look amused.

Or irritated.

"Fine. Not just the engagement ring. I might have stolen a bit more than that."

No, definitely not amused. He looks *furious*.

"Don't get mad at me, the so-called King of Diamonds is a real piece of shit, and everyone knows you can't polish a turd." I shrug one shoulder. "He got what he deserved. Don't feel bad for the man. He's horrible. You'll see." It comes out slightly defensive.

"You were betrothed to... a horrible... man?"

I cross my arms against my chest, hugging myself. "I was younger. He seemed like an easy mark."

Seemed was the operative word.

I touch my ribs reflexively. They didn't heal as fast as the rest.

"He has a crew of mercenaries and thieves?" The Sword strokes his chin, the shadow of a beard there.

"Yeah. His treasury is very well-guarded."

"You've been inside it?"

"Of course I have. Why do you think I told him I'd marry him?"

The Sword's jaw twitches.

"Fine, I get it, you don't like that I broke off my vow to marry him and robbed him blind. I'm so bad, evil thief and all that." My cheeks puff out as I blow out a breath.

"You know how to get inside the treasury?"

Oh. He's not asking about my broken engagement. "Yes, though I doubt it's the same as when I lived there."

A vein ticks in his forehead. "You lived with this... King of Diamonds?"

"Engaged, remember?" Gods, he must be ancient if he thinks unmarried people don't live together. Ancient and out of touch.

He's ancient and waiting for an answer, his bare foot tapping impatiently on the floor.

"Ugh. Yes. It was horrible." I shake my head, my hair falling all around me. "He throws so many lavish parties, but he's incredibly dull. He gave himself that name, you know? Who does that?" I dust off a spot of gods-knows-what from my green cloak. "He puts on an elaborate masquerade every winter; it's this ridiculous overblown ball with all the nobility of Heska coming from miles away, and a two-day feast..."

He's staring at me with increasing intensity. I nudge a rock on the floor with my boot. Ew. Still sticky.

"A midwinter masque?" he asks.

"You have heard of it!" I throw my hands up. "Why would you let me go on and on about it if you already knew it was called the midwinter masque?"

"I didn't."

I pause. "I told him to change the name, that it was too on the nose—"

"Kyrie," the Sword grates out my name, and I go still. Maybe it's the magic he worked through us, maybe it's the vows we've sworn... maybe it's something else, but I don't finish what I'm saying.

I wait, and I listen.

"When is midwinter?"

My nose scrunches, and I mentally tabulate the days since I left Lara's cottage.

"Two weeks," I say on an exhalation, slapping my forehead.

"That's when we'll steal Sola's Crown."

"Why do we need it?" I ask. "You haven't told me what it's for. How do you even know we need it?"

"We need something of Sola's to break the curse. Pure chaos."

My mouth twitches to the side as I consider it. "Huh. They didn't teach us magic like that."

"Then I suppose it's good you found me." His dark eyes find my gaze.

"Two weeks. Midwinter masque, steal the crown from his treasury. It could work, Sword. It could be a great plan." I tap my finger against my chin, thinking hard. "We need four more. Ugh. Six is so many people."

He smiles at me, his teeth even, and a dimple creases on his cheek.

My knees go a little weak. It's the first time he's smiled at me.

I didn't expect it to completely melt my brain.

I definitely didn't expect the dimple.

"Four more," he says, walking down the steps. "Four more to join us for a masquerade ball, where we will steal Sola's Crown from the King of Diamonds."

"I really hate that name. So tacky."

"Any ideas on who should join us?" The Sword swaggers past me to a huge stone statue in the back of the room, one whose face is covered in darkness, the wode light failing to fully illuminate it. The only thing visible is the massive broadsword in the statue's hands, the tip of which rests on the stone floor, between two bare feet.

A huge stone casket rests behind it, and that's the coffin the Sword now busies himself about, moving the stone lid off, his muscles straining.

I fan my face.

I've never been averse to a good show. The one he's putting on, all glistening skin and rippling biceps and deep grunts... it's pretty damned good.

"Do you need help?" I finally ask, pink tinging my cheeks. He doesn't bother looking at me, thank goddess, because if he did, he might realize that I've been staring at him this whole time. Ogling him, even.

"No," he says tersely.

The direcat coughs, and it sounds suspiciously like a laugh.

"Suit yourself." I'm not miffed by his refusal. Nope. He might be a bigger jackass than Mushroom, but he *is* nice to look at. And if I can appreciate his very masculine beauty and not work up a sweat, all the better.

Conserving energy and all that.

His muscles strain again, and I raise my eyebrows. If I lick my lips a little, so what?

Finally, unfortunately, the lid of the casket moves far enough that he can access whatever's inside.

My interest piqued, I amble over to him, half expecting him to have that typical sweaty-man stink, but one sniff proves different. He smells sweaty, yes, but... he smells good.

I squint at him, slightly off kilter.

"Are you about to introduce me to another rotten friend?" I pause, grinning at my joke. If I can't depend on myself to be my own best audience, then who can I depend on? "You know, I've probably said that before but I've never meant it literally. Thanks for that."

He doesn't answer, and I glance past his ridiculously handsome face into the tomb.

"That's more like it," I say, rubbing my hands together. "No bones about it, huh?"

He shoots me a pained look.

There's no body in this one—instead, it's full of... weapons. And at first, I thought that shiny stuff was silver or jewels or something fun.

It's not, though, it's armor. Not like any armor I've ever seen before, though.

My nose scrunches as the Sword pulls out a pair of gleaming gauntlets, then a matching pair of pauldrons with unlikely spikes protruding from their tops.

Greaves and cuisses follow, though they're less showy, more solidly functional. I stare at the pile of steel on the floor, the Sword still rooting around in the tomb.

"You seem to be missing a few key pieces."

He grunts.

"Besides your poor conversational skills, I mean. Where is the breastplate? The helm? Also, you're not exactly going to blend in with these." I nudge the spiked pauldrons with my foot. Then regret it because they hardly move and now my inner thigh hurts in return for my effort. Ugh.

"I don't need them."

It takes me a minute to register what he's said, still hanging over the tomb, pulling strange things out.

"What? You don't need a breastplate?" I snort, tapping my fingers along my arms. "Of course you don't. It's not like that's where the important bits are stored."

"I'm not like you," he says in a low voice, and I puzzle over that for a second before laughing again.

"Yeah, I know, you're not human. But Fae still bleed. Or elves, or whatever it is you are." I peer at him. "What are you, anyway?"

"Not like you," he repeats.

"Thank goddess we're adding some members to our team. Your powers of conversation are sorely lacking."

"I have other powers," he says, and a heap of leather joins the armor on the floor.

"Yes, that very handy power of calling spirits to communicate. I have to say, it was a lot showier than what my friend Lara does."

The statement triggers a realization about his powers. He isn't human. His magic doesn't work the same way.

Something about that... is important, and I work at it, trying to gauge why my mind's fixated on that, when a cloth pouch clinks onto the floor and the sound completely banishes any philosophical wanderings.

"Money," I say on an exhale, crouching and scooping it up. "Heavy." I weigh it, my lips twisting to the side, trying to calculate exactly how much we're looting from this crypt. "Do you often desecrate the houses of the dead?" I ask conversationally. "I thought followers of Hrakan respected these places."

"The dead have no need of it. The god of the dead knows that better than anyone."

My brow furrows because that's not what we were taught in Chast. The followers of Hrakan are known to be territorial about their sacred crypts and barrows.

I guess because they're using them as storage stations.

Clever.

"Do all the barrows in Heska have treasure waiting for Hrakan's followers to use?"

"What I am allowed to do and what a follower of another god is permitted to do are not the same," he answers, voice devoid of emotion.

I shrug. "Just curious, Sword. Just curious."

"You are planning to loot the tombs as soon as we are able to complete the chalice's curse."

"You mean cure the chalice's curse," I correct. I loose the drawstring on the coin pouch, dipping a hand in and testing the weight of the coins, then let them slip back into the pouch. "Ah, my favorite sound." We should be able to hire help with the King of Diamonds with this much money. Four more won't be a problem. Neither will buying food, and I breathe a sigh of relief.

I love it when a plan comes together. I love it even more when I have money to spend that isn't mine.

"Complete, cure. Your Heskan language is not the same as mine."

I narrow my eyes at him, tying the heavy coin pouch onto my knife belt. For safekeeping. "Completing the curse means I die. Let's not complete it. Those are very different words, no matter the language."

"How many languages do you speak?" he asks.

Oh gods. He's taken off his threadbare shirt. His chest is a latticework of scars, standing out in stark relief against his muscles.

"Like what you see?" he asks in a harsh voice.

For the span of an inhalation, I think he's realized I'm attracted to him, which, frankly, is disgusting. He's awful.

"The work of your sisters," he adds, violence in his voice.

"Oh. No," I shake my head, embarrassed in earnest now. "No. Wait. What do you mean, my sisters? Didn't you get those scars at Cottleside? From Lojad's followers?" The god of order and war is known to be a harsh one. There's no middle ground, no nuance with Lojad. I could see them meting out punishment in his name all too easily. "They've done the same to me."

He shakes his head, but I'm already moving, curious to see if the writing of Lojad's worshippers is the same on both our skins.

I tug up my blouse, not an easy task, considering everything needs a good washing and the fabric's stiff with grime and sweat. I sniff at the hem experimentally. Gross. Maybe I should have done a snow scrub last night, too.

"See?" I ask, turning my cape over one shoulder, hiking my blouse up. "Lojad's poetry." I point to the worst of the scars. "I earned this one when I was sixteen. I ran away from Sola's Sisters in Chast, slipped over the border to Sylsip, and was unlucky enough to get caught stealing from the kitchens of a lord who'd sworn himself to Lojad." The scar runs along my ribs and disappears into my lower back, and I trace it with my finger. "It was such a great meal. I was starving. Hadn't eaten in days."

The Sword exhales noisily, and I fall silent.

My gaze jumps from the white scar to his face.

His eyes are fixated on my ugly scars, and not just the one I was showing him. His chest heaves, and he takes a step closer to me.

A different, new energy dances around him and I freeze, unsure of what's wrong. "I mean, I believe you," I bite out, nervous. Which is... weird. I don't *get* nervous.

I absolutely do not get nervous around jackasses who go by the name "Sword," for crying out loud. No matter how handsome he is. No matter he's looking at my bare skin, sending waves of heat over it.

"Ugly, right?" I choke on an awkward laugh, hurriedly pulling my blouse back down.

His hand brushes against mine, sending that echo of our shared power streaking through me, making me still, hardly breathing.

He pulls the hem of my blouse back up. I'm holding my breath, captivated. Wondering what he'll do next.

"And the rest of these scars?" His voice is a low caress, sending goosebumps pebbling across my skin.

This is dangerous. He's too close, too large, too interested in the marks that tell the story of my upbringing with the Sisters of Sola, like they're some code to be deciphered.

Like they're the key to understanding me.

I start to elbow his hand away, but then he touches me—touches the scars that ruin the smooth, freckled skin of my back—and I can't move.

"This is the work of your goddess." It's not a question, and I don't need to answer.

Not like I could, anyway.

"Her handmaids, at least," I say, my voice thin and breathy and not at all like me.

I step back, and the strange spell breaks.

"Lovely people, your sisters," he says in a voice that tells me he thinks anything but that.

"Don't get much of a say in family," I shrug. "My fate was sealed when they slit my mother's throat in front of me."

Live, little bird. Live.

His gaze never leaves my face, dark eyes boring into me, no hint of the smile that transformed him earlier.

This is the Sword.

This is the male that slaughtered dozens upon dozens of my sworn sisters.

There's no sympathy there to even look for.

"Right," I say, choking out a laugh. It sounds like a sob. "Sorry about that."

He reaches out to me, like he might hold my chin in his hand, like he wants to touch me—but draws back.

"This is not your fault to apologize for."

I tear my gaze away from him, feeling like some piece of me's been stripped away, raw and tender.

Vulnerable isn't an emotion I'm familiar with.

Vulnerability gets you killed, or hurt, or whipped by the

women who raised you or the man who caught you, starving, with a crust of bread.

"Right." I clear my throat. "What else do you need from here? We don't have a lot of time to gather a crew and make a plan for the midwinter masque."

He hasn't looked away from me.

I can't tell what he's thinking.

I can usually read people very well.

He's right about one thing, though. He's not human.

"Just one thing besides all this." He waves at the armor and packs on the floor, then tugs the black shirt in his hands over his head.

"Alright, where? What is it?"

I avert my eyes as he pulls his prison pants off, donning a pair of soft black leather trousers. He doesn't answer right away and I turn around, out of sorts and still... warm from the way he touched me.

He keeps touching me.

Last night, when he held me, keeping me quiet after the direcat.

Today, when he held me against him, using our combined magic to wake the dead.

"You," he finally answers.

My molars grind together at the simple word.

"You're the key to my plans," he continues.

"Then let's get them started," I call over my shoulder. The armor's over his shoulder, black leather boots climbing his calf, a broadsword I missed now slung in a sheath between his shoulders. The pommel stands out behind him, a black stone set in the center, a stark contrast against his silver white hair. He looks good in black.

He's the key to my plans, too.

Finding a cure is the only thing that matters.

14

KYRIE

The days spent descending from the Hiirek Mountains pass quickly. We hardly spoke to each other as we trekked downhill, navigating the snowy passes in concentrated silence, then too tired to do more talking than necessary at night.

He didn't touch me again.

Not once.

Not in our shared tent, and not when I nearly broke my face open on a patch of icy gravel, tearing open my palms for my trouble.

I don't want him to touch me again, anyway.

That would be stupid of both of us. There might be something... physical there, but we couldn't be worse for each other. Our gods would never approve of any dallying between us, either.

In fact, they'd probably make our lives more hellish just to amuse themselves.

Not that I even like him.

I frown, holding the reins of my horse too tight. We managed to find a home nestled in the wild Hiirek foothills willing to sell us two horses this morning. The direcat made itself scarce as soon as we approached even that far-flung bastion of civilization, and I'm surprised to find I miss the furry cat already.

The horse under me snorts, flinging its head. There's no way either horse is the three years they claimed them to be, but the Sword and I managed to barter them down from their original, outlandish price.

"We could have stolen them tonight," I tell him from the ancient saddle they threw in. It's good leather though, and comfortable. Mushroom follows complacently behind us, loaded down with the Sword's armor and the rest of the things we liberated from the tomb.

"They would know it was us." His horse is massive, likely a former farm animal, with black feathered hoofs and a greying muzzle.

"That's half the fun. I have a reputation to uphold." I toss my hair, and he looks at me for a half-second too long.

"We don't have time to wait till nightfall. We're running out of time as it is."

"I mean, what's the worst that could happen if we don't make it to the masque on time?" I haven't said this out loud, but I'm worried. "We could steal the crown any other time."

He doesn't answer, and I glance over at him.

It's a lot easier to talk now that the horses are doing the hard work. My mare's gait is entirely different than Mushroom's, though, and I have a feeling my ass is going to be sore later. Still. Better than slicing my face and palms open on the Heskan ground.

I need my face. It's my best asset. Everyone trusts a pretty face. It's human nature.

"Not answering isn't really doing a lot for my confidence." A tickle starts in my throat and I cough once. Twice. A few more times, for good measure.

The fit finally stops. I exhale slowly, strangely tired.

I feel him staring at me, and when I look over at him, his brow is furrowed.

"What?" I ask, all aggression.

"You have been doing that a lot."

"Coughing? I have not."

"You have. Since we woke up yesterday morning."

"Well, I've been wandering around in the fucking snow for a week now." It comes out defensively, and his brow just furrows more. "I probably sucked up some dead body dust when I smashed your corpse friend's face in."

My nose wrinkles, and I really wish I could unthink that. I don't want to have any dead body dust in my not dead body.

"That's not why you're coughing," he says, then swigs from a canteen.

"Thank the gods," I say expansively. "I really don't like the idea of parts of your old pal making me cough."

The Sword grins and I smile back, unable not to thanks to that damned dimple.

Could I even be getting used to him?

He seems more normal. Something about living with him the past few days, even silently existing with him, has rubbed off most of his otherness.

I mean, yes, he dislikes me, that's still clear, seeing as how I catch him watching me with murder in his gaze more often than not. But we've reached some unspoken truce, and now he's smiling at me.

Things are looking up.

"No, it is not grave dust that's been making you sick—"

"Why do I get the feeling you're about to tell me something I don't want to know?" All my good feeling towards him stops abruptly.

"You are not stupid. You know why you're coughing as well as I do."

"I don't *know* anything," I tell him grumpily. "Not for sure."

"Fine. You may not know it, but you can guess, can you not?"

I blow a breath out, sending wisps of my red hair flying. "Nope."

"Pretty little liar," he says, still grinning at me... until the smile melts off, that murderous look back as he remembers what I am, the goddess I am sworn to, the fact we're enemies.

Annoying. I am starting to like that smile.

Frustrated with everything, I rake a hand down my face and shrug.

"Fine. What do you want me to say? That it's the chalice's curse? That we're running out of time not just for the midwinter masque, but because that stupid drink is killing me faster than I thought?"

He doesn't answer, just kicks his heels into his horse's side, sending the great black horse pounding down the snowy trail towards Lara and Effingwich.

It's answer enough, even if it's not the answer I wanted.

Not at all.

15

THE SWORD

Effingwich.
 I haven't been here in... two centuries, I think. Maybe more. Time passes differently for me.

It certainly did not look like this the last time I was here.

Or maybe it's Kyrie next to me, on the chestnut mare that's every bit as spirited and alive as she is. Maybe it's seeing it through the mortal's green, wide-eyed gaze that endears me to it.

The village, a three days' journey from the barrow, sits in the cradle of the Hiirek Mountains, a snow-dappled valley housing the town that's somehow become much larger than I remembered.

Thatched roofs on homes rise from the Heskan earth like forest mushrooms. Smoke plumes from hundreds of stone chimneys, the scents of humans and food and all sorts of animals living in close proximity growing stronger the closer we ride to the small city.

The noise grows too, the sound of music and happy singing evident as we approach the hold.

"Is there a festival?" I scour my brain for a memory of what festival would fall now, this close to midwinter, but the knowledge eludes me. Another sign that I am not who—or what—I once was.

Letting myself fall victim to Sola, letting the lure of vengeance blind me, led to this.

I am a victim of my own hubris.

Kyrie's voice tugs me from my dark memories.

"No festival. A market day, from the looks of it." One glance shows she's positively gleeful at the prospect.

"No thievery," I tell her.

Her smile disappears, replaced by a pout. "Why not? They're only too happy to part with their coin."

"I have coin. What do you need more for?"

She coughs again, the hacking worse than ever, and when she catches her breath, her face seems paler than ever.

Fear spikes through me.

Not for her though—for me. For all of Death's followers. What happens if we don't secure the Crown of Sola in time and perform the ritual, stopping her curse?

What happens to me?

That must be why my chest aches with the thought of it.

"I'm fine," she says, all grouchy lies.

"Right. Is it a tincture you're wanting to buy?" I know the question will needle her and it does, causing her to scowl. "A health draught? An unguent?"

"Shut your mouth," she says, sassily throwing her head. Her hood slides off as a result, her hair shining in the light of the setting sun, picking up all the colors in the sky, blazing with them, brilliant and bright.

Breathtaking.

"I didn't expect you to listen," she glances sidelong at me and I belatedly snap my mouth shut, embarrassed to have been found staring at her.

The sooner we steal the crown and perform the ritual, the better. She'll hate me when it's over, and that will cure me of any rogue infatuation I have with the woman.

"Tell me about Lara," I deflect. The horses' hooves beat a staccato against the uneven cobblestones as we enter the town proper, people parting as we ride through the streets.

"Ask anything you want," a voice calls out from against one of the stone walls. "I'm always happy to host a friend of a friend."

Kyrie pulls her horse to a stop, smiling broader than I've seen the whole time I've been with her. An ugly emotion surfaces, and I frown.

"Lara, you're here to meet us," she says, clearly thrilled.

"Occupational hazard," the woman says, taking Mushroom's rope from where the mule is tied to Kyrie's horse. "Come on, you two, we have much to discuss. It will be better to do so in the warmth of my home."

"But, but—"

"No," Lara and I tell Kyrie at the same time. The raven-haired seer throws a look of amusement my way—one that fades nearly immediately, smile replaced by furrowed brows.

She knows.

A mage gifted in precognition. Of course Kyrie's closest friend would immediately see to the heart of who I truly am.

I stare at her, my lips a thin line across my face, and she dips her head in unspoken acknowledgment.

She will not tell Kyrie my secret.

Misgivings crowd my thoughts, tinged with bitter shame.

We follow her through the crowded streets to her home on the outskirts of town. Kyrie prattles at Lara nonstop, and I wrestle with the discomfort of how Kyrie's closest friend would willingly lie to her. Because Lara *knew* I wanted her to do so.

It's for the best, for the greater good. It's what's *right*.

That's what I've always told myself.

So why isn't it enough now?

❄

Lara's home is instantly familiar. The thick stone walls, the thatched roof overhead, the snug furniture and cozy fire. I set our bags inside the door, my armor clanging where it sits.

I still haven't put it on.

The main difference between Lara's home and the cottages I've been to in the last century is the size—it's rather large compared to them. There's a front area that piques my interest, done in luxurious purple cloth, the color Nakush, god of magic, prefers. Lara quickly ushers us through, but not fast enough that I miss the pantheon statues featured on a shelf near a window.

The figurine of Hrakan stares at me, sightless, as I follow the women into the interior of the cottage.

Hrakan. God of death, of time, unknowable and a fact of life nonetheless. The Friendless One, they called Hrakan.

I swallow, my attention drawn to the two now-silent women in front of me.

If Kyrie is the blazing sun, then Lara is the moon, with sleek, near-black hair and luminous brown eyes. They are near opposites, Lara's round, pretty face so different from Kyrie's sharp, angular features. Reverse sides of the same coin.

So young, too, in the way all mortals are. Smooth, unlined features, clever minds at work behind eyes full of hope.

I have few lines, too, despite my age, but compared to these two... so full of life, so new—

I feel ancient. And so very, very tired.

"Are you alright?" Lara asks. "Should we eat first? I know we're in a hurry."

Kyrie's watching me, perceptive little thing that she is. "Food is good. We are in a hurry—wait. You said we. I told you it's freakish when you act like you already know what we're going to say."

"We don't have time to waste on your preferences, Kyrie," Lara says loftily, already setting the knotted trestle table dominating the main area of the room. There are two wooden doors, and based on the exterior of the home, I assume two bedrooms that branch off from this, the main living area.

"You have done well for yourself, mage," I interrupt. "Thank you for inviting us into your home, for the hospitality of bread and salt." Formal words for a formal request.

Lara shrugs one shoulder, her hair shining like midnight where it falls over her shoulder. Kyrie's waves stand out next to hers, like they have a life of their own—outsized, like the woman who wears them.

"It's an honest living," Lara replies. "Unlike some. You're welcome to my hearth and home."

She completes the ritual words, a small magic Kyrie doesn't even seem to clock, but one that will ensure we three can trust each other here, in this space.

"Don't be rude," Kyrie huffs at her, setting a loaf of still-steaming bread on the table from where it sat cooling on shelf.

Lara swings into motion, too, the two of them clearly participating in a dance they've done countless times, weaving around each other as they place a hunk of cheese on the table, a carafe of crimson wine.

Lara pulls a pot from the fire, revealing a fragrant broth and some sort of fowl swimming in it, skin brown and crisp.

"You really outdid yourself," Kyrie tells her, smiling into the pot.

"I wasn't sure when you'd last had a good meal."

"That means a lot," Kyrie says slowly, her voice soft, and then surprises me by pulling Lara into a warm embrace. "Thank you, Lara."

Her eyes meet mine over Kyrie's shoulder. The concern I see there reflects my own.

"Already?" Lara asks me, the word mournful.

I nod.

"Stop it," Kyrie says, then coughs a little. "I am fine. We can do this."

"I thought you had more time." Lara pulls away, holding Kyrie at arms' length, staring into her stunning face like it holds the answers.

Maybe it does. Sometimes it feels like it might.

"Imagine that, a witch who can see the future who suddenly can't see your future." Kyrie gives her a lopsided grin. "Comforting."

"Your future is clouded to me. Full of darkness." Lara's voice skips an octave or two lower, and the hair on the backs of my arms stands up, Nakush's magic washing over me in a lightning rush.

I roll my head on my shoulders, trying to shake the feel of it. It's like they're here with us, like they've given their blessing for Lara to join us. I tilt my face up, letting the power flood me, refresh my senses after a hard few days on the road, and after a decade of living without the touch of magic in Cottleside.

Nakush isn't here, though, and the feeling fades a half-second later.

"Full of darkness," Kyrie repeats. "You always know just what to say to make a girl feel better."

Lara doesn't respond though, and I know why.

I know why Kyrie's future is full of darkness, too.

Better darkness than nothing, though—and the thought gives me strength.

Kyrie's future will never be full of nothing, no matter how much she hates me for it.

She turns away, grabbing several goblets from a wooden shelf, and Lara turns her sorrowful gaze on me.

There's not a shred of a doubt in my mind, not anymore.

Lara knows.

16

KYRIE

I'm fit to burst. We haven't made time to cook since that first night after I rescued the Sword from Cottleside, and we made do with the hard bread I've carried in my pack for weeks, vegetables that had seen better days, and the remains of my peppery smoked jerky.

"Lara, I love you," I tell her, rubbing a hand over my swollen stomach. "This was so good." The urge to cough hits me and I cover my mouth, trying to swallow around it.

I take a long drink of wine, letting the alcohol burn my throat and relax my chest.

I don't fool Lara or the Sword, who both watch me with matching concern.

"I don't want to talk about it," I tell them once I put my goblet down. "We're doing everything we can."

"Did you want me to pretend like I don't know why you're here, or can we cut to the chase?" Lara asks, uncharacteristically bunt.

"We can cut to the chase," I say with a sigh.

The Sword is silent as the grave.

I close one eye. Well, that expression has a different meaning since our little necromantic experiment in the barrow in the Hiirek Mountains.

"Are you drunk?" Lara asks me. "You've barely drank any wine."

"No, just thinking about how chatty the Sword's friends are," I bat my eyelashes at him and he sighs heavily, rolling his eyes in disgust.

Ah yes, back to normal, then. All's right with the world.

"Cutting to the chase," Lara says, lacing her fingers into each other. "You need the Crown of... *her* crown."

I blow out a breath I didn't know I was holding, relieved Lara didn't say the goddess's name.

"The King of Diamonds has it."

Understanding rushes across Lara's plump face. "I didn't see that. I saw a ball, dancing, you and a few others, and the crown being placed on your—"

The Sword shifts next to her, and Lara falls silent.

"On my head?" I finish for her, leaning forward on my elbows. "Why? I drank from the cursed chalice and now I have to wear that bitch's crown?"

Lara sucks a breath through her teeth at my curse. "Careful."

"She's not fucking listening," I say, pouring myself more wine. "If she is, she's enjoying my torment."

"I doubt that," the Sword says. His lips are turned up in grim amusement.

"That's because you think I lie about everything," I tip my glass at him, and a bit of wine sloshes out. Okay, maybe I am a little less sober than I assumed. "I promise you this. If the goddess that stole my life away is watching us, then she is enjoying every minute of me trying to escape my fate."

"Your life has only ever belonged to one," the Sword says, face more animated than I've seen, his teeth clenched. "It does not belong to her. Never has. Never."

I stare at him. Does he mean my life's been my own? After they slaughtered my mother, my whole family? After they stole it from me, made me swear oaths I didn't believe in?

"I never expected you to be outright cruel," I whisper. It *hurts*, too, the cruelty of his words, when he's seen the damned scars, seen the truth of my feelings, my life.

He blinks at me.

"That was beneath you." The words are jagged in my throat. My life has *never* been my own.

"I did not—" he starts.

Lara clears her throat, and he closes his mouth.

"You know the visions aren't always exact, Kyrie." She purses her lips, then refills her own goblet. "It doesn't matter. Do you worry about being so close to Alaric? What if he—"

"Alaric?" the Sword interrupts.

"That's the King of Diamonds' name." I pick at my nails, still too annoyed to look at him. "Alaric Stone. A little too much, if you ask me, but he never was one for subtlety. Or taste."

"And you agreed to marry him." The Sword leans back, crossing his arms over his chest.

I glare at him. "No, I agreed to be engaged to him, then made off with a bunch of his stupid shiny shit. And look where it got me." I look down my nose at him, a hard task considering our size difference, but I'm up to the challenge.

Lara rubs her forehead with two fingers, heaving a sigh.

My words come out through clenched teeth. "I'm going to die if I don't steal from him one more time. I have to work with a man—no, a Fae male—who clearly thinks the worst of me, and I have to bring my best friend along and hope none of us get killed for the trouble."

The Sword's shoulders sag. He doesn't seem angry anymore, or cruel. He's frowning, yes, his dark brows drawn, but he's... sad.

I am too; I'm so upset about all of this that it makes my chest hurt.

Unless that ache's just the curse.

I push my goblet of wine further away, slicing a hunk of cheese off the wheel in front of me just to give my hands something to do. And my eyes.

I don't want to look at the Sword.

"You are being so selfish right now," Lara bursts out.

I nod my head, raising both hands in gratified surprise. "Finally, someone who agrees with me—"

But Lara's pointing a finger and it isn't directed at the Sword. It's at *me*. I blink, staring open-mouthed down at her hand.

"Don't you see?" She makes a disgusted noise. "This is about more than you, Kyrie Ilinus of Sola. This is about more than the curse—look at the wheels the gods have put in motion. The game board is set."

I attempt to arrange my face into the closest approximation of innocence I can muster.

"Death." She jerks her head at the Sword, who is as silent as ever. "Chaos." This time she gestures to me. "Magic." She points to herself. "That's a whole lot of power from the pantheon who's been at war for a very long time, tearing Heska apart in the process."

"Heska is..." I stop, because I was going to say Heska is fine.

Heska is not fine, and maybe she's right. Maybe I've deluded myself into being as selfish as Lara claims I am.

Lara raises her eyebrows, clearly waiting for a response.

"Heska has a few problems," I admit.

"The pantheon has been at war for a century," Lara says in a quiet voice. "You dance around it because you were taught to, and you make the most of it because that's who you are. You make the most of what you are given. It is your greatest strength and your greatest weakness—but you have to see past it."

A smart remark is on the tip of my tongue, but I close my mouth.

My silver tongue's done enough damage to everyone here. Including me. Including my now dead family.

"Throughout Heska, the gods' territories are all but at war with each other," Lara continues, her gaze a knife in my chest. "And Doston is on the fringes, watching us weaken, watching the magic wane, and waiting to strike a blow that will fracture Heska and our ways of life forever. This is about more than you, Kyrie. And it always has been." She glances sidelong at the Sword, who doesn't move a muscle, just watches me. Waits.

"That was... You've been holding that in a while?" I ask lightly.

"The time wasn't right," she admits grumpily, tugging at the straps of her teal and cream corset. "It is now, though."

That rush of power enters the room again. Magic hovers along my skin, so strong it seems to vibrate along my awareness. Every instinct screams to run, the feeling building to an almost unbearable crescendo.

I drag in a breath.

Lara's eyes have clouded over.

A chill goes down my spine. The fire in the hearth gutters, the candles on the table flaming higher, sparking purple at the wicks.

My fingers find the daggers at my hips reflexively. I've seen her in the grips of magic many times over the course of our strange friendship, but not like this. This is… different.

Nakush is here.

The Sword gently puts a hand on my wrist and I force the daggers back into their sheaths at his silent admonishment.

"Listen now and listen well," Lara's mouth says, but it's not her voice, not even close. My stomach churns. "One to lie, one to kill, one to see. Three more will join your party of deceivers, and the future hangs in the balance. One to heal, one to shield, and one to light the way. Six to retrieve the crown. Two to perform a ritual, one to bleed. Fate leads four astray."

Lara's shoulders slump as an uncanny breeze blows through the room, though all the windows are shuttered, and the candles snuff out at once.

"One will die," I choke out. "Great." I cradle my head in my hands, overwhelmed. Fuck. I don't want anyone to die. Not me, not Lara… ugh. Not even the Sword.

"Three more to find," the Sword repeats. I peek at him from between my fingers.

Lara's knuckles whiten on her glass and she raises it to her lips, draining it dry. "I know where to start."

"Less than two weeks," the Sword adds, blowing out a breath.

"Well," I drawl, shaking my arms out. "Let's see if we can play another rousing rendition of prophecy deciphering," I say with faux merriness. "I'm the one who lies. You're the one who kills, Sword, Lara, you see. So… we need one to heal, one to shield and one to light the way." I tick off my fingers. "That last one feels a little inadequate, but who am I to question a god?"

"You do it all the time," the Sword says dryly.

"That's different," I tell him. "That's the one I was forced to swear myself to. Goes with the territory."

"We need to start out at first light." Lara's tone is brisk, brooking no nonsense. "We must sleep. I will be ready at dawn."

"Ready for what? Who do you have in mind?" I furrow my brow in confusion.

"He'll be here any—" Lara's lips twitch into a smile as a knock sounds from the front room door. "Second," she finishes.

"Oooh." I wiggle my eyebrows and fake a shiver, though it's not too hard after the fucking god of magic essentially possessed Lara.

Don't see that every day.

She rolls her eyes at me, then sashays into the front room where she conducts most of her business.

The Sword and I trade a glance as she opens the door. Magic still gambols around the room, her house rife with it.

"Lara Tross?" a low baritone voice asks carefully. "I received an order to seek you out."

"Morrow Vossen," Lara says, and I can hear the smile in her voice. "You're right on time."

She opens the door wider, and a bear of a man steps into the front room. He towers over her, not as big as the Sword, but built wider, like a brawler, barrel-chested and massive, with none of the Sword's graceful, elegant bearing.

He's good-looking enough, though, strawberry-blond curls wreathing a guileless face, a thick red beard covering his jaw. Morrow Vossen looks around the room with wide blue eyes, and all I can think is he would be an excellent mark to pickpocket. My fingers twitch at my side.

"What do you mean, I'm right on time?" He seems desperately confused about what's going on.

He'll fit right in with me.

He glances around the front room, gaze pausing on the pantheon of statuettes Lara displays for her clients before stopping on where the Sword and I stand in the entryway to the main house.

"Let me guess," I say slowly. "Sworn to Lojad?"

The knight—because it doesn't take a seer to deduce what the man is—nods once.

"I didn't realize you'd have guests," he tells Lara in that deep voice, bemused. She gives him a wide berth as she closes the front door behind him, and the lock slots into place with an ominous click.

"You come to seek your fate, sent by Lojad," she tells him in her sweet, regular voice.

He blinks, surprised by her words.

"I get the feeling," I tell him, scrunching my nose up. "It's uncanny what she does, and that's not even the worst of it. If you'd been a few minutes sooner, you would've shit your pants. I almost did."

Lara glares at me, but when I glance at the Sword, expecting his usual serious frown or maybe a grimace to spice it up, he's grinning, his shoulders shaking with silent laughter.

It hits me like a punch to the gut.

He's laughing with me.

Unfamiliar warmth blooms through me and I smile back at him for a moment... until I remember we don't like each other.

"Why do I feel like I have stumbled into some inside joke I don't know?" Morrow asks, sighing as though he's resigned to it.

"That sounds like a personal problem, but if you're looking for adventure, you're in the right place." I raise an eyebrow.

His lips twitch to one side.

Lara puts her elegant hand on his wrist, which makes it look teensy in comparison. His focus homes in on her, and whew—something heated crosses his face. I force myself not to look at the Sword.

"My friend Kyrie has a quest, and her fate—and the fate of our world—hangs in the balance." Lara's voice is so soothing I'm nearly lulled by it, until she hits that fate of our world part.

I still don't see how stealing Sola's Crown from the King of Diamonds will do anything to save the world. Maybe that's just step one on our world-saving itinerary.

"Are you healer, shield, or warrior?" she asks him gently.

"Shield," the Sword answers for him.

"My power lies in protection, not death," Morrow confirms. The huge knight's clear blue eyes are full of something like wonder.

The Sword nods.

I tilt my head, like that will clue me in on whatever these two men are seeing in each other. Maybe it's just the fact they're both massive and clearly built for battle. Maybe there's some silent warrior code I'm not privy to.

"Will you join us, of your own free will?" Lara asks him solemnly.

Morrow's focus swings back to her.

She steps closer, her voice quiet. "It will not be an easy journey. Your life may be forfeit. You may have to kill others on this quest. But you will become a legend, a hero, your name sung by bards the world over."

He nods once, and I try not to laugh at how thick Lara's laying it on. I don't, though, because she doesn't look like she's joking.

She is completely serious.

I pinch the bridge of my nose.

"I will," Morrow answers. "Lojad calls, and I answer. I am faithful to Lojad. I will be your shield, Lara Tross."

The Sword crosses the room, sucking up all the energy into his black-clad body, and offers Morrow a hand in greeting.

JANUARY BELL

Lara's gaze sweeps over me, and I'm not sure she's all here, or if she still has one foot caught in Nakush's magic snare.

Am I the only one who doesn't really understand what in the hells is happening?

I've made a life of staying one step ahead, until I drank from that damned chalice.

My weight shifts and I lean my forehead against the door jamb, watching Lara, Morrow, and the Sword talk in low voices.

I have missed something vital, and it makes me uneasy. I will not be Sola's pawn in whatever it is that's going to happen, destiny be damned.

I refuse to give that bloodthirsty goddess one more ounce of my energy.

The Sword is wrong. My life has not been mine; never have I been free of her yoke. I might not have lived my own life, but if I die, it will be *my* death—I will not give my life in service to a goddess I despise with every fiber of my being.

17

THE SWORD

Guilt gnaws at my bones, a hungry dog I can't get rid of.

The fire crackles in the hearth, wet wood popping and smoking. Shadows dance along the whitewashed stone and mortar walls.

I have never been deceitful.

Even though I'm not outright lying to Kyrie... it feels close enough. It *is* close enough.

Despite my eyelids growing heavy, I can't seem to shake my misgivings.

Morrow, the newest member of our preordained group, seems to be a trustworthy companion, though he's most definitely not wary enough of Kyrie, who would rob him blind given half a chance.

If she were up to it.

I sigh, rubbing my forehead and staring into the fire.

It's increasingly clear that she's unwell, though she thinks she can hide the hacking cough by holding it in, her shoulders shaking with each new bout.

A week and a few days until the midwinter masque.

I need her alive for the ritual.

Heska hangs in the balance.

"Why are you staring at me?" Kyrie asks, glancing up from where she sits by the fire, brushing her hair out. She's exchanged her uniform of brown leather trousers and loose blouse for an oversized sweater the same color as a storm-tossed ocean. Her muscled legs are tucked beneath her, and my gaze keeps skipping to the creamy expanse of her exposed calves and ankles.

Morrow's accompanied Lara to where the horses are stabled, and I'm all too aware of the fact Kyrie and I are alone, and for the moment—safe.

"Stop it," she mutters, turning back to the crackling glow of the fire before her. "You're making me nervous."

Something about the way she pronounces the word sends a bolt of wonder through me. Is she truly nervous, or does she... feel the same attraction I do?

The fire pops, and I scowl at it.

Unlikely. Impossible.

Kyrie's made it clear that putting me off-balance is her favorite pastime. Even if she does... feel anything towards me besides distaste, acting on it will only make things harder.

She's humming under her breath, the sound of it filling the small living area. I close my eyes, leaning back in the chair, letting the sound of her hairbrush and the fire and the notes of her song lull me.

❄

My head lolls back, then snaps up straight, my body responding to some stimulus and shaking me from sleep before I know what's woken me.

Whimpering sounds, from the pile of blankets near the fire.

I focus in on it, the red curls of Kyrie's now dried hair giving her sleeping form away.

A pale limb tosses the blanket aside and she thrashes for a moment, a pitiful keening coming from her lips.

I can't stand it.

I'm moving before I've had time to think it through.

"Please," she begs, her eyes moving quick behind her still-closed lids. I bend over her and her fists curl into my shirt, the same one I've worn for two days, the one from the crypt.

She shouldn't have to touch it. She shouldn't have to seek comfort in the arms of death.

A second later, she's in my arms.

She's so small and warm against my body, her face and chest glistening with a sheen of sweat. Her hands clench and unclench the fabric of my shirt. A stream of unintelligible nonsense comes from her mouth, and the only thing that's clear is that whatever she's dreaming about is terrifying her.

I watch her fight in her sleep for a long moment, simply holding her in front of the dying fire. This, comforting another, is so far beyond what I know and am used to.

These hands are used to dealing death, not holding another.

I lean closer, trying to suss out what she's saying in her sleep, like knowing will unlock the secret of what her power over me is.

Her skin's so pale, paler than usual, blue veins standing out on the delicate skin of her eyelids, her lashes dark blonde and twitching. I'm so close to her, the scent of the lye in the soap she used to wash before falling asleep in front of the fire fills my nose and mouth, but it's not strong enough to block out the scent of her, that smell that's tantalized me for days now.

My exhalation sends the fiery hair across her forehead flying, and I inhale her again, the subtle sweetness of her short human life better than anything I've ever known.

I don't know why the impulse seizes me, but I act on it like it's the most natural thing in the world. Like it's inevitable. My lips brush against her forehead, velvet night crowding out the sun.

She goes still, her small, clenched fists loosening on my shirt, and fear grips me—fear like I've never known—that I've woken her and that now I'll face her human wrath.

Her eyes are still closed, though, and it's not a scowl that greets me on her face.

No, Kyrie is smiling in her sleep, a faint shadow of her waking mirth, but a smile all the same.

I clutch at her, emotion welling tight in my chest, too much to hold in, overwhelming.

The urge to take her back to the chair I slept in, to hold her through the rest of the darkness, to soothe her into peaceful dreams and keep her nightmares at bay, tears at my willpower to keep my distance from her.

Clenching my teeth, I set her carefully back down on the nest of blankets, tucking her, watching her, unable to look away.

I stoke the fire, wanting to keep her warm. My embrace won't be welcomed in the light of day.

Mortals prefer to be held in the dark of night, to be embraced by death unknowing.

I keep watch over her, jealous of the way dawn's fingers caress her skin as daylight slowly creeps through the windows.

18

KYRIE

We leave the slumbering town of Effingwich soon after dawn. Of course, it takes us longer to get on the road than Lara would like, but I can't stop yawning.

I slept well enough last night, I think, cozy in front of her hearth. It's probably that I've never been a morning person, unlike Lara, who seems as well-rested and ready to take on the world as ever.

My horse prances a bit, and a little grin kicks the sides of my mouth up at her obvious joy at being out and about on this crisp winter morning. The sun is shining, and despite my sleepiness and the heavy task ahead, the world seems full of possibilities.

Morrow rides a destrier, a dapple-grey warhorse who looks like he'd be as much at home in front of a cart as he is with the massive warrior astride him.

As for the Sword, he barely looks at me this morning, which... I think I prefer.

Especially since I had the strangest dream about him.

My fingers flutter over my forehead, and I can almost feel his lips there. My cheeks heat at the memory of the dream. Probably a fever dream, compliments of the chalice's blood curse.

Didn't realize I'd be having vivid sex dreams from drinking it, but if that's a side effect, I can think of worse.

Even if it does make a certain knight of death appealing to me. I frown. Odd, though, how real his touch felt. It's almost as if I can still feel the imprint of his kiss on my skin.

Ridiculous.

I shake my head and take a long draught of cold water from the flask slung across my chest.

Still, the memory of my dream persists no matter how I attempt to dislodge it from my brain, focusing on the bright red plumage of the winter birds flitting to and fro. Counting the number of silver birch trees doesn't help, my attention continually slipping to the silent, black-clad knight.

The horses' slow pace isn't helping, either.

Time is running out faster than we can travel, the path through the foothills of the Hiirek Mountains too narrow to risk the horses by prioritizing speed.

Still, speed is the only thing that matters, if the dark pressure in my chest is any indicator. It's as if the chalice's curse is sitting on my lungs, making me cough. My thoughts are cloudier than normal, like the word I want is right on the tip of my tongue but I can't quite think of it. Like there is something I'm missing but I can't figure out what, or even why I think that.

It makes me worried.

I *hate* being worried.

Huffing in annoyance, I dig my heels into my mare's sides, trotting closer to where Morrow's warhorse picks its way over the ice-slicked ground.

"Good Morrow," I call out to him by way of greeting, grinning at my own feeble joke.

He glances back at me, a mild expression on his face, and I realize he's likely heard some variation of that every day of his life.

Irritation rises.

It's the Sword's fault. He shouldn't have kissed me in my dreams last night. It made me distracted.

"Sorry," I tell him, and Morrow's brows rise a fraction. Now I'm apologizing? "Do you do this often?" I ask him.

"Ride my horse? Yes."

Lara laughs from where she leads our little group.

"Get called on quests by Lojad. Take up with a band of strangers for reasons you don't fully understand."

Any hint of warmth in his expression cools, and he looks me up and down.

"I understand Sola favors those who lie and cannot trust, but Lojad's chosen are loyal and just." The censure in his voice rings through each word, and my scowl deepens. "I am here because his hand is upon me, as Sola's gifts are upon you. We each have a role to play in what's to come."

He says the last three words with a certain gravitas that makes me sit up straighter in my saddle. My horse continues to mince across the ground, clearly beyond pleased with herself.

"What's to come?" I repeat. It doesn't seem like he means me curing myself of this curse. "What is to come?"

"I do not have the gift of prescience," he hedges, and I roll my eyes skyward.

"Lara, what is he talking about?" I yell at her, knowing full well she's listening.

The Sword chuckles from where he brings up the rear, Mushroom on a lead between us.

"We stand at a crossroads. Which path will be taken is yet unknown," she says lightly.

"Thank you so much," I call back. "That was incredibly illuminating. So helpful."

"You're welcome," she sings out.

"Where do you expect to find the other two we need for our merry band of thieves, by the way?" Lara's been incredibly cagey about how we're supposed to add two more people to our party.

This is why I don't work well with others.

I like to handle things. I like every possibility and outcome sorted out. I haven't felt this out of control since I was so *lovingly* adopted into the tender embrace of the Sisters of Sola.

I *hate* it.

"They will find us," Lara assures me.

My lips twist to the side and I find my gaze darting to the Sword before my cheeks go hot and I immediately look away.

"Right." I drag the word out. "So we're just going to... make our way to Nyzbern, figure out how to infiltrate the midwinter masque, and pray that we stumble upon the last two people we need to fulfill the prophecy you delivered last night?"

The Sword laughs, but there's an edge to it. I ignore him. I thought I was getting good at that particular trick, but the urge to turn around and see the smile on his face, sarcastic or not, is strong.

Damn his dimple.

"That's the plan," Lara says easily.

"Prayer. The plan is prayer," I repeat, beyond annoyed. "I don't know if you remember who I'm supposed to pray to, but—"

"Every god has two faces," Morrow interrupts, quoting the

most popular Heskan prayer book. "Pray you get the one you want, and not the one you need."

I decide I don't like Morrow very much.

"Hey, Sword, old friend," my tongue nearly trips over that descriptor, but I forge ahead anyway. "Maybe we could desecrate some more graves. Ask your rotting friends for help." This time, I turn around as fully as I can in the saddle, watching carefully for his response.

"You would call upon Hrakan?" Morrow asks seriously.

Morrow is much easier to ignore than the Sword, but I answer him anyway.

"Oh yeah, me and the Sword, we live for that shit," I lie easily. "Maybe our new friends the gods want us to work with are already dead." I bat my eyelashes at the Sword over my shoulder.

"I think you just want to share power again," the Sword says easily, and I go all tense and hot at once, remembering the way he felt against me.

His lips on my wrist.

His mouth on my skin.

His arm around my waist, holding me tight.

Goddess, I shouldn't have said anything.

"You shared power?" Lara asks sharply.

"It wasn't a big deal. Some corpse needed a little Kyrie juice. Special blend of smartass and magic. Irresistible, apparently."

The Sword makes a choked noise, and I can tell he's trying not to laugh.

It makes me grin. It makes me feel like I've won a prize.

"You are, by far, the most heretical person I have ever encountered," Morrow mutters.

"Did Lojad murder your family so he could turn you into his perfect chosen one?" If acid drips from my tongue, so be it.

Power builds, a tiny knot in my chest, and then I've unleashed it before I realize fully what's happening. "Maybe you should just shut up about things you don't understand."

"Maybe I should," Morrow agrees readily, falling silent.

"For Nakush's sake, Kyrie," Lara hisses at me, turning around in her saddle. "We fucking need him. Don't *do* that."

"Do what?" I shrug one shoulder carelessly.

I feel anything but careless.

Disgust roils my stomach. I shouldn't have said anything, much less blasted him with a dose of my horrible power just because I was feeling cranky.

I might be an asshole, but that's too far, even for me.

"What's done is done," the Sword says in an infuriatingly calm voice. "No reason to continue fighting amongst ourselves."

The path widens slightly and I urge my horse forward, walking alongside Morrow's huge beast of a mount, guilt scraping me hollow inside.

"Morrow," I say his name nastily. Well, you can take the liar out of Sola's sisterhood, but you can't make her play nice, or something. "You can say whatever you want. You don't have to listen to my directive..." I trail off, but Lara gives me a warning look. "You can say whatever you want," I finish awkwardly, the words infused with my magic.

Morrow gives me a thorough sidelong look, and I ignore the tree branches clawing at me.

"Kyrie," Lara prompts.

"I'm sorry I used my power on you," I grit out.

"I'm sorry I assumed your experience was anything other than what it was," Morrow says agreeably.

My nose wrinkles in annoyance.

Leave it to Lojad's follower, our shield, to be patient with me to the point of boring. I expected an outburst. I expected outrage. I didn't expect... an apology.

I glance sidelong at him. At least he's kind, I suppose.

"Do you smell that?" the Sword asks suddenly.

My mouth opens automatically to make a childish joke, until I catch wind of it, too.

"Smoke," Morrow says, his voice thick with concern.

Tension descends on our group, and we urge our horses into a faster pace. Their hooves drum the half-frozen ground and we all go silent, the knot in my chest growing tighter.

A pervasive sense of wrongness saturates the world all around, as though the landscape's suddenly shifted left.

I want to ask if anyone else feels it, but one look tells me all I need to know.

Their expressions are set, Lara's pinched in worry, Morrow's gaze far away and concentrated. The Sword looks as grim as ever.

It sets my teeth on edge.

The screams begin soon after. A bell tolls somewhere not too far ahead.

"A village is under attack," Morrow calls out, unnecessarily. Obviously there's a village under duress, or they wouldn't be ringing their bell. We wouldn't smell smoke, and we wouldn't hear screams.

The question is, what the hell is attacking it?

Lara looks back at us expectantly.

"Do you feel the gods' hands in this?" she asks.

A chill goes through me, and I grimace.

"No," I snarl. "And if the gods are the ones responsible for attacking that village, then they should go fuck themselves." My pulse pounds in my head, my anger peaking at these so-called gods of ours who see us as playthings and puppets.

A laugh booms out from behind me, and it takes me a second to realize it's the Sword.

"Kyrie has a point there," he says mildly. "For one raised to lie, she doesn't mince her words, does she?"

The ground vibrates. The screaming gets louder, and birds take flight en masse from the fir trees all around.

"Wait." Morrow holds up a hand, closing it into a fist.

Waiting is a good idea, as would be figuring out whatever the hells we're going to ride into.

From the sound of it, we might not ride back out.

We do as he says, an odd clicking screech echoing off the tree trunks.

"It's a fucking manticore," the Sword growls. "I can smell the poison."

"We cannot leave them to fend for themselves," Morrow says, the very paragon of virtue.

I sigh. "We absolutely could."

"Kyrie," Lara reprimands.

"What? I am a thief, not a fucking warrior. I lie, I cheat, I steal. I am not going to go running into a situation that's almost guaranteed to get me killed. How are we supposed to fulfill your prophecy if we all die?"

The ground vibrates again and my teeth grind together in my head, a scream getting louder before suddenly cutting off.

My blood runs cold.

"I cannot in good faith leave these people to their doom," Morrow says gallantly.

I glare at him. "What happened to letting prayer guide us all?"

"Kyrie!" Lara snaps. "What happened to your anger? All that righteous indignation at the gods and yet you can't find it in you to help? How are you any better than Sola?"

That stings. I wince.

"A manticore should not be here," the Sword intones. "Morrow is right. We can't let it ravage this land and my—our—people."

I'm outnumbered, clearly. Traitors.

"Lara, do you plan to use your foresight to take down the manticore?" I ask her sweetly. "Or are you going to sit back and let us do the dirty work?"

"Don't be a bitch, Kyrie. I have a few offensive spells. You don't know everything about me." She bares her teeth at me, and it doesn't take a seer to tell she's pissed. "You, however, are great in a pinch and quick with your daggers. What better time to see how we work as a team?"

"We need to move," Morrow demands, another pitiful shriek cutting off too abruptly.

I sigh again, tired, that knot of darkness in my chest pressing heavily on me.

"Fine, fuck it. I'll help. But don't get used to it," I snarl.

Lara beams at me like she's forgotten my selfishness. The look quickly dies as the ground shakes again, causing the horses to stamp their hooves nervously.

Except Morrow's horse, who looks like he could nap at any minute.

Lara takes off down the forest path in the direction of the chaos, Morrow pressing his horse into a fast canter after her.

"Kyrie," the Sword says suddenly. "Be careful."

He holds my gaze for a long moment, his dark eyes boring into me like they see straight through me. I think he might.

"I'm always careful." I grin at him.

He doesn't return it.

We both know it's a lie.

19

THE SWORD

Manticores have long been banished from this world, one of many creatures deemed too fickle and dangerous to be allowed to roam wild, hunted to near extinction. Like the Fae, in that respect.

Only one thing could have let this monstrosity back into this world. A god... or goddess.

We canter until the forest thins, giving way to farmland and rolling hills dotted with the occasional uncleared tree. A small town sits on one of the hills, and as soon as the path evens out, the horses stretch their legs long, canters turning to furious gallops.

"They don't have much time," Morrow roars over the noise.

He reminds me of someone I used to know, another of Lojad's faithful from a different lifetime.

Morrow won't stop until he's dead or dying, and I can't let that happen.

Kyrie needs him. She needs him, and Lara, and me, and whoever else is destined to fall in with us.

I sigh. Fucking Nakush. He couldn't have given us more direct instructions, could he?

It doesn't matter that the smoke thickens the closer we get, that the sounds of chaos and terror are louder with every hoofbeat on the packed dirt road. None of it helps lessen my frustration with the gods.

Which is how I managed to get myself in this desperate situation in the first place. Instead of airing my frustrations in the correct ways, I took them out on Sola's followers.

I have never regretted it. My vengeance upon her was richly deserved.

Now, though, with Kyrie riding flat out in front of me, I feel the first threads of remorse. Her horse's legs stretch long, eating up the terrain. Dirt flies in icy clods where its iron-clad hooves strike. Kyrie's life—her destiny—hangs in the precarious balance... and shame snakes through me.

My lust for vengeance will extinguish every spark of life in her.

That is her destiny. Because of my choices.

I grit my teeth.

"Yah!" I urge my own horse forward and it snorts before reluctantly surging forward. Kyrie's faithful pack mule brays, racing alongside us.

Kyrie pretends not to care, not to hurt; she pretends to be everything the Sisters of Sola raised her to be. Corrupted her into being. Or tried, at least.

Red hair streams behind her like a banner, coming undone from her long braid, as wild and unruly as the thief herself. Her green cloak floats on the wind. When she glances over one shoulder at me, that cocksure smile firmly in place, my heart skips a beat.

She smiles, but I see through her bravado. There is worry in her eyes, etched across her forehead.

She cares deeply. She hurts.

And not just for herself, but for others. Mushroom the mule, her friend Lara, the direcat, her poor long-dead family—for the people in this small forgotten town being laid siege to by a beast that should have stayed forgotten.

Life has taught her to wear indifference like armor.

I wonder what Death will teach her.

Knowing I will witness the result doesn't bring me any joy.

I submit myself to the rhythm of the horse, to the sound of a woefully unbalanced battle being fought ahead, and to my fate.

It doesn't matter who I am, or what I am—fate will have her way with us all.

20

KYRIE

The manticore is straight from a nightmare. The incredible, putrid stink of it will haunt me the rest of my life, I'm sure of it.

"It's fucking huge." I'm not even aware I'm speaking out loud until I hear my own voice.

Bat-like, leathery wings stretch from its strange, furred hide, each segment tipped with a talon so dark they seem to absorb the light. It's larger than the direcat even, and I'm grateful that creature took its leave of us in the Hiirek foothills rather than battle this thing. Shaggy dark-brown fur hangs in tangled mats all over it, a grotesquely long whip of a scorpion's tail lashing behind it.

When it turns towards us, though, revealing its face, fear plunges icy hands into my heart.

Its nearly human features take us in, wide, cat-like eyes intelligent and crazed all at once, its features too monstrous to be human and too human to be truly monstrous.

It is horrible.

Lara's horse rears and she dives forward, grabbing fistfuls of mane to stay on, then manages a surprisingly elegant dismount.

The Sword reins in his horse, and the manticore seems to smile at the sight of him, revealing fangs the size of my forearms. Ropes of saliva dangle from its mouth, and it roars a challenge.

"Right then," the Sword says, sounding slightly bored.

My gaze darts back to Lara, who's drawing a circle at least twice as wide as she is tall in the ice-glazed dirt.

The town's belltower continues to ring, and the manticore shakes its great shaggy head then roars again, attention diverted from our small company. My stomach lurches as I realize what's happening.

"The bell," I mutter, glancing back at the Sword.

My mouth goes dry. He's shirtless, pulling on his armor, spiked pauldrons glinting in the hazy winter sun.

I shake my head. "The bell," I say more loudly. "The noise—look." I point at the manticore, willing them to see what I'm suddenly having trouble putting into words.

Morrow's horse prances underneath him, nostrils blowing. "What do you suggest?" he asks casually, as though I've offered him a tray of sweets to choose from.

"We need to stop them ringing the bell," I say, looking to Lara for support. Lara's busy, though, etching all sorts of unrecognizable symbols into the dirt. An iridescent globe shimmers above her, and though her mouth's moving, I can't hear a word she's saying.

Right. No help there.

"The bell could be a good distraction from our attack," the Sword says calmly. How the hells he's able to put on armor without any help, I don't understand, but how everyone is so damned relaxed in the face of this thing is even more perplexing.

It pisses me off.

"There is a monster right *there*," I point at it, in case they missed it, "and it's going to decimate this place unless we get them to stop ringing the gods-damned bell."

I almost call them all idiots, but I restrain myself. Barely.

"So you want to risk your neck riding for the bell tower... past the beast?" Morrow asks. He grins. *He's smug.* "Or do you want them to be the distraction, so we have an easier time?"

"Oh, fuck you, Morrow." I shake my finger at him. "Don't think I don't see what you're trying to do. Don't make me out to be like you. I am not a hero."

Something changes, energy pulsing through the air.

The bell stops ringing.

The Sword's attention whips over to Lara and I follow his gaze. She's chanting, still silent, at least to me, but there's no doubt that's where the power emanates from. A glowing blue chain of light pours from her palms, stretching all the way to the bell tower, where it disappears from view under the bell.

"I like her," Morrow says.

The Sword doesn't say anything.

He looks at me, though, and there's a sadness there, an inevitability I don't know how to describe.

I nod at him once. "Guard Lara," I yell at Morrow and spur my horse towards the manticore. Despite the sudden silence from the bell tower, the town is still in chaos, multiple pillars of smoke rising from many small fires.

The manticore screams, an eerily human noise, then attacks the building nearest it again. Sparks fly through the billowing smoke as its claws rake across the stone. A split second later, the acrid smell of the beast triples.

"Watch out," the Sword yells at me just as fire explodes around it.

Reflexively, I throw my arm over my face, pulling my horse away from the massive ball of flame unfurling from the creature. Heat sears my skin, my mount screaming in fear.

I can't put the creature through this. It certainly didn't ask to be put in harm's way.

"By Sola's fucking teeth," I swear, dismounting as carefully as I can from the panicked horse. "Mushroom," I yell out, feeling idiotic, but continuing on anyway. "Calm the horse down." I swat at the horse's flank, but it doesn't need any urging, already streaking away from me and the fiery manticore.

"How in the hells did it manage fire?" I shout over to the Sword, who's done the same, his mount kicking up dust behind us. Through the smoke and the sweat dripping into my eyes, I catch sight of Morrow, a strange transparent green film shimmering across his flesh.

"Lojad's shield," the Sword explains, watching my focus. "Lara will be safe with him."

I nod once, grateful for his reassurance, slightly ashamed that he picked up on my concern for her. If I were a good little Sister of Sola, though, I wouldn't even be in this fucked up mess.

I pull my long daggers from their sheaths, enjoying the way they glint in the manticore's fire, knowing I'll like the way they look coated in its blood even more.

"I'll have to invest in a proper bow after this," I yell at him above the din.

He nods once, a slight smile on his face, the huge black-pommeled broadsword in his hands, sweat dripping down his chiseled chest.

"I'll draw its attention," he tells me, a serious look in his eyes. "You circle from behind. There's a bundle of nerves in front of its tail. Its sting is poisonous, though. It won't kill you. Well, it shouldn't kill you," he amends, a dark eyebrow cocked, his silver hair floating on the chaotic hot wind. "But with the curse, it might put you over the edge—"

"Don't get stung, got it. Let's get this the fuck over with," I grit out.

That real smile blooms across his face, the orange flames reflecting in his fathomless eyes, and for once, I let myself really look at him. His lone dimple. His even teeth. The cut cheekbones, the strong jaw.

He looks right back at me, understanding glimmering under my perusal.

"Now," he growls out, and I spin away from him, sprinting around to out-flank the beast.

The manticore's tail is too long, overly agile, and it whips around behind it, the scorpion's stinger dripping with some foul poison.

Yeah, I don't think I need the Sword to tell me that I should avoid that particular end of it. Seems pretty obvious.

All I need to do is cripple it, make it easy for him to lop its head off. Bundle of nerves in front of the tail. The tendons in its legs—I'll hamstring it. Quick feet, in and out, slash.

I've been doing this since I was a child, and for once, I'm glad the Sisters of Sola taught me to fight, no matter how many deep cuts I had to stitch up myself at night.

That might just keep me alive today.

From my angle behind the manticore, the Sword's onslaught is apparent.

He's faster than he should be in that strange spiked armor, weaving in and out, slashing at its horrible, uncanny face with his huge sword. I'm so entranced by his dance as I sneak behind the beast, I nearly miss the tail whipping towards me.

"Shit," I curse, fear making my heart slam into my chest.

Breathe, Kyrie. The command echoes in my mind, the words dark and masculine.

Okay. A bad time to start hallucinating, but at least the advice is solid.

I inhale deeply.

Time seems to slow, then still, and I bend back, the scorpion tail snaking over my chest. I slam onto my side on the frozen muck of the ground, then scramble to my feet.

The sick, fetid stench of the manticore's fire breath hits me and I gag.

"Fire," I scream, trying to get the Sword's attention. "It's going to breathe fire!"

The Sword glances up at me, time still strangely slow, muddy even, as he swings his broadsword into the beast's face.

A glimmering wind pushes at me, blowing more hair from my braid.

From behind Morrow, Lara's gaze is glassy, her lips still moving soundlessly, purple glittering smoke pushing from her.

"Focus," the Sword roars at me. "Damn it, Kyrie, *focus.*"

My teeth rattle as the beast lunges towards him, shaking the ground. A stone dislodges from the top of the building, and I manage to dive into a roll and avoid it at the last minute.

"Fucking shit," I curse.

Slick with sweat, my daggers are slippery in my hands and I tighten my grip on them. My senses are overloaded with the sick smell of the manticore mingling with brimstone and fire, the sounds of terrified people in the village, the tingle of Lara's magic pressing against my skin, and my own terror.

I don't want to die. I'm not ready to die.

Everything becomes crystal clear as I chant those words under my breath, and I ignore the burning pain in my shoulder where something's grazed it, sprinting back towards the body of the beast.

The tail's not the only place the manticore is weak. It's moving so quickly though, even with the odd sensation that time itself has slowed, which is impossible.

The only type of magic that could slow time is that of Hrakan himself, and I highly doubt the death god gives two shits about whether any of us live or die.

"Fuck the gods," I say, slicing my dagger across the manticore's legs.

I bound away, mud and muck coating every inch of me. The green cloak's getting in my way, and a quick cut to the neck has it floating away from me. The burning pain's dulled, though the ache spreads down my arm and into my fingers, turning my hand numb.

The injury must be worse than I thought.

I grit my teeth against it.

I'm not going to let this motherfucking manticore get the best of me. Or the curse, or any fucking thing else.

Because I might be an asshole, I might be a liar, and selfish —but more than any of those traits, I am stubborn to a fault.

My blood throbs in my hurt side and I cough once, spitting out something dark and wiping my mouth with my wrist, tasting blood.

The manticore's tail whips towards me again and the Sword roars my name, the sound echoing off the building, loud enough to cause the beast to shriek with rage.

Well, that makes two of us that are thoroughly pissed off.

I'm tired. So tired, and that's not like me. It's rare I pick a fight that I can't win, though, and even rarer that I give up.

With that thought held tight, I race back towards the manticore, sliding on my thigh and hip as I meet it. One foot steps on my bad arm and I stab up, up, with my daggers into the thick furred hide and its tender stomach.

The thing screams again and this time, it's not fury, it's pain.

Magic builds inside me, filling me up tight.

"Die already," I shriek right back, pissed off and hurt myself.

A half-second later, steaming entrails drop onto my legs, followed by the weight of the massive beast.

Darkness and exhaustion and pain compete, the sudden silence and pressure of its body blocking out nearly all coherent thought.

All I can think is that I hope the asshole Sword saw what I did because I just know it's going to piss him off that I got the killing blow.

21

THE SWORD

For the first time in my life, I am so stunned by what's happened that I can't do more than stare at the slain beast.

Morrow brushes past me, heaving at the dead animal, and Kyrie's blood-and-muck-covered hand appears, fingers wriggling.

I finally breathe.

She lives.

She did the unthinkable.

Her silver tongue magic is more powerful than it has any right to be, and the truth of that knowledge, of what she did to the manticore, means that destiny was leading me to her this whole time.

It should be impossible.

I drop the broadsword on the ground, helping Morrow heave the huge beast off Kyrie's body.

Faintly, I can hear her cursing up a storm under the

massive dead creature, and when her shoulders emerge, her red hair unrecognizable, I seize her under around her chest and pull.

Morrow grunts, and she slides out from beneath the beast with a disgusting suctioning sound.

I fall back at the sudden shift in weight, unused to the balance of my armor and the woman in my arms.

Kyrie is alive, blessedly warm against my bare chest.

I can't bear to loosen my arms from around her. Her shoulders heave, she's covered in the gods only know what from the monster, but so am I, and I have never been so glad to hold a life in my hands as I am in this very moment.

Hot blood trickles from my nose and I swipe at it, an aching pain behind my eyes.

It cost me.

The fight, ensuring Kyrie had enough time to attack. It cost me more than it should have.

"We smell like shit," she says in a muffled voice.

A laugh trickles out of me in spite of myself.

It was worth the price. She will be worth every price.

Even if she hates me when all is said and done.

"Is it dead?" A crowd has gathered around the body of the beast.

I don't need to look at it to know.

"It is dead," I confirm.

"It better fucking be dead," Kyrie snarls, her sharp elbow catching me in the ribs as she gets to her feet.

My chest is cold without her against it.

"We owe you our lives," a woman with a trembling chin says. "There are no thanks we could give that would be enough."

"We will feast in your honor this day," a man yells, and the crowd circling around us cheers, the sound weightless with relief.

"All of Mossbury will thank you," another calls out.

"I could eat," Lara says, leaning heavily on Morrow. The crowd cheers.

"I need to bathe. Desperately." Kyrie sniffs herself experimentally, her blood-soaked hair hanging in wet strings around her face. "Immediately."

She coughs.

"There is a hot spring in the middle of town," an older woman says. "You two come with me, we will get you cleaned up and take care of your horses."

Kyrie coughs. Twice, her eyes watering, shoulders trembling.

The woman's eyes go round.

"Sorry," she says with a bright smile. "I think that thing crushed my chest a little. I'm not sick."

It's a lie, I can tell immediately, and not just because I know about her curse, or because I recognize the potent sting of her magic—but because I know *her*.

Her silvered words work, though, and the woman smiles back at her. "The waters will help with that too, I expect. Our Mossbury hot springs are famous, blessed by Heska herself."

Someone is already rounding up our horses and the mule, and Morrow helps Lara through the hard-packed streets of the town proper. Kyrie's still breathing hard and seems to be favoring one side, though she puts on a brave show.

Until she stumbles.

"Kyrie." I'm at her side in an instant, but when I catch her with my arm around her waist, her eyes are wide, and not with pain.

With interest.

"Thank you," she says softly, one arm tangling around me,

the other hand pressed to my stomach. "Sorry. I'm a little tired, I think. You know why." She winks at me, and some of the worry melts away.

I do know why. For one, she used a massive amount of power willing the beast to die, something I'm not even sure she realizes she did, nor am I sure it would have worked if she hadn't already made mincemeat of its stomach.

Her body, though undoubtedly muscular and strong, feels so small up against me. So human, so frail.

The urge to protect her surges through me, and when she loses her footing again, I take full advantage of my own strength and lift her into my arms.

"Ohhh," she says, batting her eyelashes in that infuriating way of hers that only seems charming with her like this. Her arms wrap around my head and she watches me through heavy-lidded eyes as I carry her in the wake of the woman taking us to the town's hot spring.

There are patches of smoldering embers all around, and those not following behind us are already putting their town to rights after the manticore's chaos.

A wooden sign in the shape of a beer stein swings overhead.

"That's the local inn and pub," our erstwhile tour guide says cheerfully. "Old Craig will put you up for free, I'll see to that."

"We'll meet you here when you're done," Lara says. "You alright, Kyrie?"

Kyrie smiles widely at her. "Never been better. This is much more comfortable transport than a horse."

Lara's eyebrows rise with worry, and I know she hears the lie as well as I do.

"Take care of her?" she asks me.

"Always," I tell her.

She looks set to argue, but shakes her head, smiling wanly up at Kyrie before heading inside.

Always.

It's the truth. I will take care of her to the best of my abilities, no matter what.

The only promise I can give to any of them.

The hot spring isn't far from the pub, as it turns out, behind a sort of ramshackle round wooden door.

"There are soap and towels in there already. I'll gather some fresh clothes for you both—"

"No, that's not necessary," I interrupt. I hate to think of these folk giving us any of their hard-earned belongings.

"Nonsense." The older woman beams up at me. "We can't have you going around shirtless, or you'll start a riot worse than that manticore did."

Kyrie's laugh rings like a bell. "She's right about that, Sword."

"Sword?" Recognition dawns on the woman's face. "Well, I can't say I expected to see you. I'll leave you two to it, then."

With that, she scurries off, stopping me from asking any further questions.

She recognized my name.

It happens, and it shouldn't alarm me as much as it does.

Kyrie wiggles in my arms and I kick open the door, walking through and shutting it again with my foot.

Suspended lanterns cast a warm glow throughout the natural cavern, and just as the woman said, there are several cakes of wax-paper-wrapped soap next to a statue of Heska herself, the mother goddess, the patron of love—and of hate.

Every god has two faces.

Odd to find a statue of her here, in between Nakush's and Sola's territory, of all places. A small dish sits in front of her, with a bevy of coins. Donations, I assume.

I make a mental note to drop some of my own coin here afterwards. Offending Heska would only make things harder for all of us.

"Lavender," Kyrie says suddenly.

"What?"

"Lavender soap." She points a filthy finger at one of the soaps, and I pluck it from the pile.

I take a few steps forward, past the rustic table piled with soap and towels, then stop again.

"There's only one." The hot spring doesn't allow privacy—none at all. There are no convenient rocks to hide behind, no set of pools or dividers.

"I can wait, if you want to go first," Kyrie says softly. "Just plop me down and I'll close my eyes."

Her fingers are trekking up my neck though, one after another. Her palm cups my cheek, and I swallow hard, my throat bobbing.

I shouldn't be selfish. I should not give in to this... feeling of closeness to Kyrie.

"You could join me," I rasp, my voice deeper than usual.

White teeth flash as she bites her lower lip, something I suddenly, desperately want to do, to taste it, too.

"Are you sure that's a good idea?"

"No," I say shortly. "It is not a good idea."

Her hands move down my neck to the buckle fastening my pauldrons together between my shoulders.

"Wouldn't want them to rust," she says, her green eyes focused on the task at hand.

I groan. I want her. I want her fiercely, the adrenaline from battle still singing through my veins.

I set her down, working quickly to shuck off the armored barrier between us, giving in to the very mortal need that has me so firmly in its grip.

Kyrie's breath is coming sharp and fast, and her eyes are glazed.

"I'm going to wash up," she says mildly, her voice shaking. I close my eyes because gods, just the thought of this happening, of her coming to me willingly, is enough to get me hard.

Her ruined clothes fall on the floor, bruises blooming all over creamy thighs and hips, marks of a warrior. Kyrie's back is a map of twisted scars, and it pains me to see the proof of her past written in her skin.

Her torso is too soaked with blood and muck to see much of anything. I force myself to work on removing my own boots, anticipation leaving me lightheaded.

When I look up, my breath catches in my throat.

Kyrie's managed to slough off most of the blood and mud already, standing in waist-deep water. "Come on in," she says breathlessly, her emerald eyes full of wonder and hot with a lust that reflects my own.

I've never seen anything as beautiful and wondrous as her naked, steam curling around her.

22

KYRIE

It's hot. So hot.

The Sword is naked, and I'm on fire.

"Want you," I say, dizzy with it. I rub soap in my hair, knowing it's going to take forever to dry, but not wanting one more second of the manticore's disgusting fluids on me.

Manticore.

A stabbing pain goes through my arm and I suck in a breath, moving my hair from the shoulder that's suddenly throbbing again.

The Sword's in front of me, and the pain recedes in the face of him.

Huge.

It doesn't seem to matter how much time I spend with him, the fact that he's practically twice the size of me hasn't ceased to be impressive.

"I want you," I say again, because gods, this need is all-consuming.

He's naked. "I'm naked," I tell him, running my hands down his wet chest.

"This isn't right," he says, tilting my chin up, staring into my eyes.

Gods, yes, he's going to kiss me, I need him to kiss me... everywhere.

"You can start with my mouth, but if you don't put your tongue between my legs, I'm going to die," I tell him, and I mean every word.

Heat. Too hot. I'm on fire.

He's not kissing me though, he's staring at my eyes, his own expression growing cold and distant.

"Kiss me," I order, sobbing on the words. "You have to."

"Gods damn it all, Kyrie," he swears. "Your pupils are blown. No wonder... I am a fucking fool."

"No, please, I need it, you don't understand."

"I do understand," he says savagely. "I see exactly what's gotten into you, Silver Tongue."

"I want you to get in me," I plead, reaching for my powers, trying to convince him. I come up emptyhanded. There's nothing there. I'm all out. "Deep in me."

"Fucking hells, woman." He pulls my long, wet hair from my shoulder, and I nearly scream as his fingers run over the tender spot, choking on it instead. "The manticore stung you."

"I don't care, just fuck me, please, please, I need it."

"You don't want me," he shakes his head. "This is how the poison works. It's numbing the pain by lighting up other parts of your body, and then it will kill you while you're distracted, or your heart will give out."

"Why do you hate me?" I rage, punching his shoulder. It should hurt, but he's right, I don't really feel it. "Can't you see I need you?"

"I see it alright," he says darkly. "I'll give you what you need, Kyrie."

He takes me by the throat, turning my head to one side and pulling me close until I'm flush up against his body.

"Oh gods," I sob. "Yes."

A moment ticks by and he's shaking against me, and I've never wanted anything as badly as I want this impossible, stubborn, rude male.

I wrap one naked leg around him. His cock jerks as my inner thighs rub against it, the water sloshing around us. I try to line him up with my entrance as his lips travel down the side of my neck.

Then his mouth covers the wound on my shoulder, sucking it so hard that I scream.

And immediately black out.

23

KYRIE

Pain pulls me from sleep and I sit up, gasping for air.

"Relax," a deep voice says.

The Sword's sitting in a cane chair at the edge of the bed. Dark circles tug at his eyes, stubble climbing along his jawline like he hasn't slept or shaved in days.

Confusion clouds around me, and I tug the thick quilt up to my chest.

"What happened?" I ask, my voice hoarse. "Where are we?"

A strange look crosses over his face at my question. I swallow, feeling like I should remember something... anything about how I got here.

"We're in the inn above the pub in the village we saved from the manticore—Mossbury, they call it. It's around..." he drifts off, glancing past me at a window. "It's before dawn."

"Dawn?" My scattered brain clutches at that. "How many days did I lose? How long until the midwinter masque?"

"Ten days. You were out for two."

"Fuck." I collapse dramatically back onto the bed, then wince because my fucking shoulder is hurting like hell.

"You've had a rough time of it. We can afford to lose another day."

His voice sounds far away.

My shoulder. His mouth on my shoulder.

Heat rushes through me as the memory slams into my consciousness.

The manticore's stinger, the poison that made me... well, ready to fuck the Sword until I died of it.

Unless I'm remembering incorrectly... the Sword was just as into that idea as I was.

A slow smile spreads across my face, and I flutter my eyelashes at him.

"I *doooo* remember," I tell him. "I remember everything." My gaze drops to his hips, and I wiggle my eyebrows meaningfully.

"Oh, do you?" he asks acidly. "Do you remember me holding back your hair while you threw up so much bile we thought you were going to die?"

I pause, pursing my lips. That explains the disgusting taste in my mouth.

"Here," he rasps, holding out an earthenware mug. "Drink."

"Should I swallow?" I ask, arching one eyebrow suggestively.

"Shut up," he says, standing so abruptly water sloshes over the rim of the cup as I take it.

The water tastes heavenly on my tongue, cold and fresh and perfect. The fact that the Sword all but threw it at me in an awkward rage makes it taste even better, too.

"You wanted to kiss me," I say in a sing-song voice.

"I wanted you to live," he growls, suddenly over me, one

hand slamming into the wooden headboard, his face so close to mine I can scent the sweat on his skin. "To *live*, Kyrie, and you could have told me sooner that you were hurt. But no. You were as stubborn and intractable and infuriating as you always, *always* are."

"I didn't know I was stung." An uncomfortable tightness settles deep in my chest and I make myself look away from him, outside that same window where the sun is slowly rising.

"If you hate me so very much, Sword," I swing my gaze back towards where he's pacing along the wall, silver hair shining in the growing light. "Why do you want me to live so badly? Wouldn't it be better for you if I were wiped off the board completely?"

He stops walking. Turns his head to me.

So preternaturally still, he doesn't even seem to be breathing.

"I swore an oath to you, you fool. You made me, if you remember correctly."

"The oath didn't cover any kind of accidental death or damage," I say, narrowing my eyes at him, suspicion growing. "You do hate me; you aren't denying it. So why, Sword? Why do you want me to live?"

He's within a hairsbreadth of my lips again in an instant, the bed sagging under the weight of his knee on the mattress.

"Because you are my burden, Kyrie of Sola, my responsibility to bear, no matter how much I pray I could be rid of the torment you so willingly hand out on a daily basis. The mere sight of you is punishment for every misdeed I've ever committed."

I flinch as though I've been slapped.

The door flings open and the smallest woman I've ever seen glides through it.

The Sword immediately backs away, ducking through the door behind the woman, leaving me reeling on the bed.

Not from the manticore's poison, or from the memory of what we nearly did together in that damned hot spring.

From his words, his vicious tone, and the clear truth in every syllable.

The sight of you is punishment for every misdeed I've ever committed.

It hurts. It hurts more than the remnants of poison in my shoulder.

"I didn't think he'd ever leave," the small woman says.

"What?" I ask, finally taking her in. She has green-tinted skin, long greenish-blonde hair falling in gentle waves to her waist. A wreath of tiny white flowers sits on top of her head, giving her a girlish quality, though she must be at least my age. "What do you mean?"

"That male. The Sword? He hasn't left your bedside in days. Took his meals in here, too. I thought he was going to murder me if I didn't take care of you."

"You're a healer," I say, then tilt my head, studying her strange appearance. "Are you a dryad?"

"Half," she says, a sad smile on her lovely face. "If I were a full dryad, I wouldn't be here, would I?"

She doesn't wait for an answer, but busies herself by grinding up a potent blend of herbs in a black mortar on the bedside table.

I sink back into the pillow, my eyes stinging with tears I refuse to shed. I'm not going to fucking cry because the Sword is a horrible bastard murderer without one ounce of gratefulness in his stupidly gorgeous body.

I'm not going to cry because I'm apparently the worst person he's ever met in his entire long life.

I am not going to cry because I don't give a shit what he thinks of me.

I am going to live, if for nothing else than to spite him by doing so.

Asshole.

"You alright?" the dryad asks, pulling the quilt down, a slip of a nightdress not covering my arms or chest in any real way.

The wound is... grisly. Black around the edges, with black lines running down the veins of my arm and chest. I hiss in a breath as she packs the herbal poultice on it, chanting quietly under her breath.

"I am always alright," I finally answer, and it makes me tired to say.

I have to be alright. Always. No one but me cares if I am.

The pain increases, and I grit my teeth.

"You don't have to pretend to be strong, you know?" The dryad's watching me closely. "There's no one here but me."

"It fucking hurts."

"Good. That means it's working." She grins at me, laughing, and her tongue's also green.

"You're a healer," I repeat slowly. "You're *the* healer."

She cocks her head at me, then presses a hand against my forehead. "Are you feeling feverish?"

"No." I shake my head. "How do you feel about going on a quest?"

"If I had a silver coin for every time a patient asked me that." She laughs again, and the sound of the spring wind rings through it.

It has to be her. She's the healer Lara prophesied, I just know it, deep down.

"I didn't mean like that, and also, disgusting, I'm sorry people treat you like that." I wince again, because didn't I just treat the Sword like that?

Stupid, stupid Sword.

Ugh.

"What's your name?" I ask her.

"You've asked me that every time I've woken you. It's Caedia. Caedia Wood."

Right. Of course I did.

I clear my throat, trying to refocus, but the effort's exhausting me.

"Can we hire you to come with us? We have a task in Nyzbern," I say. Why haven't the others recruited her yet? I don't understand. "Er, we're doing something dangerous, to be honest, but I think we need you."

"I go where fate takes me. My life is one of a leaf on the winds of destiny." She says it in a strange voice and I sit up clumsily, clutching my sore arm against my chest.

"You are supposed to come with us," I tell her, and I don't think I've ever been more serious in my entire life. "Those winds of destiny you're talking about, they brought me to you."

"If I didn't know better, I'd say you were using your silver tongue powers on me." Her green tongue flicks out like a snake tasting the air. "But you're not. You really mean it. Why?"

"There was a prophecy. Nakush spoke through Lara, she's the witch in our group."

"One to lie, one to kill, one to see. Three more will join your party of deceivers, and the future rests in the balance. One to heal, one to shield, and one to light the way. Six to retrieve the crown. Two to perform a ritual, one to bleed. Fate leads four astray." Lara's in the doorway, the words of the foretelling rolling off her tongue.

Caedia dips her head in greeting, silent.

Can't say I blame her. There's not much to say to *that*.

"That's the prophecy," Lara tells her. "We weren't sure if

we should tell you about it, but it seems like Kyrie thinks she knows best, as always."

The words land like a blow on the part of my soul the Sword's already rubbed raw.

Lara's eyes narrow at my response... or lack thereof.

"Is this why you were trying to secure my services to accompany her?" Caedia asks, her lilting voice sharp as thorns. "You needed another body for your prophecy and you thought, sure, the half human—"

"You are the one we need," I interrupt. "I don't know how I know that, but I do. I can feel it."

Caedia makes a scoffing noise.

I huff. "Please. You were just telling me that you blew on the winds of fate. This is the wind blowing you." I gesture between the three of us with my good hand.

I don't even make a joke about being blown by fate, which shows exactly how serious I am.

"There was a manticore here," I continue, undeterred by the pinched look on her green-tinted face. "It stung me. You were here to heal me. How often does that sort of coincidence happen? This is fate."

I can *feel* the truth in the words, the power in them, similar to Sola's magic of lies—but there is no godly magic here. Only the truth.

The dryad's expression turns wide-eyed, her nostrils flaring as she inhales. "I expect to be paid," she says slowly.

"We can arrange that," the Sword says from the door, where I hadn't even noticed him.

Now, though, noticing him makes my chest ache in a way that has nothing to do with the manticore's poison or the curse.

I'm really having a bad month.

The Sword is watching me. I don't look at him, keeping my focus on Caedia, but I can feel his gaze hot on my skin.

"We leave after breakfast," I say quickly, needing to fill the silence, to push everyone towards what's next instead of what's just happened.

I don't want to think about what's just happened.

Ever since my family died, thinking about the past only leads to heartache in the present.

"You aren't ready to be on horseback," Caedia finally replies, skewering me with a look.

"Good thing the Sword is paying you handsomely to come along, then," I say smoothly.

He grunts from the doorway and I ignore the way saying his stupid name hurt, too.

"Ten days," I murmur to myself, swinging my legs over the side of the bed.

Lara's there in a flash, thankfully, because damn it, they're right, I'm unsteady and off balance. A brush lies on the nightstand, strands of red hair running through it.

Confused, I put a hand to my head and sure enough, my hair is smooth, not knotted or tangled like it would be if I'd been sick on my own.

"Thanks," I tell Lara.

"I wasn't going to let you fall, you ass," she says, laughing and squeezing my waist. "I'm glad to see you awake. You scared the shit out of all of us."

"I meant for brushing my hair," I explain, pointing to the hairbrush. "You know what a pain in the ass it is to get knots out."

"I didn't brush your hair," she says gently, a soft, sad smile on her face.

I glance behind me at Caedia, who's gathering medicinal supplies from the table next to the bed.

It's a lot of supplies.

I must have been really sick.

"Don't look at me," she says. "I didn't brush your hair, either. He wouldn't let me near you except to work on your wound."

My attention slides back to the brush, shot through with long red hair.

The Sword brushed my hair?

The realization is an uncomfortable one. I hustle away from Lara, leaning on the wall as I make my way to my leather satchel in the corner. My pants and blouse are neatly tucked inside it, freshly laundered, too.

"He didn't wash those, in case you're wondering. He did, however, pay the innkeeper's daughter to. She mended the cloak I gave you as well." Lara's voice is thick with an emotion I don't know how to name.

"I don't understand. He said he hates me." Didn't he? He said I was his *punishment.*

Lara's hand is warm on my bare shoulder. "I don't know if he understands, either."

I force a smile. "Well, I suppose I'll have to keep up my methods if it produces these results."

Lara laughs, but it ends on a sigh.

She opens her mouth like she wants to say something else, but I turn away, tugging my clothes on carefully.

"Breakfast will be downstairs, and then I suppose we'll be on the road."

"Got it," I say in a voice that I hardly recognize.

"Be careful, Kyrie," Lara says.

She's gone before I can ask her what she means.

24

THE SWORD

Our horses are rested and loaded down with food and supplies the people of the town were only too happy to offer up as thanks.

They wouldn't even take payment, which rankles.

I do not like the idea of a debt unpaid, though in the end, only one debt ever truly comes due.

Kyrie's singing as she rides out at the head of the group, Morrow at her side, who has a warbling bass that complements Kyrie's light soprano all too well. Caedia rides behind them on a snow-white mare the likes of which I haven't seen in an age.

The music is as pretty as Kyrie, but the sound of her harmonizing with Morrow makes me grit my teeth.

I hate this even more than I thought I would. Being in Cottleside for a decade was better than this torture.

Kyrie is all I can think about, insufferable, beautiful Kyrie, with her whip-smart humor and devil-may-care attitude. Her fearlessness, her stubbornness, the hidden kindness she thinks no one sees.

The worst part is, I see so plainly now why she hides it. She's been punished for it before. She thinks it makes her weak.

I want to show her how wrong she is, but I know I'll only prove her right.

And that, *that*, more than anything, is a blade straight to my dark heart.

"You are quiet." Lara's mellow voice jerks me out of my reverie, and I glance sideways to find her riding alongside me, Mushroom trotting behind her happily.

"The quiet suits me."

"I am sure it does," she says, a meaningful look on her face.

"How long have you known?" I ask her. I've been debating for days on when to ask her, or if I should even pry, if her knowing even matters.

"As soon as I knew she drank from the chalice." She pats her horse's neck. "She was marked before that, though, as I'm sure you know too. It's what drew her to me, drew us together. Our fates have been entwined as long as yours."

"You haven't told her?" I narrow my eyes in suspicion.

She shrugs a shoulder, but her expression and the sadness in her eyes are anything but cavalier. "It is not my place to interfere in the will of the gods. I am the instrument of Nakush. Unlike Kyrie, I put my faith in my god."

"Kyrie considers you a friend." It comes out a snarl, and her horse tosses its head at my tone.

"I am her friend."

"You would lead her like a bull towards—" I shake my head, angry. Angry at Lara for doing exactly what she should be doing, and keeping secrets from Kyrie.

Mostly, though, furious with myself for keeping secrets from Kyrie—and for doing what must be done.

Lara simply watches me, our horses keeping pace behind Morrow and the thief, who are now singing a rollicking shanty about what to do with a drunken soldier.

"I do what Nakush bids. I trust in their judgment. I trust in fate, and I trust in Kyrie, who is my friend, who has *always* been my friend." Her words are thick with emotion. "Just because I submit to the will of the god of magic does not mean that I want my friend to suffer. I have faith, *Sword*." She spits the word out like the falsehood it is. "I have faith that good will come of what she chooses to do. I have faith in the good in her, more than anything else."

I chuckle, but there's no mirth in the sound. "Then you have more than I do."

She raises her chin, her dark brown eyes redolent with magic, holding mine firm, and I see more of Nakush in this woman than I'd like.

"That makes me sad for you. Of everyone here, you should have the most faith. You almost have as much to lose as Kyrie should fate's great plan falter." Lara's voice is not her own and I dip my head, acknowledging the god who's chosen her.

Nakush is right, as is Lara, who speaks their words.

Only time will show the full hand we have been dealt, that the humans have been dealt, thanks to my choices.

Fate's great plan may yet break us all.

25

KYRIE

I avoided the Sword on our cross-country ride. Now that we're stopping for the night, only to rest our horses—and unfortunately, my own wasted body—it's harder to avoid him.

Impossible, even.

I sigh, settling next to the campfire and staring around at the four tents constructed around it. There's not enough room to do anything but sit and eat the food Lara's happily making.

A rabbit turns on a spit, mushrooms Caedia foraged roasting on a skillet underneath it with chunks of potatoes and herbs. The fat from the rabbit hisses as it splatters onto the vegetables below, flames licking up the sides of the skillet.

"It looks much better than what I made at camp the past few weeks," I tell Lara. "Thank you."

She grins at me as she turns the spit. "I always was the better cook."

"I brought strawberry wine," Caedia trills, sitting alongside me. She's so petite, I feel like an ogre next to the green-skinned woman. "Made it myself two springs ago. I thought we could celebrate our first night with a glass. Or two."

"Never thought I'd be drinking strawberry cordial with a dryad, much less the most beautiful witch I've ever seen." Morrow threads another rabbit on a second spit, adding it to the fire as Lara's cheeks turn red.

I grin. Morrow's grown on me, like one of the fungi in Lara's dish, and he seems much more amiable to me after I took out the manticore.

"Wildest thing I've ever seen in a fight," he told me as we rode together. "You were utterly fearless. Slid under it like a snake, and then boom! It was dead. Incredible work."

It's clearer than the sparkling night sky that he likes Lara, too, and it makes me giddy for them. They would be darling together. Lara, however, treats him as she does everyone else. Polite, tolerant, cold at times.

Well, everyone except me, but that's a privilege I've earned.

I have a feeling Morrow's not the type to give up easily, though.

"How's your shoulder?" Caedia asks, handing me a wine skin.

"It's sore, but fine, really." I take a swig from the skin and flavor explodes across my mouth. "By Sola's fingers, this is incredible." It's like summer dances down my throat.

"Of course it is. I'm a dryad." She rolls her eyes at me, then wiggles her fingers. "Let me take a look at it."

I turn towards her, obedience coming much easier with the strawberry wine in my mouth, and pull the blouse over my head. I fold it neatly on the green cloak next to me, chilly in my chemise alone.

"Ooh, it looks like it's doing well, really," Caedia says happily, cold fingers pressing at it gently.

"You couldn't do that in a tent?" the Sword rumbles from across the fire.

"Oh, did you want her to learn to see in the dark? Would that be more reasonable?" I bark.

Lara and Morrow's quiet conversation stops at our sharp words.

"You two need to get along," Morrow finally says. "We have a long road ahead, and picking at her won't make it any easier, Sword."

"Picking at her?" The Sword stands up, his handsome face bathed in shadow despite the warm firelight. "You think I'm picking at her?"

"The girl needs medical help. I don't see why you're making a big deal of it. Don't look if it bothers you," Morrow tells him, gallant even in the face of the Sword's ire.

He rises in my esteem even more. I smile at him.

"Oh, it's fine, Morrow," I tell him sweetly, knowing exactly what to say that will piss off the Sword even more. "He can't stand the sight of my bare skin because it reminds him of how much he liked touching it just a few days ago."

"Fucking hells," the Sword swears, turning his wrath on me.

I smile sweetly up at him. Caedia studiously ignores the drama, tending to the dressing on my shoulder instead.

"It's true, isn't it? Or is the sight of my bare shoulders really that offensive to you?" I wink, pulling down the strap of my chemise so it hangs off my good shoulder.

"Kyrie," Lara says, a warning in her voice. "Stop. Morrow is right. Stop aggravating him. And you, Sword, leave her alone, for fuck's sake."

Mushroom whinnies loudly in agreement, breaking some of the tension.

"Traitor," I mutter. If the Sword wants a fight, I'll give him a fight.

Caedia tightens the bandage and I suck in a breath. Maybe we should fight tomorrow, though, because I'm not sure I'd win tonight. Unless I played dirty.

"Caedia," I say innocently. "When do you think I can use my daggers again?"

"At the rate this is healing, tomorrow, I'd think."

"Kyrie, don't you dare," Lara sighs.

"Sword, how about we train tomorrow?"

"I wouldn't train with the likes of you."

I bark a laugh, glaring at the knight of death and assholes across the fire. "Why? You know I would kick your ass?"

"I know you'd cheat to win, and I wouldn't give you the satisfaction."

I stand up, swigging from the strawberry wine, then hand it back to Caedia, who seems highly entertained by everything. Good. I do so love a captive audience.

I cross to where the Sword's standing, glowering at me like his entire being depends on it.

"You couldn't handle me." I poke his chest and he frowns harder. "You couldn't handle me if I fought dirty, or if I fought clean." I let a slow smile curl my lips. "Dirty is always more fun, though."

"Enough." Lara's voice rings out. "That's enough. I want to enjoy this meal."

"You two should fuck already and get it over with," Caedia says frankly.

I startle. The Sword glowers.

And Morrow coughs, clearly offended by her rough suggestion.

"Is that your healer opinion?" I ask lightly.

"It's my 'it's going to be a long trip' if someone doesn't give in to this sexual tension' opinion." Caedia snorts.

Morrow makes another embarrassed noise, then pulls the first rabbit off the fire. "We should eat."

"What?" Caedia asks, her eyes wide and innocent. "I can't be the only one that's thinking it."

"*Enough.*" Lara pulls the mushrooms and potatoes off the embers. "Fill your mouths with food instead of insults, you pair of idiots."

Seems like a good enough compromise to me.

Besides, I got the last word, and from the look on the Sword's face as he stares at me, he's still thinking about it.

I grin at him, daring him to do something about it.

I'm disappointed when he only finishes eating and goes inside his tent. I'm not entirely sure why, either.

❋

LARA'S SNORING in her sleep like a hog in a mud puddle.

I toss and turn, but that only makes the pain in my shoulder worse.

"Fuck this," I mutter, but the words are lost in the wake of Lara's absurdly loud snoring. Surely snoring like that can't be healthy. I cast a concerned look at her, but other than the ludicrous sawing noise, she seems perfectly content.

I drape my cloak over my bare shoulders and chemise, not bothering with the blouse folded up next to our packs.

A small part of me knows it's dangerous to go alone at this time of night, so I fasten on my belt of daggers as a nod to self-preservation. A moment later, I'm through the tent's flap, tucking my feet into the fur-lined boots that are starting to look a little worse for wear, thanks to the manticore.

"Fucking monsters." I kick at a rock, annoyed and frustrated and full of a pent-up emotion that I'm not sure I really want to put a name to.

Maybe that's the reason I can't sleep. Maybe it's Lara's ripsaw snores, or maybe it's the fact I slept for two days straight, fevered from manticore poison.

Maybe it's the fact that no matter how hard I've tried to push the Sword from my mind today, I keep returning to the hairbrush on the nightstand, full of my hair.

He never left my side.

I don't understand it.

I suck in a deep breath, closing my eyes and trying to ground myself, to quiet my mind. A cough starts up in my chest, but whatever medicine Caedia's given me helps calm it nearly immediately.

The winter wind's not as harsh tonight, though the night is chill enough that I hug the cloak around myself. The scent of the air holds the promise of snow and I inhale it again, feeling more relaxed. Pine sap and wet earth, campfire smoke. The musk of a great cat.

My eyes fly open.

Sure enough, two glowing eyes stare out at me from the depths of the thick band of trees barely held back by the common road.

"Is that you, kitty-kitty?" I call. My nose scrunches because am I seriously calling the direcat kitty-kitty? Well. I didn't name him the last time he was around, so maybe kitty-kitty is better than nothing.

The eyes blink once, twice.

I decide to take my chances.

There's a dreamlike quality to the quiet night, especially once I move further from Lara's incredibly loud snoring.

"Kitty-kitty?" I murmur. Wretchedly unoriginal.

The eyes are close now, and the great rumbling purr of the direcat is like a balm to my soul.

"I missed you, you big bag of bones," I say softly, holding out a hand to the huge beast. I did, too, the truth of that statement surprising me. "I fought a manticore. It got ugly. I'm glad you weren't there to see it, but I would have liked having some company when I was recuperating."

I frown and the direcat butts against my hand, as if he senses my dismay.

Because I did have *some* company.

Just not company I understand. Not at all.

"I'm glad you're here," I say again, scratching under his ears until his eyes close in contentment. "I would have brought a few extra rabbits for you if I'd known you were going to show up."

I run my hand over his rumbling chest, expecting to feel bones—and I do, but not nearly as prominent.

"You've been eating well, huh, Fluffy?" My nose twitches. That's not a great name for him. "I'm glad you're doing better."

I lean against the giant cat and he rubs his face up and down my back, nearly knocking me off balance.

"He's marking you as his."

I nearly yelp in surprise, stopping the noise just in time.

The Sword emerges from the dark, moving without a sound.

"I don't mind," I say, too shocked that he's followed me to come up with a smart remark. "I just wish I knew what he wanted." His fur is so soft and warm I want to bury my face in it.

"Direcats were created as battle partners for the Fae."

I glance back at him in surprise. "I suppose you were there when the Fae fought with them by their sides, considering how ancient you are."

"I was there," he says simply.

"What was it like?" I ask before I can stop myself. I shouldn't pay attention to him at all, much less ask him questions. He's been extremely clear about how he feels about me.

And yet.

And yet—here he is. Standing in front of me, half-dressed despite the cold, his chest just as perfect as the last time I saw it at the hot spring, ready to tell me about the Fae.

About him.

"It was glorious and horrible all at once." He tilts his head up, staring at the stars dotting the night sky. "They were the kind of the days legends are made of, that great songs are composed about. There was nothing great about them, though. Just a lot of senseless death. Blood and violence, all because of the petty quarrelings of the princelings of the Fae."

He falls silent and I keep stroking the direcat, grateful to have something to do with my hands because I can't seem to look away from him.

"Did you know they say the gods were Fae once?" His words are so quiet I have to strain to hear them.

I frown in earnest, confused. "I have never heard that."

"No, you wouldn't have, would you?"

"Because I'm so incredibly young compared to you, is that right?" I ask on a low laugh.

"You have no idea," he agrees, his attention finally moving from the constellations hanging in the night sky to my face. "You have no idea," he repeats.

"Why don't you explain it to me, then?" I ask, and the question takes us both by surprise. "If I have no idea, then why don't you help me understand? Because I want to. I want to understand."

The pure anguish that furrows his brow takes my breath away. He hangs his head, then rakes a hand over his face.

I wait, anticipation building. It surprises me how much I want to understand him. How much I do care about him, despite him being a total fuckhead most of the time.

I'm one too, after all.

"We should get some sleep," he says instead.

I let out a long exhalation, relief and disappointment warring within me. I want to understand him, but the idea of... setting aside our petty nonsense scares me a little.

I don't know what we might have without it.

I don't know how to *be* without it. I should tell him that. I should tell him the truth.

"I can't sleep in that tent," I say instead. "Lara sounds like she forgot how to breathe."

"I did notice that." He looks past me at the direcat, who really, truly, very much needs a name. "You could sleep out here, with the direcat."

"What's the Fae word for it?" I blurt.

"For what?" His brow furrows in confusion.

"For the direcat. What did you call them, when they went into battle with you?"

The Sword sighs heavily, then surprises me by approaching the massive feline, holding out his calloused hand.

The cat sniffs at it, whiskers twitching, before raising its head slightly. The dimple appears on the Sword's face as he obediently scratches at the direcat's fluffy brown and white jaw.

"Osgotvorn," he says quietly, and the huge cat chuffs. I laugh at the sound, as well as the way the Sword startles at his response.

Our eyes meet and we share a smile for a moment.

"I'm not calling him that," I finally say, breaking the spell.

"That's probably for the best." He nods solemnly. "It translates to organ-eater of my enemies. Hardly rolls off the tongue."

I bite my cheeks. "Lovely."

A night bird coos somewhere in the trees above, and a yawn cracks my jaw.

"Sleep."

"I told you, there's no way I could with Lara making all that noise—"

"I meant here. With the organ-eater." He doesn't take his eyes from the cat, whose purring, I have to admit, is a much more soothing alternative to Lara's snoring.

"We can't call him that."

The Sword sighs, then points to the sky above. "You see that star up there? The one at the tip of the bow constellation?"

I crane my neck until I spot it. "The bluish one?"

"The Fae called it Filarion, named after a prince of our people. He was said to have been so fierce in battle, the gods took him as one of their own, jealous of his abilities. The gods are nothing if not a jealous sort," he muses. "We would send up prayers to our prince Filarion on the eve of battle, asking him to watch over us. Much like this creature keeps wanting to watch over you."

"Filarion," I repeat, running my hands through the cat's fur. "As much as it pains me to say you've picked a good name, I like it. What do you think, Fil?" The cat butts me and I smile at him, indulging his request by scratching behind his ears. "Fil it is."

The noise of something small scampering over the snow sets his tufted ears to twitching.

"Did you believe it?" I ask suddenly.

"Believe what?" The Sword scratches the scruff on his jaw.

"That the gods were Fae once?" The question feels important, feels necessary. "Did you believe Filarion watched over you when he was gone?"

"Filarion never felt the need to watch over me," he says darkly.

I narrow my eyes at him until the cat bumps my hand, asking for more scratching.

"Sleep well, Kyrie of Sola," the Sword says, still watching the star twinkling overhead. "I will watch over you, with Filarion's help."

I don't know if he means the star or the Fae prince or the cat, but I do know the words are truth. The Sword will watch over me.

Hasn't he been doing that since the moment I found him in Cottleside?

Confused, I try to think of a response, but exhaustion crashes over me like unruly waves on a beach before the storm.

I blink, sleepy in spite of myself, and somehow, Fil seems to sense that too, lying down and stretching out long on the ground.

It does look cozy.

"I've never been one to follow directions," I muse out loud. "I don't know why I am now."

Fil chuffs again, and if the Sword's still there in the dark, he doesn't answer.

The direcat's fur is soft and warm, and his purring lulls me to sleep.

26

THE SWORD

She is so very, very young.
The direcat kneads the dirt, clearly pleased with himself for comforting Kyrie into sleep.

"Filarion would laugh to know I've named you after him," I mutter to the cat. The prince would likewise be amused at my feelings for the human thief.

He would be disgusted with what's happened to me, though, what I've become—what I've done.

Kyrie's lids flutter in her sleep, her breathing soft and even. I envy that about her: how easily she can relax. I've watched her sleep since the day we met, and the contrast between her stillness in repose and her constant movement while awake never ceases to amaze me.

With the manticore poison in her, she wasn't still at all. Moving, muttering, sweating and crying out in her sleep. The only thing that seemed to soothe her was when I'd brush her hair, singing lullabies my mother used to sing to me, words half-forgotten, the melodies ingrained in my very heart.

I know I shouldn't get close to her, I know I shouldn't care for her, that it will only make everything more impossible than it already is—but I cannot resist her.

I meant what I told her, even though I watched it fracture a piece of her when I said it.

She is my punishment, my price for every crime.

Sleep never finds me, and dawn's first fingers of light turn her hair to molten copper.

I doubt I'll ever get to touch it again.

27

KYRIE

I feel fucking great. With five people, it took us no time at all to disassemble camp. Hard bread and sharp cheese put the fast in breakfast, and by noon we've put the forested foothills of Hiirek behind us, trading them for open road.

Without the shelter of the hills and woods, there's an uncomfortable bite to the air that even my cloak doesn't quite keep from nipping through.

A grey thicket of clouds blankets the sky, and before long, tiny dots of ice-cold snow prickle along my cheeks and nose.

"It's going to get worse," Morrow calls from the lead. "We need to push harder so we don't lose any more time."

Time. We all feel the weight pressing down on us of making it to Nyzbern in time for the distraction of the midwinter masque.

I cough, the tension in my chest ever tighter. Before we set off, Caedia handed me a flagon of some kind of herbal drink and I swig from it now, the taste bitter.

"He's right," the dryad calls from her white horse. "This storm is coming fast. I can feel it."

The Sword nods, as distant as ever, hardly sparing me a word today, even after our... mild truce last night. Well, maybe not a truce, but we weren't at each other's throats for once.

I've caught him looking at me, though. Throughout the morning, and even now, his gaze weighs heavy on me.

Fil the direcat was nowhere to be seen when I woke, but the ground was still warm where he'd been lying. Even now, trying to outrun the snow, I can't shake the feeling he's not far from us.

The world turns quiet as the snow begins falling in earnest, smothering out color and making the horses steam with their efforts.

There's no time for chat as we do our best to outrun the worst of the snow.

"We need to find a place to stay for the night," Lara yells, the wind nearly drowning out her words.

The horses' hooves sink in the snow. To our left, the Hiirek Mountains hide behind a veil of icy lace, a bride of jagged peaks. I blink through the snow gathering on my lashes. The tip of my nose went numb an hour ago, and the reins feel frozen in my hands.

"There," Morrow booms, and one of the horses screams in terror at his sudden sound.

Lara's right. The sooner we get our animals out of this storm, the better.

I squint, trying to make out whatever Morrow's seen, but my horse slips, losing her footing on the icy frozen ground.

"Fucking hells," I yelp, grabbing fistfuls of mane and trying to stay upright. My horse squeals, a high-pitched noise of pure terror. My heart jumps into my throat.

I don't want her to break a leg. Gods, I don't want to break a leg, either.

"Woah, girl, it's alright, it's alright." I'm shouting, the wind so loud I can hardly hear myself.

Finally, I regain control of her and she stops prancing, her sides heaving. I slip off her back, determined to lead her on foot, but one look around tells me the worst.

I've lost sight of everyone else.

The storm's only worsened, and all I can see are white sheets of snow in every direction.

I blow out a breath, the air so cold now it's sharp against my lungs. The horse nudges my shoulder.

Well.

Maybe it won't be the curse that kills me after all. I huff a laugh, but there's no humor in it.

"Kyrie," a voice bellows to my right. "Kyrie, where are you?"

It's the Sword.

Of course it is. He's stalking towards me, his hair so bright it shines even against the snow, his black clothes a blot of inky night against white.

I'm so happy to see him, I could cry. Except my tears would freeze in my eyelashes, and that would be truly embarrassing because he would know without a doubt I was crying.

"Don't think for a minute you're getting out of this that easily," he says roughly.

"How did you even see me?" I sputter. He grabs my horse's reins with one hand, and his other arm wraps around my waist. "I can't see anything in this."

"There's nowhere you could go that I wouldn't find you," he says.

With that, he heaves me over one shoulder.
For once in my life, I'm rendered utterly speechless.

28

THE SWORD

Morrow's proven useful, I'll give him that.

The abandoned cabin is tucked in the thicket of evergreen trees at the very start of the ancient forest that bleeds into the Hiirek Mountains. Dust coats the interior in thick layers, and cold air seeps through the uneven door, but it is out of the storm, and for that, I am immensely grateful.

"Thank Lojad for steering you here," I tell the knight. I set Kyrie down on the planks. It takes great effort, though, for I'd rather keep holding her, ensuring she's warm.

He inclines his head, humble enough to avoid looking too pleased with himself.

Caedia's singing softly to the horses, who we've managed to coax inside, and Lara's taking their tack off. Kyrie shoots me a strange look, then scurries off to help them.

"How far back was she?" Morrow asks quietly. "It's odd she fell behind."

"Far enough to make me worry," I tell him.

It isn't odd though, not to me.

It's to be expected. Sola may not have the same immediate reach as I do, or that of Nakush or Lojad, but she has a hand in this all the same.

All too easily could she have thwarted us. All too easily could she set the storm in motion that could have undone all our efforts.

"We should take care of our mounts," is all the knight says, though his eyes are narrowed as he scrutinizes my face.

A sigh tries to escape from my throat, but I swallow it down.

Being around these humans nonstop has caused me to pick up some of their mannerisms, I fear.

My own horse seems well off compared to the others, and Mushroom is as easy-going as ever, so it's almost natural that I find myself beside Kyrie again, helping her tend to her mare.

"She's pulled up lame," Kyrie says, and when I glance at her from the corner of my eye, I see a tear roll down her cheek. "It's my fault. I wasn't paying attention, and—"

"Hush, Kyrie," I tell her fiercely. "Did you call down the blizzard? Do you have some elemental powers you were hiding this whole time?"

Comforting her is as strange as it suddenly seems second nature.

A reluctant chuckle follows my questioning and she spares me a slow, grateful smile. "Of course not." The smile fades just as quickly as it graced her lips, a hint of warmth in winter. "But if I hadn't drank from the chalice, she wouldn't be hurt. None of you would have to do this with me."

"Is that... guilt I hear?" Lara pipes up, and I clamp down on the urge to snarl at her to shut the hells up.

Kyrie doesn't respond with her usual devil-may-care repartee.

Instead, she crumples, flinging her arms around me.

"I shouldn't have done it. What have I done? I don't want any of you to get hurt because of me."

I freeze.

She's so cold, the tip of her nose ice where it meets the fabric of my shirt.

Lara's eyes widen, and Caedia simply ignores everything, tending to her white horse like Kyrie crying isn't anything to worry about.

"Get a fire started, Morrow," I order. "Caedia, heal her horse."

Caedia shoots me a disgruntled frown.

"Please," I tack on.

As for Kyrie, I pick her up again because, Heska help me, I can't seem to keep myself from touching her. Not for any comfort it gives her, but because of the comfort it gives me.

The reassurance that she's real.

There's a small door in the floor near the stone fireplace and I kick it open, carrying Kyrie down into the cold dark beneath.

The dark's never bothered me, and I know Kyrie well enough to know she doesn't want to be around the others right now.

The door slams behind us and the only noise is that of the horses and quiet conversation above, muffled by Kyrie's full-on sobs.

"I am sorry, Sword, I am so sorry." She's shaking her head, her hands tight around my neck, like she's afraid of what will happen should she let go.

I don't want her to let go.

She blinks up at me, eyes swollen and red as her frost-bit nose, and it's clear she can't see as well as I can in the dark.

I shift her, settling us down on what's undoubtedly a filthy cellar floor, not caring, the need to comfort her overriding everything, always.

"Why, Kyrie? Why are you sorry?"

"Be-be-because someone is going to die. Someone I care about now, even stupid Morrow, I like him too, I don't want him to die."

My shoulders tense. I don't want her to like Morrow.

"I'm not stupid," he yells from overhead.

"Shut it," Lara says, and dirt slips through the cracks between floorboards as they walk around above us.

Blessedly, Caedia begins singing, a song I thought lost to time.

It makes me tighten my hold on Kyrie.

I don't want to lose her.

I can't.

"Why did I have to drink from it?" She drags a hand across her face, wiping the evidence of her tears away.

"Kyrie of Sola," I say softly, wanting my words to be for her alone and not any that may listen above, gods and humans both.

She stares up at me, her eyes huge and luminous, the red rims only making them seem even more unearthly green.

My breath stalls and I force myself to breathe through the sudden desire rushing through me.

"Kyrie," I finally manage to continue. "Think. Could you have kept yourself from it?"

"Shouldn't I have been able to? If no one else has been stupid enough to do it but me?"

"Did you consider, Kyrie," *my Kyrie*, "that you did it because you had to? That you were the one the draught was destined for?"

I'm getting dangerously close to revealing too much. The truth is right there, dangling before her, and all she need do is reach out and grab it.

But if there's one thing I've learned about mortals in all my years, it's that they are so often blind to what is right before them—they don't want to see it, don't want to upset their fragile notions of where they belong in this life.

And the next.

"Why would I be destined for it? I'm nothing special. Just one of Sola's many blood orphans."

"You are, for better or worse," I say slowly, trying desperately to help her see it, knowing I cannot tell her plainly, "the *only* one special enough to drink from that chalice. The silver tongue, the first blessed with such power in an age or more. You are the distillment of magic and chaos, the embodiment of all that Sola holds precious."

"Fuck Sola," she says, and I know I've lost my opportunity to help her understand.

This is going to kill me. It's slowly ripping the shreds of my soul further and further apart, and for the first time in my memory, I want something other than my old self back.

I *want* Kyrie.

I want her smiles, and her terrible jokes, and her mischievous looks, and I want to earn the heat and desire she lavished on me in that small, gods-forsaken village in the Hiirek foothills.

For better or worse, for my ruin and hers, I would sell what's left of my time on Heska to have Kyrie beside me forever.

"That's why you had to drink from the cup," I tell her, shaking my head, because lies don't come easily to me. Not now, not with Kyrie in my lap, tired and cold and so sad it makes my heart ache. "You."

I almost tell her then, the truth that will end us both so savagely that it will change the course of history.

She had to drink from the cup because Kyrie, with her chaotic sunshine warmth, is the only one I could love.

"The mare is going to be fine, Kyrie," Caedia shouts. "Come up here, you two."

"We have the fire going," Morrow rumbles. "There's food."

I look past the flame-haired beauty in my arms to the barrels all around us.

"Morrow, you're going to have a headache tomorrow," I call back.

"What? I don't think you should threaten him," Kyrie says tiredly, without any real heat.

"I'm not." I can't help but huff a laugh at her. "These barrels?" I knock on one, and sure enough, it's not empty. "They're full of *something*. Based on where we are, on the outlands of Chast, I'm going to guess rum or whiskey. This is probably a bootlegger's stash."

Her pretty lips form a round O, and I *barely* resist hugging her to me.

"Then we should celebrate being alive while I still can," she says, and though her lips smile like it's a joke, it doesn't quite reach her eyes.

The worst part is, I can't disagree.

29

KYRIE

Morrow's singing again. Caedia is too, and Lara's dancing around, clapping her hands as a fire crackles in the hearth. Morrow grabs her by the wrists as he sings, and she laughs uproariously as he spins her around.

Aside from an occasional ear twitch, the horses and Mushroom pointedly ignore us, just like we're pointedly ignoring the fact we're rooming with them until the worst of the storm passes. As for Fil, he's braving it on his own somewhere, and the thought makes me worried for the huge cat all over again.

Lara invents a ridiculous verse about the drunken soldier, making Morrow boom it out, too.

"What would you do with a drunken soldier," he belts, "when you tie his boots together?"

Lara dissolves into giggles, barely able to stand on her own.

I'm laughing too, but it all too quickly turns into a cough, a cough I can't seem to get the better of, gasping for air, my eyes watering.

"Here," Caedia says, putting my hands around a cup of steaming tea.

"I didn't realize you were making this." I sniff it cautiously.

"Well, you were pretty busy making the most of the poison you found in the cellar."

I cough again, and she tips some into my mouth, causing me to sputter.

The coughing fit immediately ceases, and I make myself swallow the foul mixture.

"She's getting worse," Caedia tells the Sword.

"She can hear you," I slur, grumpy and slightly drunk.

But gods, I'm alive. I'm alive, despite the white-out blizzard, despite the curse, despite the manticore, and to spite Sola her fucking self.

"You should sleep," Caedia says with a smile. "You need rest."

"I can't sleep while they're making all that noise—" I gesture at Morrow and Lara, but they've stopped making noise.

My jaw drops open. She's kissing him. *Oh.*

"Come on," the Sword says, a hint of amusement in his deep voice. "We can give them some privacy."

"Don't tell me you're taking me down to the cellar again," I say. The Sword's been in and out of there, hauling up barrels and other things he's found beneath. How the hells he's able to see down there, I guess I'll just have to blame on his Fae heritage or his allegiance to Hrakan or, if that fails, maybe he's conned some spirits into being his eyes and ears in the dark.

"It's not so bad," the Sword says, and when his dimple flashes, I shrug one shoulder.

Hard to argue with that dimple.

I follow him down the dark steps on my own this time, warm and fuzzy from the liquor, from being safe from the storm outside, and from... whatever the hells is going on between me and this huge male I thought hated me.

When I reach the bottom, the Sword flips the door overhead closed, and I gasp in surprise.

He's set up a little room down here.

"I didn't notice you doing this," I say slowly, turning around and taking it all in. The stone cellar walls are hung with sconces I didn't notice before, but now they're lit, fire dancing merrily in their iron basins. Shadows chase each other across the small underground room, and the dirt floors are covered in our sleeping supplies.

I chug the rest of the scalding tea, even though it makes my eyes water worse.

He's watching me carefully, his dark eyes narrowed as he scrutinizes every expression that passes over my face.

"Sword," I say quietly, tearing my gaze away from the pallet he's set up on the floor... for us.

I swallow hard.

"I thought you might sleep better away from everyone. Lara and her snoring in particular," he says roughly, scratching the scruff on his jaw. "Caedia said you need rest, and I don't want you wandering outside tonight in these conditions."

"Sword," I say again, this time grinning up at him. Gods, he's so huge, he eats up nearly all the air in the room. I step closer, poking his chest. "I would almost say you're worried about me. Are you going soft on me?"

A muscle in his temple twitches, and I keep my finger on him for a moment before placing my palm in its place over his heart.

"Would you rather I be hard for you?"

My eyes widen. Are we going to—is he... confusion tangles my thoughts.

I really thought he hated me.

You're my punishment, he told me.

That's not how he's looking at me now. No, I was mistaken. It's not hate—maybe it never was. I shift closer to him, watching him so, so carefully.

I bite my lower lip, running my palm up the hard plane of his chest.

"What are you doing?" he asks, his warm, rum-scented breath a caress against my forehead.

"What I think we've both wanted for a while now," I answer, standing up on my tiptoes. My palm slides up to his cheek and he sighs, leaning into it in a sweet way I never would have expected from him.

It makes me feel vulnerable.

"It doesn't have to mean anything," I blurt out, scrambling to blot out that weak sensation.

"Is that what you want?" he says, that heat in his eyes growing. No, not hate at all. Intensity, yes. Scary, also yes, a little. But hate? No.

"Isn't that what you want?" I tilt my head, tickling my fingers along his cheekbone. "Or are you afraid you're too old to keep up with me?"

His expression darkens at the reminder of how fundamentally different we are and I go still, nervous I've pushed too far.

Until his arm goes around my waist, dragging me into him, his fingers digging into my hip. His other hand pushes at my unbound hair, tucking it behind my ear before clasping the back of my neck.

"I have thousands of years of experience," he drawls in a slow, lazy tone I haven't heard before. A shiver of anticipation goes up my spine. "I can make you come in ways you never even imagined."

"Mmmmm," I say, twisting my lips to the side. "Never imagined? I think you're underestimating my creativity, oh ancient one."

"I doubt it," he murmurs, his lips brushing against my forehead, my cheek.

I melt into him, my fingertips tracing the hard edge of his cheekbone.

"Are you sure?" he whispers into my ear, his hand dipping into the waist of my pants.

"If you are, I am," I answer easily. "Caedia's right, we should get it out of our system, you know? Have a little fun."

"It wouldn't be just a little fun with you," he murmurs, and I moan as his teeth scrape against my earlobe. "I would ruin you for all others."

"Well, you could certainly try," I say, gasping as his fingers run lower, nearly touching me where I'm wet and wanting, teasing me.

"No," he says, matter of fact. "I would not just try. I would succeed, and it wouldn't be for *fun*, or to get it out of your system. And I think until you can admit that to yourself, you should keep your distance from me."

I reel as his hands leave my skin, leaving me cold and trembling.

"I'll sleep upstairs. Don't even think about midnight wandering," he says.

I've never disliked him more than I do right now, in this moment, when he closes the door to the cellar, leaving me open-mouthed and half-drunk and impossibly frustrated.

"Fuck you, Sword," I yell up.

"In your dreams, maybe," he yells back.

Oooh, I'm going to kill him for this.

30

THE SWORD

I am a fool.

I lie awake, the sound of the fire crackling in the hearth competing with the raging wind blowing snow outside.

My self-control is slipping around Kyrie, everything about her a siren's call to my very soul.

Just as fate knew she would be.

My opposite in so many things, both attractive and infuriating for just that reason. A light against the darkness, everything I've needed and been resistant to all at once.

The blizzard rages outside, as loud as the swirling thoughts inside my head, usually neat and ordered. The taste of her skin's still on my tongue, and I know all I would have to do to sate my need is go back to her side.

I won't, though. Not like that.

No, if Kyrie ever comes to me again, it will be with the full knowledge that she is mine, and mine alone, forever.

JANUARY BELL

Even if she hates me for it.
My molars grind against each other.
I don't sleep.

❄

The worst of the storm's spent itself by the time everyone else awakes, bleary-eyed and hung over, save for Caedia, who is as chipper as ever.

Likely due to her dryad metabolism, faster than the humans and better equipped at processing all kinds of poisons, including nearly a hundred-proof bootlegger alcohol.

The cellar door creaks open, and Kyrie emerges. She covers her mouth with a delicate hand, yawning.

"Good morning, Morrow, Caedia, Lara. And the horses of course," she says in her musical voice.

I shift, amusement and irritation warring within me at her heavy-handed attempt at ignoring me.

"I see the storm's stopped." She peers out the thick, crude window into the bright white snow.

"Your mare is in good shape, by the way," Caedia tells her, handing her a hunk of bread. "Right as rain."

Relief crosses over Kyrie's face, quickly hidden by that mischievous smile.

My throat constricts. I loathe that stamp of Sola on her— that she thinks she needs to hide the best parts of her under a mask constructed by the sisters who raised her.

Despite everything, though, that kindness, that soft heart of hers shines through.

I see her.

The chalice, the curse put on me by Sola herself...

Perhaps it's been my biggest blessing. The only blessing.

Morrow nudges me with his elbow. "Seems you pissed her

right off," he says conspiratorially, with a dark look at the raven-haired witch.

Lara's studiously ignoring him, too, though they were both snoring by the time I left Kyrie alone in the basement last night.

"We might be in the same boat, Sword," Morrow continues, then shoves a piece of dried fruit in his mouth, chewing aggressively. "Looks like my woman's displeased with me as well. We're a right pair of idiots."

"Speak for yourself," I tell him. But a bolt of warmth shoots through my chest, and my lips stretch into a conspiratorial smile.

The last time I had any sort of true companionship was with Filarion and our old unit of Fae warriors. My friends, now wiped from the face of this world, only seen on clear nights shimmering high above in the heavens. The memories sober me and I sigh deeply.

Morrow finishes chewing, giving me a long look.

"I wouldn't dare call someone who allowed himself to be caught and put in Cottleside for ten years an idiot," he says.

"Just as I wouldn't call Lojad's chosen an idiot." I find myself smiling again, the muscles in my face twitching from the strangeness of it.

"I'm not the one who worships Death." Morrow snorts, tearing off a hunk of bread with his teeth.

"Death doesn't need worship. Death and time are inevitable," I say. My gaze strays to Kyrie's laughing face, deep in quiet conversation with Lara while Caedia inspects her wounds.

One of the horses stamps its feet and we both glance back at where they're crowded by the cabin door.

"There's something out there," Caedia says suddenly.

Morrow's up in a flash, muttering a cantrip under his breath. Red flashes across his skin, and he rolls his shoulder.

"We face a fork in the road," Lara murmurs, so quiet even I must strain to hear her.

The horses tug at their makeshift tethers, nostrils flaring as they blow out frantic breaths.

A snarl, inhuman, rattles the door.

"What the fuck? By Lojad's fucking beard, what the fuck are you?"

A catlike sound of pain and anger follows a thud.

"It's Fil," Kyrie says, leaping to her feet.

Her feet slam against the floorboards as she sprints to the door, tugging it open. Violence radiates from her in tangible waves.

I leap to her side, pulling my sword from the sheath on my back. A tall, lean man outside the cabin surveys Kyrie with obvious interest.

My lip curls into a snarl.

"Get the fuck away from my cat," she hisses, her daggers flashing in the harsh winter sun.

"Well, hello," the male drawls. "And what, exactly, are you and your horses doing in my cabin?"

"Considering murder," Kyrie says, her voice deadly calm.

Morrow's beside her in a flash, one hand on her shoulder, a gesture that might appear to be calming, but the red now flashing across Kyrie's skin signals it's anything but.

Morrow's just transferred his ward to her.

I dip my chin at him in gratitude.

"Your cabin," Kyrie repeats in a low voice that promises bloodshed.

"That's right, Red," he says to her, wicked amusement playing across his face at her clear distaste for his nickname.

"Lucky you're still here, by the way, considering Lojad came to me in a dream last night and told me to find you."

Morrow heaves a sigh of what can only be relief.

"You won't be so lucky if you touch my cat again," Kyrie snarls.

"Put the daggers away, Kyrie," Lara calls from beside the fire. "He's our sixth."

The man stuffs his gloved hands into his pockets, strolling past Kyrie and me with an air of studied nonchalance. "Thank you, lovely maiden," he tells Lara.

Lara remains expressionless.

Once inside, he pauses, taking in the horses in the corner, raising one eyebrow in distaste.

"I see you've made yourselves at home," he says mildly, then dips his upper body in the faintest hint of a bow. "Sampled the goods, even?" His gaze floats over the open barrel of alcohol, then catalogs the rest of the barrel crowding the room. "The name's Dario. Dario Krauss." He tosses his brown shoulder-length hair. "I'm sure you've heard of me."

Lara and Kyrie share a confused look. Morrow shifts his weight, one hand on his sword pommel, and Caedia outright laughs.

"No one has heard of you," she tells him, matter of fact.

"Lojad told me I needed to smuggle you into Nyzbern," he drawls.

"Did he tell you why?" Kyrie asks. Fil stands beside her, rubbing his whiskered cheeks on her shoulders.

"Of course he did," the man sniffs with disdain. "To save Heska and unite the gods."

My fingers grip the pommel of my sword even more tightly. "Unite the gods," I repeat.

"Well, I hate to break it to you," Kyrie trills. "But all we're really doing is stealing something from my ex-fiancé. I'm sure you've heard of him. Alaric, King of Diamonds?"

Dario considers her, taking in her red waves and still-defensive posture.

"You," he says slowly, his face blanching suddenly. "*You.*"

"Me," she tells him cheerily, clearly enjoying this. Or at least pretending to for his benefit. Kyrie steps closer to him, and he shrinks backward. "And you kicked my cat," she tells him.

Fil bares his teeth, snarling. I grin. His namesake would be proud.

"Kyrie," Lara says in a warning voice. "We need him."

"The King of Diamonds," Dario says, taking us all in, deflating slightly before putting his hands on his hips. He's missing his third and fourth finger from his left hand. "You need to steal something from the most dangerous man in Nyzbern?"

"Yes. And like you said..." Kyrie trails off, like she can't quite bring herself to say it.

"The fate of the world hangs in the balance," I finish for her.

She doesn't look at me.

It doesn't negate the truth of it, no matter how much she wants to lie to herself about her unwitting role. Or how much she's afraid of it.

31

KYRIE

I take a bit too much satisfaction in the knowledge that Dario knows who I am.

"Regardless of destiny, or the damned gods—"

He flinches at my blasphemy.

"We have a job to do, and if, like you said, Lojad sent you, then he must have a reason for it." Suspicion builds in me. "Why are you really here? You don't strike me as one of Lojad's faithful."

His gaze shifts sideways to where the Sword stands, the very picture of menace.

I yawn. "I can make you tell us."

Dario flinches. A tiny thing, less than a second, but I caught it. Spreading his hands wide, he smiles blandly.

"Silver Tongue, I know you can. All who remember your reign of terror at the King of Diamonds' side do."

"It was advantageous for me." The words sound dull, bored, but my stomach twists in disgust at the memory of those months at his side, at the way I used my power to convince people to do whatever we—he—bade. All so I could unlock the mystery of Alaric's many vaults and help myself to what lay within.

"I'm sure it was," he agrees, every inch of him projecting calm yet again. "You know," he says, narrowing his eyes at me. "You aren't the King of Diamonds' favorite person. In fact... I think he has a bounty out on you. One thousand gold marks."

"One thousand?" I echo. "That's all?" I sigh in disappointment.

"That's a fortune," Caedia interjects, her strange eyes glimmering. "You stole enough from him to warrant that kind of coin, and you dress like that?"

Offended, I glance down at my clothes. "What's wrong with how I dress?"

"What did you steal from him, Kyrie?" Lara asks.

"Whatever looked good. Whatever looked like something I might want." I shrug a shoulder. Lara's staring at me though, and I wonder how much Nakush has whispered to her about me, how much she knows in spite of my best efforts.

She might be my only friend, my closest friend, but I keep my secrets even from her.

Anything to protect the truth of what those stolen goods went to fund. Anything to protect those people.

Dario scratches his beard, considering. "The best time to steal from him would be the—"

"Midwinter masque," Lara and I chime in together.

"Good thing I have a standing invitation." Dario smiles, all charm, but I'm not buying it. There's something slippery about him, something I don't trust.

Not that I trust many people, anyway.

Still. It puts me on edge. Fil rubs his cheek against my head and I reach up to scratch under his chin.

"How do you feel about traveling into Nyzbern via a barrel?" he asks me. "The rest of you won't have a problem getting through the gates." He jerks his chin at me. "Silver Tongue is a different story."

I preen. "It's so nice to be recognized for my hard work."

"A barrel?" the Sword asks, dubious.

Aw, is he worried about me? Not that it matters, the huge asshole.

Dario sizes him up like he's just now seeing him, and a flash of who Dario really is appears, vanishing just as quickly, replaced by that smarmy smile.

"I'm the official supplier of liquor to His Majesty, King of Diamonds," he says in a mocking voice. "Beyond pleased to make your acquaintance." The words are tinged with a familiar air of self-deprecation. "Silver Tongue, I know, though I daresay you don't remember me. The rest of you, though, are new to me."

"How did you lose your fingers?" Caedia asks him with her usual off-beat bluntness.

"I gambled them in a card game."

I can taste the lie, and despite all my promises to myself not to do so, I glance over at the Sword.

He's watching me. Not Dario, who he should be watching.

Nope. His gaze smolders over me and I quickly look away.

"How soon can you get us into Nyzbern?" I shift my attention back to Dario. "We need as much time as we can get to prepare for the masque."

"What are you stealing?" he asks.

Lara opens her mouth, but I interrupt before she can get a word out.

"Whatever I feel like," I answer with a shrug.

No matter what Lara says about him being our sixth, I don't trust him.

That strange, hyper-intelligent gaze trips over me, replaced by smarm in less than half a second.

I tilt my head, studying him. The oily sweet-talking version, the fake one.

Takes a liar to know one.

I just hope whatever I saw under that facade isn't even worse.

"I can certainly get you lot inside the ball, but as far as stealing from the King of Diamonds, I'm afraid I won't be too much help. He keeps his treasures in a vault below ground, guarded with both magic and traps."

The Sword takes a step closer to Dario, menace simmering in his body language.

Dario shrinks back slightly.

"You say you know nothing of his vault?"

"Of course not. I do know some things. Like where the entrance is in his keep," he stammers slightly, as though the Sword terrifies him. "I told you I was sent by Lojad. Why would I lie?"

"Why would you lie, indeed?" I repeat, my eyes narrowed. "And his keep?"

"Things have changed since you were last in Nyzbern, Silver Tongue," Dario says meekly. "The King of Diamonds has fortified his palace…" he trails off, looking at me expectantly. "Likely because of what happened the last time you were there."

I preen a little. "It's nice to know your hard work's been appreciated."

Lara waves a hand at the Sword and me, an annoyed rush of air sighing out of her. "Nakush says he's our sixth, so he's our sixth. He can get us into the city, and into the masque. The gods provide," she says.

I wince. The gods provide. Ugh. How many times did I hear

that from the Sisters of Sola after I begged them to stop hurting me or the few friends I had? The goddess provides, they'd say.

I learned to stop asking for mercy.

Sola's mercy is little different from her punishment.

Swallowing, I dip my chin in acquiescence. I extend a hand, smiling through my misgivings.

"Welcome to the team," I say, and he takes my hand in his gloved one. A truce.

And a sign of how I'll keep him exactly at arm's length because I don't trust him, and I certainly don't trust the damned gods.

❄

Nyzbern by night is just as ostentatious as I remember, the jewel in Sola's city-state of Chast. Smoke rises from the chimney spires within the city, candles flickering in windows as the sunset's blaze dies behind the Hiirek Mountains. Nivor Forest creeps around and behind the city walls, massive trees with trunks as big as three grown men casting harsh shadows in the dying light. The newer copper shingle roofs gleam under patches of snow in the waning light, the older buildings' copper shingles the trademark Nyzbern green with verdigris.

My hand goes to my throat, the air suddenly hard to breathe.

I didn't think I would ever come back here. Not willingly, at least.

A sarcastic smile turns my lips up because I suppose I'm here on pain of death, just as my ex-fiancé would like. Alaric's palace is just visible near the center of the walled city, and I stare at it for a long moment.

"What have you done with your treasures, Alaric?" I murmur to myself.

My chest tightens at the thought of seeing him again. At risking it.

I haven't been brave enough to tell the others just how much he hates me, though I'm sure the Sword can guess, what with his firsthand experience with me.

"Time to get in," Morrow tells me, jerking me from my reverie. He takes the reins of my mare so I can climb down. Lara grimaces, then checks herself and gives me a wan smile.

The Sword says nothing, but I can feel his attention on me. Snow falls again in pretty, soft flakes, settling in his hair before melting away.

"I lined it with a quilt," Lara tells me for the millionth time.

"Here," Caedia says, handing me a flagon. I uncork the top and sniff it, making a face and gagging slightly.

"What the hells is this?" I should know better than to smell anything Caedia gives me at this point.

"We can't have you coughing in the barrel. Drink it and keep your mouth shut, if you can."

"You know, I could just use my magic to convince the guards to let us through," I say uneasily, eyeing the barrels in the back of the wagon we helped Dario load up this morning before setting out to Nyzbern.

"Not an option," Lara says. "You can't enchant everyone who sees you, and from what Dario says, you're well known in this city."

I roll my eyes, then blow out a breath because she's right, and I hate it.

Gingerly, I step onto the wood surface of the wagon, slick with ice and snow from the day's ride to Nyzbern. The empty barrel is in the middle of the wagon, towards the front.

"And you don't think they'll check this one?" I ask Dario again.

"Don't worry," he says smoothly. "They know me. I'll take care of it."

I take one last look at the green and copper roofed city through the gently falling snow, then watch the direcat slinking towards the forest encircling the city.

Fil's the last thing I need to worry about, but I can't help thinking I'd feel better with him at my side. Creature comfort, I guess. Even I have to admit, though, that the huge cat might raise some red flags around Nyzbern, and the fewer flags we put out, the better.

"Hurry up," Caedia demands, pushing the flagon up. "Drink."

I do as she says, because what option do I have? I'm dying, and I might be murdered by the guards if they hear a barrel of rum having a coughing fit.

Might as well drink the nasty potion and put off the inevitable while I can.

"That was gods-awful," I tell her, trying not to hurl, then pass the flagon back to her.

"Hurry, someone is coming," Lara hisses.

"Here goes nothing," I mutter. I take one last look around, sincerely hoping my plan doesn't go to shit.

The Sword's gaze is still fixed on me, and my eyes widen in surprise as I see something there I haven't before: worry.

Concern.

"Not for you, Kyrie," I tell myself, putting one leg in the barrel, then another. I fold myself up, knees as close to my chest as they can get, still tasting the foul bitterness of the medicine on my tongue.

The barrel reeks of alcohol, and I think I might get half drunk on the fumes alone.

"Ready?" Dario asks, not waiting for an answer as he closed

the lid over the barrel. I flinch as he hammers one nail, two nails, then three into the lid.

I close my eyes and wish I had a god I trusted to pray to.

I don't dare invoke Sola. She would no doubt make things worse for me for her own amusement.

My stomach churns with every rut and bump the wagon hits, and my teeth chatter from the cold, despite the heavy quilt padding the interior and the tarp they threw over the barrels.

"Halt," a guard's voice calls out, and I blink into the darkness, clamping a hand over my mouth. "What's in the cart?"

"Rum for the King of Diamonds' festivities," Dario says in an unctuous voice. "And clients of mine in for his masque."

"Show us," another guard says in a bored voice. My stomach clenches.

I don't like this. I don't like being cooped up in here, unable to see what's happening and entirely at the mercy of my companions' quick thinking... or not-so-quick.

Torchlight flickers through the seams in the lid of the barrel, the tarp overhead thrown aside.

"Would you care for a taste of my wares?" Dario asks, and the clink of coin filters through the thick wood. "And a donation for your outpost this eve," he adds.

"Open that one," one of the guards commands, I stop breathing as he knocks on the lid of my barrel.

Until the urge to cough hits me.

I suck in a small breath, trying to swallow the coughing fit that threatens. Gods, if even Caedia's potions aren't working against the stupid chalice's curse, how long do I have?

"Of course, of course," Dario says, and the cart wobbles as a body jumps onto the bed. One of the cracks goes dark. "Though the King of Diamonds may not be pleased to know his supply has been tampered with."

The implicit threat hangs in the air, and for a second, I think I'm totally fucked, that I'll have to enchant these two guards no matter what, and I start gathering my power, letting it filter through me.

"Fine. Move along," one of the guards says easily. "Give the King of Diamonds our respects."

"Will do, gentlemen."

Minutes pass like molasses and I bite down on my wrist, my lungs burning with the need to cough.

Finally, the barrel rocks slightly as the wagon begins moving again.

The sound of the Night Market of Nyzbern fills the barrel, and nostalgia winds through me. I used to love this city. The chaos of the Night Market especially, all the vendors with their colorful wares, the musicians busking on every street corner, and the scent of spiced meats and all sorts of bread and goods.

The light changes from the smokey oranges of the gate's torches to purples and greens and pinks, the multicolored markers of the different types of merchants. Purples for fine jewelry and top-tier silks and satins, greens for herbalists and potion makers, and pinks for food stalls. Blues for blacksmiths and armorers, oranges for booksellers and scrolls, and bright red for goods that would be illegal anywhere else in Heska, save for Nyzbern.

We pass under one such lantern, and Lara hisses in distaste so loudly I can hear her from inside the barrel.

"Come on then, gents, ladies, care to sample the flesh of the newest imports to Nyzbern? We have anything you might want, any race, any color, any age."

I close my eyes, sickened by the sound of an all too familiar voice.

Has it all been for nothing, then, if he's still here? Despair winds through me and I brace one palm against the inside of the barrel, glad I chose to get inside of it because that vendor would sell me out to Alaric as soon as he saw me.

Motherfucking flesh traders, and that one is the worst of them all.

I crack my neck, stretching out as much as I can in the small space.

Maybe I should put the flesh-traders permanently out of business... and wipe him off the Heskan continent for good.

I bare my teeth, relishing the thought.

Maybe I'll do a bit more crime than I originally planned on while I'm here.

32

THE SWORD

Raucous. Overwhelming. There are too many scents, too many people, too much.

Nyzbern is chaos, and it's no wonder it's the capital of Sola's city-state.

I tug the dark hood of my cloak lower over my face, the flesh-monger leering at me from under the glowing red lights of his brothel.

Only the fact I don't dare draw attention to any of us keeps me from pulling the sword from under my cloak and running him through.

How Kyrie stood this place long enough to carve out a home here is beyond my ken. Disgust curls my lip, and I breathe a sigh of relief as we move past the red lights and onto an emptier side street.

Despite the evening wearing on, there are plenty of people milling about, the sour smell of unwashed skin mingling uncomfortably with the scent of yeast breads and spiced meats.

Dario leads the way, his cart rumbling slowly along the cobblestones, gas lamps lighting the way.

Morrow's rigid in his saddle and Lara sneers at nearly everything she sees, but Caedia's staring around open-mouthed, the healer clearly overwhelmed.

I don't remember Nyzbern like this. The flesh-mongers in the open, their red lights brash as they call out the people for sale—it was not like this before.

Sola may be the goddess of chaos and lies, but this is beyond even her.

I was in Cottleside for years, yes, but the rate at which this city's declined into open depravity far exceeds any expectations I had.

"How long have the flesh traders been in the open?" I ask Dario in a low voice.

He glances sidelong at me, tilting his head as he considers the question. "As long as I can remember."

I wince, guilt flooding through me. There is so much I should have been doing, should have been fixing, instead seeking vengeance and then punishment.

My time in Cottleside is nothing compared to what the people of Heska have been through during my selfish tantrums.

The barrel where Kyrie's hiding sits quietly among the rest of Dario's illicit stash and I tear my gaze from it, from where I can scent her, even through the stench of wine and the foul tonic Caedia brewed for her.

What have I done, turning a blind eye to the suffering of the people I should be shepherding through this life and the next in favor of revenge?

I have been a fool.

Shaking my head, I settle back in the saddle, angry at Sola for allowing this in her city. Angry at the people for committing such atrocities against each other.

Most of all, though, I'm angry at myself. Resolve stiffens my spine.

I *will* make it right.

Kyrie and I will fix this.

The first step is retrieving the Crown of Sola, then performing the ritual. There's no doubt in my mind she will loathe me for what we must do, but it's the only way.

Then, and only then, we can turn our attention to correcting the fraying threads of fate all around us.

"Here we are," Dario announces, pulling up to a large estate at the western wall of town. Behind the wall, the skeletal trees of Nivor Forest reach their snow-covered branches skyward, towards the stars hanging above.

A few servants rush out of the house at our arrival, ushering the horses—and Mushroom—into a connected stable.

The servants begin offloading the barrels too, and I shove my way between them, grabbing Kyrie's barrel without bothering to give them an explanation.

A cough sounds as I pick it up and I cough, too, to cover it.

The chalice's curse is advancing faster than it should, just like the evil festering across Heska.

Holding the barrel over one shoulder, I ignore the mystified looks the servants shoot my way, following Dario and the rest into his opulent home.

Candles glint all along the hallways, more servants rushing about on black and white checkerboard floors.

"You've done well for yourself," Morrow remarks, scratching his red beard. A clod of dirt falls off his boot behind him and Dario closes his eyes.

"I am but a humble merchant," Dario finally says. "I've been lucky."

"Right," Lara says, staring up at the ceiling painted with all manner of legendary creatures. "Lucky."

"Where did you find the luck?" Caedia asks in a sing-song voice. "We dryads often find it in unexpected places."

Dario blinks at her.

"What now?" Morrow asks, looking at me.

"You'll find a wing of rooms up those stairs," Dario answers before I have a chance to say anything. Which, frankly, is fine by me. "The servants will draw you baths, and I highly suggest that you indulge in that particular hygienic exercise." He sniffs.

"Tonight I'll send word to the... appropriate people. Architects, tailors, et cetera. I'll meet you down here in the morning, and we will begin the work needed to, ah, relieve *him* of the necessary items."

With that, he stalks off down another candlelit hallway, a liveried servant scurrying after him.

"Right this way," a plump woman calls, her cheeks pink and a cherubic nose on her face. "Been a long trip, by the looks of it. We'll get you settled in."

In the barrel on my shoulder, Kyrie inhales sharply, and the need to pry the lid off now and pull her out consumes me.

I grit my teeth and carry her, in the barrel, up the stairs.

Keeping her hidden for now is keeping her safe.

Even if it's killing me to imagine how uncomfortable she must be in there.

33

KYRIE

"I don't think I've ever smelled this bad in my life," I moan from my prone position on the floor. My feet are still in the barrel, my legs and arms tingling, half asleep.

"You smelled pretty wretched after the sewers under Cottleside," the Sword offers.

"I'm surprised you could smell anything other than *yourself*," I mutter. "Frankly, I'm surprised you could even walk."

I peel myself off the expensive silk carpet a little, narrowing my eyes at him.

How was he able to walk? Barefoot in the snow, up the Hiirek Mountains?

"Fae are made from sturdier stock than humans," the Sword answers my unspoken questions a little too quickly.

Morrow glances over from where he's closing curtains and checking locks. "Humans are plenty sturdy," he says.

"I would have frozen my toes off if I tried what he did," I

tell him, forcing myself more upright, massaging my cramping thighs.

"Then it's lucky you had shoes, even if you didn't think to provide any for me."

Ouch. I glare at him. "I didn't see you getting yourself out of prison, you ingrate."

"Stop calling names," Lara thunders, slamming down the satchel she'd been busy unpacking. "I am sick of you two being at each other's throats."

Caedia flinches from where she's laid out her stock of herbs, already busy grinding up her next foul medicine, I assume. My heart squeezes a little.

It's nice to be taken care of.

Even when your friend is yelling at you.

"Well?" Lara demands, throwing her hands in the air. "You have nothing to say for yourselves?"

"We should do some trust-building exercises," Morrow interjects.

I burst out laughing. "Trust-building? You do remember who I am, right?"

Morrow frowns at me, but when Lara points a witchy finger at my chest, I flinch.

"Sorry," she says, lowering her finger... then points at me again. "See? We all need to trust each other, or this isn't going to work. I'm not going to hex you, Kyrie," she huffs. "Stop looking at me like that."

"I don't trust Dario," Caedia offers up, still grinding away. "Should we go get him?"

"No," I tell her too quickly. "I don't trust him either."

"Stop trying to distract everyone," Lara shouts, stamping her foot. "If we want this to work, if we want to help reunite Heska and keep Doston from conquering any more bits and pieces of our country, we need to work together."

"I just want to live," I mutter. "I don't care about the rest."

"What?" Lara bites off the word, her eyes gleaming with fury.

I roll mine. "I just want to live. That's what I said—"

"I do not give a fuck what you said," she whispers, the sounds harsher than her shouting. "What kind of world do you want to live in? One where things like what we rode by tonight happen, where people are forced to trade sex for coin and are sold like fine wine?"

My eyebrows rise.

"Of course not—" I start, fury building in me.

She has no idea. None of them do.

No idea of what I've done, or where my ill-gotten funds went, or who I am.

Because... I didn't trust her with those parts of me. I blow out a breath, staring down at my filthy leather pants.

"Fine," I murmur. "You're right."

"You never let anyone in and—"

"I said fine," I repeat.

She stares at me, the anger in her warm brown eyes cooling slightly. "Fine?"

"Yep. Morrow and you want to trust me, and I agree. It will make things easier for... what we have planned."

I'm afraid to say the word heist. Who knows who's listening in this strange suite of rooms?

"This is a nice place, you know?" I ask awkwardly, already at odds with having to trust. And we haven't even started whatever hellish shit Morrow has in mind. It is, too. A huge white stacked stone fireplace dominates one side of the living area, a trio of arched windows providing a view of the winter forest. The whole place is tastefully decorated, from the silk rugs I'm still lying on to the luxurious chairs and divans spread about.

"There are four bedrooms," Caedia tells us with authority. "The wood they used for the beds speaks to me." She goes back to grinding herbs, humming in a low voice.

I blink at her.

Lara clears her throat.

Right. Because *that* is totally normal.

"You and the Sword are sharing a room," Lara commands.

"What?" I sputter. The Sword simply grunts at her.

Typical.

"Do the math. Caedia and I will share a room, Morrow can have a room, but you and the Sword... you need to work out whatever your problems are because I'm sick to death of it," Lara hisses, her eyes flaring purple.

Great.

"Fine by me," the Sword says.

Morrow holds a hand over his mouth like he's disguising a laugh. I bare my teeth at him, daring him to let it out.

"See?" Lara says, pointing at me.

"Stop it. We haven't even done the trust-building yet," I complain. "Put your finger away. You haven't even given us a chance to get along. And build trust. Or whatever it is Morrow is suggesting."

"Whatever in the gods' names is wrong between you two won't be solved by this," he mutters under his breath.

I glare daggers at him, then look to the Sword for support.

Shouldn't he be arguing against this too?

He's not, though, he's not even looking at them.

His attention is firmly and wholly on me, and my awareness of him roars to life.

"So," I squeak out, desperately swinging my gaze to Morrow, who seems outlandishly amused, gods damn him. "Trust exercises. Where do we start?"

"You should start with a bath," the Sword says in a low tone.

I glare at him.

Lara sighs, placing her hands on her hips.

"Enough," she tells him in her no-nonsense voice.

He straightens slightly, then dips his head.

The asshole gives me a shit-eating grin as he holds out a hand, helping me off the floor. I take his hand, only because I don't completely trust my still-asleep legs.

I'm going to wipe that dimple off his handsome face one of these days.

"Well, I would suggest something we used to do in my military officer days where we would each tell a lie and a truth about ourselves, and the rest of the group would have to guess which was which." Morrow wrinkles his nose as he glances sidelong at me.

"I won't use my power. Easy enough. I'll still win." I sink onto the green velvet chaise, running my fingers over the gorgeous fabric. They leave greasy marks. Disgusting.

The Sword smirks down at me.

"By Nakush's knees, it's not about winning, Kyrie, sweet gods above, help me." Lara rakes a hand over her face.

"Might want to pray to those below," Caedia trills.

The Sword stiffens, then sits down next to me.

My cheeks expand as I blow out a breath, keyed up, the heat from his muscled thigh warming mine.

"Fine. I understand. It's about getting to know each other better."

"Yes, so why don't you start?" Lara challenges.

Me? I blink up at her.

"That's right."

Off guard, probably because of the sick potions Caedia

keeps forcing on me along with the fact I've been in a barrel for the last hour, I say the first things that pop into my head.

"I used to frequent the brothels here in Nyzbern, and I recognized that man's voice earlier because I paid to have him killed for the unspeakable things he did to the people there. I used the money from the goods I stole the last time I was here to fund the people in that brothel's escape."

I pause, running my fingers over and over my thighs again.

Everyone's gaping at me, except... the Sword. No, his dark eyes are glimmering.

I swallow hard.

"And one more," I say, a liar who suddenly can't think of a lie. "I kept half the profits when I sold Alaric's goods on the black market."

Morrow clears his throat, then plops unceremoniously on a deep red chair that he manages to dwarf completely. "Those are your two stories for us to pick between?" he clarifies.

Even Caedia's watching me, her dryad's eyes twinkling.

Lara's mouth is an open ring of shock, and I twist my lips to the side, uneasy with the two stories I've presented.

Uneasy with how they'll judge them, and me in the balance.

"You used the money to free the friends you made at the brothels," Caedia says easily. "That's the truth. I suspect your ex-fiancé dragged you there, hm? You didn't keep any of it, which is how you got yourself into this mess in the first place, isn't it?"

Everyone turns to look at her. She spreads her hands wide, and some of the herbs fall off the pestle, glopping onto the floor.

"I admit, Kyrie does talk in her sleep a bit. She said something about it while she had a fever." She glances nervously at Morrow, who's gallantly trying to hide his astonishment behind his thick red beard and large hand. "You said it wasn't about winning, though, so I didn't think it was cheating. But I did think it might hurt her feelings if you all insisted she was as horrible as she pretends to be."

Tears threaten, stinging my eyes. I feel like a complete idiot, and I'm not sure why.

"Kyrie," Lara says softly, wringing her hands. "Is this true?"

"Caedia's right," I say, too loudly, leaning forward onto my elbows and blinking rapidly. "Who's next?"

They're all staring at me, though.

I inspect a floral pattern on the rug with interest.

"I'll go," Morrow says, also too loud, causing everyone to wince.

Gratitude wells in me. He's not very slick, but he is kind.

Morrow holds up one finger. "My best friend growing up was the girl I was supposed to marry, and when she ran off with another, I joined Lojad's ranks." A second finger joins the first. "Or, I ran away to join Lojad's ranks because I thought I could make more of a difference there than on my family's farm."

A quiet breath rushes out of me as everyone sizes up Morrow's truth and lie, and I scoot further into the divan so my back can rest up against it. The Sword touches my ankle as I tuck my leg underneath me, and there's a question in his eyes.

Like he wants to know if I'm alright.

Like he cares.

I look back to Morrow.

He's smirking, seemingly pleased that the four of us can't make up our minds about him. Except I'm so distracted by the Sword that I hardly remember what it is I'm supposed to be thinking about.

Which is a very, very bad sign.

I need my focus now more than ever before, to pull off the heist in just a few days' time.

"You have to guess," Morrow says, clearly off-put by how poorly we know him.

I'm not about to open my mouth. Nope. I am fine to sit here and let someone else be the center of attention.

"The girl who broke your heart. She drove you to Lojad," Lara finally says, one eyebrow arched in challenge.

"What," he blusters. "You don't think me the type to want to make a difference?"

"They're both true, but only partly. The trick is, you think it's all because of the girl because it makes it easier for you to handle that you weren't able to make a difference," Caedia says in that sing-song way of hers.

Morrow shrinks back as if he's been slapped.

The Sword gives me a long look, and I do my best to avoid meeting his eyes because I'm suddenly afraid I'll start laughing and Morrow will be even angrier at me.

Besides, I don't want to give Lara a reason to point her finger at me again, either. It makes me a little too nervous, especially after seeing what she was capable of with the manticore.

"Well, I never thought of it like that," Morrow finally says, a shade paler than before.

"I like this game," Caedia says, finally setting the mortar and pestle down and perching on a sapphire-blue armchair. "Lara, you next."

Lara scrunches her nose, a faraway look in her eyes.

"I make up fortunes for people sometimes when Nakush doesn't guide my hand. It's made me very good at reading more than cards." Her nose scrunches again, and her gaze flits across my face, finally resting on Morrow's. "I spent more time the last two years learning offensive magic than honing my ability to see the future."

Caedia's peering at her, one hand under her chin, foot tapping fast as a hummingbird's wings.

"The first one's the truth," Morrow says, and I blink because I thought for sure the second one was.

"There you have it," Lara says, but her smile is self-deprecating.

"The prophecy... that was true though, right?" I narrow my eyes. "Have you told us the truth about that?" And Dario, I want to ask, but it doesn't matter what she says, I haven't trusted his oily ass since the minute he kicked Fil.

That would make me question his judgment regardless, because what kind of idiot kicks a direcat?

One with a death wish, maybe.

"That was true, Kyrie," Lara answers slowly. "But the future... it's been increasingly cloudy over the past few years. Fraught with... chaos."

Everyone's gaze swings to me.

When will I learn to keep my mouth shut?

"My turn," Caedia announces, clapping her hands. "I started training to be a healer because I had a dog I wanted to take care of." She gives us a mischievous smile. "Or, I started training to be a healer so I could break every bone in someone's body, heal him, and do it again."

My jaw drops.

Morrow puts a hand over his face, and the Sword lets out a startled laugh.

Lara just winces. "I'm assuming the dog's a lie."

"I did have a dog," Caedia tells us solemnly. "But the other was a bigger motivator."

Lara catches my eye, and I scrub a hand down my face.

"Good to know," I say. "Morrow, this has been an enlightening exercise." And it has. I'm reevaluating my opinion of

Caedia fairly quickly—as well as her role in my plan. "Caedia, do you have... any dryad, er, magic besides healing?"

"Of course I do." She snaps her fingers, and one of the logs stacked next to the fireplace begins sprouting leaves.

A real smile curves my lips. "That's... perfect." I'll have to ask her how she feels about hurting people as a healer nowadays... but I have a feeling I know the answer.

"My turn," the Sword says, his low growl of a voice taking me by surprise. I was so invested in Caedia's unexpected bloodthirstiness I forgot just how close he is to me.

"I am glad Kyrie drank from the chalice," he says, his throat bobbing.

My heart nearly stops, then starts up again, pounding faster than ever.

"My real name is the Sword."

Shock winds through me. His real name isn't the Sword, there's no way.

Which means he's glad I drank from the chalice. He's glad I've been cursed to die by his god.

Seething, I stand up, ignoring the way his fingers brush my wrist.

"Are you fucking serious right now?" Lara asks him. "My gods, you *are* an asshole. Kyrie, wait." I shake her hand off.

"She doesn't *understand*," Lara hisses at him.

Caedia says something in her high-pitched voice. It bounces off me.

Unseeing, not caring, I lurch towards one of the doors branching off from the living room into the main bedroom.

The door doesn't slam behind me, snicking softly closed instead, and I lean against it, my breath coming in fast pants.

There's a tub steaming in the corner and I shuck my clothes automatically. Water threatens to slosh over the sides as I get in.

It's hot, uncomfortably so on my cold feet and hands, and I sink under the water all the way, only my nostrils breaching the surface.

I breathe in deeply.

I don't want to die. I hate that the Sword does want me to. I hate how much his truth hurts, and how cruel he was to admit it.

And, yet, everyone here thinks lies are the greater evil, when truth's the sharper weapon.

34

THE SWORD

"Why would you tell her that?" Lara asks. Caedia and Morrow have excused themselves, clearly not wanting to witness Lara scold me like an angry goose.

The fire crackles in the sooty stone hearth, and I pace in front of it.

Lara is the only one who knows the truth of it.

"I can't lie like you. I can't lie like her. It makes me sick."

"She thinks you want her dead, you absolute idiot."

"You and I know that's not what the curse means."

Kyrie's coughing in the next room, a wet hacking noise that sets my teeth on edge.

"She doesn't know that!" Lara explodes, so angry her brown hair floats around her, her irises glowing purple. "They don't know who you are, or what has to happen. Do you truly want her to hate you?" She tips her chin up, inspecting me in a way few mortals have done and lived to tell the tale. "That's it, isn't it? Will it make it easier for you if she hates you?"

My throat closes up. I nod, then shake my head, turning to the fire and away from Lara's judgment.

"I don't think there is a way to make it easier," I finally answer.

Lara's small human hand squeezes my elbow, then falls away. "I think you should do what feels right with her, Hr— Sword."

I flinch at her mistake.

"I think just because... of who you are, truly are, you shouldn't assume you can be rational about this. There is nothing rational about... our emotions."

Love. She doesn't say it, but the word flits across my mind all the same.

"I shouldn't." I want to sob the words, but it comes out on an angry snarl. "I shouldn't feel anything for her but contempt."

"She isn't what you thought she'd be, is she?" Lara's voice is so full of pain and compassion it hurts to hear.

"Did you know?" I ask aggressively, turning back to face her.

A tear slips down her cheek, and she shakes her head. "She never told me. I wondered why she kept stealing, but... I thought she was like a magpie, or it was some... internal need to steal and hoard. I didn't know she was using it to help anyone but herself."

Her face crumples, shame clear in the expression.

When she meets my eyes again, though, there's strength there.

"You two will change this world for the better, and it will be easier if she doesn't hate you when you do it. She might even find it in her secret heart to forgive you, if you can be truthful with yourself about her."

With that, Lara leaves the living room, abandoning me to my wretched thoughts and the dark guilt I've lived with for an eternity.

35

KYRIE

Sweat soaks the sheets all around me, and a huge hand holds my wrist. My dagger's in my hand, silhouetted by the full moon shining outside the window.

"Kyrie," the Sword says warily. "You are safe."

Relief wars with the sense of betrayal at the sight of him.

"I guess it would be too much to ask for me to die already," I manage, my voice hoarse like I've been screaming.

I blink. I was screaming. In my sleep.

"You were having a nightmare," the Sword continues.

I open my hand, and the dagger falls to the bed. The Sword's fingers close over the hilt.

"Are you going to slit my throat, since you want me dead so badly?"

"Kyrie," he says, and my name's never sounded so pained, so full of hope and fear.

My throat works as I swallow.

There is something I don't understand happening here, between us.

Hells, I don't understand anything between us, not at all, not one bit.

"You will ruin me," he says, and my breath catches as his attention slides down my throat to the curve of my shoulder, to where the sheets don't hide my nudity. "Why aren't you wearing night clothes?"

"I didn't expect any visitors," I manage, aiming for nonchalance and missing by a mile. Or a hundred miles.

"We were supposed to share a room." His voice is a soft murmur, and goosebumps rise along my arms.

"I didn't think you'd come to bed," I say truthfully. "I thought you'd have the sense to sleep out there." I jerk my chin at the living room.

"Do you want me to come to bed?" he asks, cocking his head at me, something like lust shining in his eyes.

Or maybe I'm just seeing what I want to see there.

Maybe I've only ever seen what I want in him.

Murderer, prisoner, captive, partner... friend.

But what is he, who is he, really?

"Why do you hate me so much?" I ask him, and the tears I refused to shed earlier spill in earnest. "Do you really think I'm evil? That I deserve to die?"

"I have never hated you. I hate... who I have to be around you." The words are careful and loaded with a truth I don't understand, can't make meaning from in this moonlit moment. "I hate that I keep hurting you, and you keep lashing out at me, and that I can't seem to learn how to... be a friend to you."

"Friends," I echo.

The way he's staring at the exposed swell of my breast beneath my collarbones doesn't feel friendly.

My lower body pulses.

"Friends," he repeats. "Do you want to be friends?" His voice breaks on the word. "My friend?"

"Friends don't usually want each other dead," I say thickly.

"I don't want you anywhere but at my side, Kyrie." It's fervent, and my magic responds to the truth in it, reverberating through me.

"Then explain—" I start, but his hand grips my cheek, his eyes fiery as his lips draw closer to mine.

"Explain what?" he asks. "How I want to kiss you so badly I wonder if I'm the one who's cursed? Cursed to need you with every beat of my heart?"

"Oh." My eyes are wide, and his other hand's on my bare shoulder, his thumb making circles. The heat between my legs intensifies, and he inhales.

"I can scent your need for me, Kyrie. Tell me what to do."

"It's sweat," I tell him weakly, lying my ass off and we both know it. "From the nightmare."

"I'll fuck the lies from your tongue, Kyrie. I will fuck you until all we have is the truth of our need between us. Tell me to kiss you. Tell me I can taste what I've forbidden myself from wanting. From needing." The growl in his voice sends a shiver down my spine, and my nipples grow hard from the rawness of it, from the energy he's radiating.

"Do it," I whisper, my eyes darting between his.

"What?" he asks, a knee going between my legs, another on the side of the bed.

"Unh," is all I can say as his mouth meets the soft skin between my neck and shoulder.

"Do what, Kyrie?"

"All of it. Kiss me, taste me."

"Is that what you want?" The hand on my shoulder moves

lower and I shudder as his thumb grazes over my sheet-covered nipple. "Is that all you want?"

"I want you to fuck me like you mean it, like you've been wanting to since I came into Cottleside and told you I wanted you for sex."

His eyes flash, and his mouth's on me in the next second.

I expect a clash of teeth, of tongues, and my hands go around his neck, his hair impossibly silver in the moonlight.

There's no clash though, like the fight's already been fought.

His mouth is soft on mine, gentle, and teasing.

It doesn't make me feel like he hates me.

It makes me feel precious and cared for—like he's holding himself back.

I don't want him to hold anything back.

I want there to be truth between us, in this, at least.

I slip my hand between his legs, feeling for his cock, and he groans as my fingers curl around his hardness.

"Kyrie," he groans.

"That wasn't what I asked for. I didn't ask for gentle," I tell him with a sly smile.

"Fuck," he says, and this time when he kisses me, it's devouring.

My toes curl and I tilt my hips up, aiming for relief from what's already building between my legs.

Our breaths are ragged as our mouths move apart and he puts his forehead against mine, the tendons on his neck standing out.

"Kyrie," he says. "You are—"

"I think it's time for me to go back to sleep," I tell him, grinning like the cat who ate the canary.

"Wait, what?" He blinks.

"You didn't think you could just kiss me and I'd forget how mean you were to me tonight, did you?" I shake a finger at him. "You want more from me, you're going to have to treat me nicely."

"I will treat you like a goddess," he says, and to my surprise, he's smiling too.

He must have bathed.

We're smiling *at each other*.

He rolls off me to the empty side of the bed, tugging his shirt off. A clean shirt.

"Did you bathe in here while I was sleeping?"

"I did."

"Pervert. I bet you loved being naked with me right here," I purr.

"I did," he agrees, his palm going to the back of my neck, pulling me close. "I can show you, if you want."

"No. You're going to have to court me."

"Court you?" he huffs a laugh.

"I can't be distracted from planning the heist, though," I tell him, rolling over to my side and propping myself up on an elbow. "So yes. You have my permission to court me. And then, after the heist, we can see where this takes us."

"I already know where it will take you. You'll be ruined for all other males. For eternity."

I roll my eyes, laughing. "I'm going to remind you of that if you fail to live up to your own inflated expectations."

He glances down to where his cock's tenting his pants. "I'll give you inflated, alright."

I burst out laughing even harder and he tucks me against him, his body warm and muscular and comforting.

"I'm sorry I made you feel..."

"Terrible?" I suggest. "Like I should be dead?"

He falls silent, but his hand strokes a steady rhythm on my upper arm.

"Death comes for us all," he says finally.

"But not yet," I say firmly.

"Not yet," the Sword agrees, pressing a kiss to my shoulder blade.

36

THE SWORD

When I wake, morning light is streaming through the window in shades of wintery gold, dust motes glimmering in the air. I reach out—but Kyrie is gone, her side of the bed cold under my hand.

Her taste haunts me. I squeeze my eyes shut, preferring the dark to the bright of day, holding onto the feel of her curves, her softness against me.

Time, ever vigilant, presses onward towards our fate.

Hushed conversation sounds from the other side of the door and I sit up, dressing in record time, splashing some cold water on my face. Mostly, I'm steeling myself for another day of shame warring with my intense attraction to the thief who's stealing my heart.

The door creaks open to the living room, the wooden knob slick and polished on my palm. A fire blazes in the huge hearth, and Kyrie and Caedia lean over a large unrolled parchment on the floor, furniture pushed out of the way to make room for it.

I raise a brow, neither of them pausing to even look up at me.

Speaking in low tones, Kyrie points at the parchment—blueprints, I belatedly realize—and Caedia nods.

"And you won't have any problems with it?" Kyrie asks her, nose scrunching in slight disbelief.

Caedia shrugs a shoulder. "No. Especially not after what you told me earlier."

"Good morning," I make myself say. They both startle slightly. "Don't mind me."

A soft, secretive smile blooms across Kyrie's face, her cheeks going pink as her green gaze holds mine. Gods, I want to kiss her. I want to pull her back into that bedroom and turn that smile into something completely different—

"Can you send for breakfast?" Caedia asks brightly. "Or are you going to continue looking at Kyrie like you want to eat her up?"

Kyrie laughs then coughs, an awkward sound that quickly becomes too real.

The half-dryad leaps to her feet, returning a moment later with a dark brown bottle that Kyrie tips down her throat between coughs.

I don't move, frozen to the spot at the overwhelming proof of the curse's efficacy.

Why would I ever tell her I was glad she drank from the chalice and sealed her fate with mine? It has only brought her pain and suffering.

It was selfish of me to hope she'd glean an insight from my thoughtless words.

It's selfish of me to keep trying to show my hand, when so much depends on playing my cards close to my chest.

"She will feel better after some food." Caedia smiles at me, but her eyes are troubled, her hand still on Kyrie's back.

I nod once, grateful Caedia's given me something to do, some small task to occupy my mind instead of the thoughts intent on ripping me apart.

Dario's home is buzzing with activity already. A maid in slate-blue linen bows her head as I walk past, only to realize I have no idea where I'm going.

I pivot back towards her. She glances at me in alarm, alarm that turns to shock as she takes me in.

Shock, and something like recognition.

She dips into a curtsy, her hands shaking in her skirts. A tocsin of warning shakes in my head, and I study her for a long moment, unsure of how to proceed.

No one has looked at me like that in a very, very long time.

"We require food brought up, miss," I tell her, gentling my voice as much as possible. It's doubtful that she does indeed recognize me, but the last thing I need is for her to have a panic attack outside the suite where Kyrie sits and plans to do exactly what I need.

"Right away, my lord Hr—"

"I am only the Sword," I interrupt before she can say anything more.

She swallows audibly, then curtsies again, walking backwards away from me, her eyes glued to the floor. "As you wish, my lord."

From behind the swoop of light brown hair, the points of her ears are barely noticeable.

It's my turn to stare.

What in the name of Heska is one with Fae blood doing here, a servant in Dario's house?

Sorrow hits me so hard that I lean a palm against the wall, bracing myself against the onslaught. This is why I must finish this with Kyrie. For the Fae, for my people, for Heska.

For what is right.

37

KYRIE

The day of the midwinter masque dawns and I blink at the sunlight, stretching like a cat from the timelines I've been pouring over, tweaking them again and again.

I have hardly stopped to breathe. The last few days have passed by in a haze of work and fear.

The Sword and I have barely had time to speak to one another, save for working out the specifics of his part in the heist.

It's better that way. I stretch out my feet, my toes tingling from being tucked under me for hours.

My stomach grumbles. Food. I'm hungry.

The others see to it that I'm fed, but I hardly sleep, taking the potions Caedia has on hand more frequently, my lungs tight and full of fluid.

Tonight, I lay my life on the line and pray to all the gods save one that I've accounted for everything.

"Did you sleep at all?" Lara asks, yawning as she strides into the living room.

"I took a catnap," I tell her. "The dresses—"

"They'll be here at noon," she tells me, smiling, though her eyes are worried. "You need to sleep, Kyrie."

"No, we need to go over the plan again. I made some changes to it this morning."

A knock sounds, and Dario strides into the room. He's been in and out of our rooms while I've been scheming and I take him in, scrutinizing his appearance.

There are dark circles under his eyes, his face pallid and tired.

I know how he feels.

"Is it done?" I ask, my voice a croak. So much hinges on what he's been doing.

"With the help of your Sword, yes. The barrels are full, and I will have nightmares for the rest of my life about the contents." Disgust winds through the words, and for the first time since I met Dario, I know he's telling the absolute truth. "What a waste of a rare vintage."

"You could still try drinking it," I tell him cheerily, biting into a piece of smoked sausage I've been nibbling since last night. "In fact, the vintage is even more rare now. Truly one-of-a-kind."

Dario turns a little green. "I don't know how you can eat while we discuss this."

"Easy. I'm hungry." The tray of half-eaten food sits on a table next to me, and I eye a hunk of cheese before popping it in my mouth too.

Cheese is life.

"The casks were delivered this morning. I just came from overseeing it," Dario says on a sigh.

Lara's watching him carefully, her fingers tightly gripping the back of one of the armchairs.

Dario settles on the armchair closest to the fire, stretching his boots out towards the heat.

"Were they delivered where we need them?" I ask carefully.

"You know I can't guarantee that. I told them exactly what you instructed me to, and if Alaric plays to type, at least one of the rarest casks will be with the rest of his hoard."

I blow out a breath, leaning my head back onto the chair and studying the ceiling. "It's a risk."

"It was always going to be a risk." Lara takes a slice of browning apple, chewing thoughtfully.

"Any chance you can see how it plays out?" I ask her.

"I can't tell you anything that might change the course of the night," she says cryptically.

"Of course not. Or, you know, you could, and the gods and fate be damned," I tell her sweetly.

She just sighs.

"You look like shit," Dario tells me.

"You would know," I snipe back.

He leans his elbows on his thighs, peering at me. "You need to be at your best, right? You said it yourself. For this to work, you have to look the part."

"You're being fucking rude," I tell him.

"He's right," Lara says.

"Fuck you too," I bare my teeth at her.

"Right, and your judgment isn't impaired at all by your lack of sleep. Just your tired, haggard face."

I roll my eyes, hating that she's right.

"She's already perfect," the Sword says, and I blink in surprise, both at the compliment and because I didn't realize he was in the room.

"Maybe I do need sleep," I admit, rubbing a palm over my face.

"I have a draught for that," Caedia says, stretching her arms overhead as she walks sleepily into the room.

"I need to be able to wake up easily," I tell her, shaking a finger in warning.

"Have I ever steered you wrong?" Caedia asks. "Don't insult my potions."

"Sorry," I say meekly. "Of course you haven't. You just steered me to drinking things that taste like manticore piss."

"Hmmph," she says.

"Why did you drink manticore piss?" Dario asks. A laugh bubbles out of me at the perplexed expression on his face. "No, seriously, what are you talking about?"

Morrow opens the door to his room, standing in the threshold with his strawberry-blond hair standing straight up. He nods in silent greeting.

"Dario, I don't have time to explain the ways of the world to you." I wave a dismissive hand at him, and Lara snorts. "I want to go over the plan again," I tell everyone. "And I need to be awake in time to get ready for tonight."

Morrow leans against the door to his room.

"Morrow, do you have the horses—"

"Everything is ready for us to ride like hell after you steal it," he says easily. "Bags packed, horses are in good shape. I have several spells at the ready to cast over us as we go."

I nod. "Right. And Lara—"

"I will be in Alaric's oak parlor, ready to scream my head off and seal all the doors."

"The jeweler will be here with the finished pieces around dinnertime," I say. "Caedia, you need to—"

"Wear the pieces and set the spells with Lara," she interrupts.

I rake through my mind, trying to figure out what it is I'm missing because something tells me there's a piece to the puzzle I haven't figured out yet.

Although, I've been feeling that way for weeks now, since I drank from the chalice.

I blow out a breath, my finger moving over the timeline in front of me. "Maximum—"

"Chaos," everyone finishes with me.

"So we start out—"

"With a dance," the Sword says, nodding. "We know."

"Get some sleep," Morrow rumbles. "No one is going to want to dance with you if you smell like that. No point in laying a trap with bait that looks half dead."

My jaw drops open. "I don't look that bad," I say mildly.

"You really do," Caedia tells me. "You stink, too. Like you've been sweating in your clothes and living on smoked sausage and cheese for three days straight."

Scowling, I take the proffered bottle from her and bravely swig it down, prepared to be disgusted by the flavor as usual.

"Oh," I say. It doesn't taste bad. "It tastes like midnight feels," I tell her.

"Good. That means it's working."

Heaviness settles over my limbs, and Lara barks out a laugh.

I smile up at her.

"Come on, little liar," the Sword says, easily hefting me into his arms. "Let's get you to bed. Tonight will be perfect. You've done all you can."

My eyelids are a thousand pounds and my jaw cracks in a yawn.

"I don't need it to be perfect. I just need us all to get out alive with the crown."

"You've accounted for nearly every possibility." He sets me down on the bed, pulling the crisp sheets up and over me.

I stretch my arms out long overhead, then stop. "What do you mean, *nearly*?"

"No human could possibly account for every possibility."

"So you admit my crime planning capabilities are godly?" I ask jokingly, my half smile melting into another out-of-control yawn.

The Sword stiffens, then turns away.

Maybe I do stink.

Two things are for certain: I'm going to take a long bath when I wake up, and the Sword and I are going to have a long talk tomorrow, once the Crown of Sola's in my possession and I can focus on something besides the midwinter masque.

※

Kyrie's joking words echo in my ears. Even as I lay the groundwork for the magic she demanded of me, I can't help but hear them over and over again.

I don't need to focus for my magic, though—I haven't since the days of going into battle alongside Filarion.

You admit my capabilities are godly? she asked.

It wasn't an accusation, though maybe closer to one than she could imagine.

I've wanted to hold onto her so badly, so tightly, over the past few days, since she kissed me back our first night here. I've wanted to stop time and spend countless hours memorizing the cant of her eyes and the perfect curvature of her mischievous smile.

Now, the night that will put an end to her smiling at me draws nearer.

How can I want to succeed so badly and to fail all at once?

Fuck Sola and the chalice's curse, and fuck my own past that's led me to this point. There is no crossroads, there is no choice to be made. It's been made for me, and for Kyrie, and all I can do is cling to this version of her and remember her like this, when she looked at me with hope, and with desire, and not with burning hatred.

Not yet, at least.

I will do everything in my power to ensure none of the mortals in my charge are hurt.

That is, of course, the whole point of this. Ensure the safety of the peoples of Heska. Satisfy Sola's punishment for my vengeance against her followers.

And make sure that the goddess of lies can never do what she's done to her followers again.

38

KYRIE

The water's so warm, the scented soap so decadent, my body so languid and relaxed that getting out of the tub is likely impossible.

I did need the nap.

Embarrassing to admit, even to myself, like I'm some overextended toddler who needs to be put to bed lest she completely melt down at the worst time possible.

I glance at the clock on the end table for the hundredth time since Dario's servants filled the bath for me.

The worst time possible is nearly at hand.

"Kyrie?" Caedia calls, then knocks.

"Come in," I say.

She's already through the door by the time I've spoken, and I grin at the dryad who clearly barely cares about little things like human ideas of politeness and definitely doesn't care about nudity.

Caedia stands over the tub, staring at me with her luminous, otherworldly eyes. Her silky blonde hair's been curled and falls in soft waves around her face, and her sage-green gown glimmers in the candlelight.

"You look stunning," I tell her.

"I want you to be careful tonight," she says immediately.

I raise an eyebrow. "Of course I'll be careful. What's... what's wrong?"

She turns, pacing along the edge of the tub, the silk of the custom gown we barely had made for her in time whispering as she walks.

"I don't know. There's something... off. I can feel it—" She stops talking, and when she pivots to glance at me, her eyes are glowing with her innate magic. A shiver goes up my back at the sight. "I don't know, though. I'm not a seer like Lara. Promise me you'll be careful. Promise me."

"I promise," I tell her.

"Good," she nods, some of the glow in her eyes dying. "Because I didn't work as hard as I did on taking care of you to have you die tonight."

I snort, unable to stay straight-faced. "Unlike the man you healed just to break his bones again?"

"He was a special case. I learned a lot about bones. You deserve to live, Kyrie. He deserved to suffer." She shrugs a shoulder, then breezes back out the door while I softly laugh.

Caedia might be the scariest of us all.

I'm glad she'll be with me when it counts tonight.

Water sloshes around as I stand, stepping carefully out of the tub and drying off. The dress we had made for me lies across the bed, sparkling in the low light.

White silk, opalescent beads. Nearly completely sheer to the waist, with delicate beading that will barely conceal my breasts and a full skirt with a slit all the way up to my hip.

I'll stand out in it, that's for sure.

"Need help?" Lara asks from the doorway. "Feeling better?"

"Are you worried?" My hair drips on the rug. A second later, a whisper of magic rushes over me and my hair dries in near-perfect ringlets. "That's a helpful spell."

"I made that one up a few years ago during that winter that never seemed to end."

"Clever." I purse my lips, finally looking at her. She's in a blue so deep it's nearly purple, her smooth raven hair half up in an elaborate braid. She has her mask on already, and the silver sets off the crimson-red stain on her lips. "You look pretty," I tell her.

Lara gives me a girlish grin. "You think?"

"I know. You're going to have the whole of Nyzbern eating out of the palm of your hand."

"Until you walk in," she scoffs.

"As the bait," I say quietly.

A moment of silence passes between us.

"I've never seen you nervous about stealing something."

"I feel like I've missed something, Lara. I don't know what. I know Alaric's palace, we have the updated blueprints, and I've planned it as much as I could possibly plan." I bite my lip, my hands holding the towel over my body.

She cocks her head at me. "Are you sure it's something about tonight you're missing? Or is it something else?"

The question turns me cold all over. "What do you mean?"

"Just that maybe you're looking for something to be wrong because so little has gone right for you."

I glance at her sidelong. I don't think that's what she meant, not at all. But I know Lara, and I know that once she's decided to be cryptic, she's going to be cryptic for as long as she wants.

"Help me get dressed?" I ask her instead. I don't want what

could be my last moments with her tarnished by trying to interrogate her.

I'd rather pretend we were getting dressed up to go have fun at a ball, instead of getting dressed up to put everyone I've come to care about in danger.

It doesn't take too long to put on the dress, with Lara's help, at least.

I smooth my hands down the full skirt, adjusting the sheer tulle sleeves whose only purpose is to be another vehicle for the gems adorning the dress.

"Not too bad," Lara says.

"It better be good enough." I sigh, fluffing my curls.

"Everyone is ready," she says softly, adjusting the bejeweled sleeve. "Are you ready?"

I inhale, closing my eyes. I would pray, if there were only a god who would listen.

I open my eyes instead.

I've never been the praying type.

"I'm ready," I tell her.

She smiles, buoyed by the confidence in my voice.

It's a silver-tongued lie.

39

THE SWORD

Morrow, Caedia and I wait at the entrance to Dario's house for everyone else to emerge. My silver mask hides the upper half of my face, but in the black and silver-threaded finery, I feel exposed.

This is not the armor and grime I've accustomed myself to over the last half century.

"Stop fidgeting," Caedia tells Morrow, who looks as uncomfortable as I feel, clothed in red and gold, a red domino across his eyes.

"Why, you two oafs nearly look presentable," Dario calls out, heading towards us from the far hallway.

I cock an eyebrow at the word oaf, but Dario is far from worth any additional effort on my behalf.

"We need to leave soon," he continues. "Where are the other women?"

"They're getting ready still," Caedia tells him. "You could have done more to yourself, by the way."

He blinks at the half-dryad's words, glancing down at his own over-the-top finery. "Caedia, you look lovely."

Morrow shoots me an amused look over Dario's head.

"Of course I do."

"Right on schedule," comes a crisp voice, and I turn from Dario in time to see Kyrie gliding down the stairs.

Her hair's a waterfall of crimson curls, an iridescent strand of pearls and gems wound through it. Her green eyes are lined in darkness, making them stand out beneath the creamy white mask.

I have never seen anything, anyone, as lovely as this white-clad thief.

I swallow hard.

The dress clings to her curves, leaving little room for imagination, the breasts I've barely kept myself from hardly concealed under the intricate, pale beadwork. The flash of creamy thigh beneath the skirts is next to draw my attention.

"Breathe," Caedia instructs, an amused smile on her face.

I do as she bids, unable to do anything else but stare at the mortal woman coming down the stairs, a vision in cream, the very picture of beauty. Hope shines in her green eyes for a second as our gazes meet.

In a few days' time, she won't look at me like that again. Ever.

"Well?" Lara asks, and I blink at where she is now standing beside me. I hadn't even realized she was with Kyrie.

"You are stunning," Morrow tells Lara, and I don't need her gift of prescience to see that the man's half in love with her already.

Kyrie sweeps by us all, hardly even glancing at me, already settling into her role for the night.

Temptress, thief, mastermind.

What would it be like if she was only mine?

40

KYRIE

The green copper-clad spires of Alaric's palace gleam in the starlight. Smoke wafts from the braziers along the cobblestone pathway.

Mushroom and the horses are stabled nearby, according to Morrow, ready for our escape.

Getting in and getting the goods isn't usually the hard part; getting away is.

I swallow some of the panic that threatens and focus on putting one foot in front of the other.

There's no hiding the sweat that makes my palms slippery, though, or the fact my heart's going to sprout wings and fly off if it beats any faster.

I do not want to see Alaric.

I never wanted to see him again.

This entire plan is a gamble. If he doesn't react the way we want him to, the way I'm gambling with our lives that he will, then this curse won't matter. I'll die in one of his dungeons.

The Sword's arm wraps around my waist and I glance up at him, startled by the movement.

"Don't," he says in a low voice. "Don't be afraid."

"I'm not." I toss my hair.

"Pretty little liar," he says, trapping a curl and winding it around his finger.

My heart skips a beat, and it has nothing to do with fear and everything to do with how badly I want this man.

"You told me," he drawls, "that you didn't want me near you until we finished this thing here tonight."

"Right." I nod decisively, my voice giving me away by cracking. "No distractions."

The Sword grins at that, so unbelievably handsome in his silver-shot black clothes and silver mask that I doubt anyone would think he's human.

He's never been further from human than he is right now, bathed in starlight and fire, his dark eyes gleaming from behind his mask.

"No distractions," I repeat, and he smiles down at me like he knows I'm saying it for my own benefit.

"As far as I remember, I am the one providing the distraction tonight."

"And I'm the worm on the hook," I tell him.

I don't mention my misgivings about Dario, but he leans closer, like he senses them anyhow. "Kyrie. Look at me."

I do, of course I do, because for some reason, this male is impossible for me to resist, same as that damned chalice I drank from, and he holds my gaze.

"You can do this. You will do this. I believe in you."

My chest tightens, an aching warmth spreading through it that has nothing to do with the curse's progression in my lungs and everything to do with the way he's looking at me like I've hung the moon itself.

"Besides," he says, pulling me closer into his side. "You're the loveliest worm I've ever seen."

I laugh out loud, a barking noise that turns into a cough. I glance back at Caedia once it finally subsides, but she just shakes her head.

I've had as many of her potions as she can give me—safely, that is—already today.

I square my shoulders, and the entrance to Alaric's palace —where I once made my home—looms ahead.

"Here we go," I say quietly.

The stakes couldn't be higher for me, personally.

And if I believe everything Lara's said, then there's more riding on this crime than I can fathom.

"You know... is it really a crime if you're stealing from a criminal?" I murmur to the Sword.

"Yes," Morrow says from behind me. "It is."

"Are you sure, though?" I ask him, batting my eyelashes. "Really, really sure?"

Lojad's knight laughs, a booming noise that catches the attention of nearly everyone in the snow-dusted courtyard.

Good.

I pull the hood of the white velvet cloak down a little bit, letting my red curls shine against the fabric.

The whispers begin nearly immediately.

The first part of my plan is in full swing.

41

KYRIE

The strangest thing about covertly trying to pull all the attention in the room is when I actually receive it.

I walk through the carved double doors into Alaric's palace, the vestibule packed with partygoers in a rainbow of colors and masks to match, handing the velvet cloak to the servant in the entryway with a smile, and let them look.

The dress leaves little to the imagination, the tell-tale scars standing out purposefully thanks to the low back.

If the King of Diamonds has any doubts about who I am, regardless of my signature hair—the scars will speak for themselves.

Anyone who remembers me from my time here will remember those scars just as well as the unsubtle message they send.

Here I am.

Come and get me.

I trail my fingertips along the round marble-topped table

in the middle of the foyer, taking my time, sniffing the vase full of enchanted lilacs.

My skin grows hot from the attention of many eyes, my ears burning from the whispers behind hands.

I pretend like I hear nothing, like I see nothing, and continue through the second entryway, a domed two-story masterpiece that offers a view of the night sky unlike any other palace in Heska.

Not that I've been to many palaces.

But still. It's nice.

I crane my neck up. There, in the night sky, hangs the constellation Filarion. Despite the dread curdling my stomach, the anxiety I feel every time I'm about to do something like this, the memory of that night with the direcat and the Sword settles over me like a warm blanket.

Filarion, both direcat and his Fae namesake, wouldn't waste time and energy feeling sick over the danger.

They would charge into battle.

This is a battle for my life and death, and I'll be damned if I let Alaric get the best of me.

A sharp smile curves my lips, and I keep my head high as I glide through the gilded archway towards the sound of music floating from the ballroom.

Conversation stutters, then stops, as I make my way to the dance floor, guests parting before me with stunned expressions.

It's so nice to be remembered.

"Care to dance?" a low voice asks, sending a shiver down my spine.

I don't bother answering, but simply extend my hand, which the Sword takes in his.

For all the time we spent planning this moment, down to our coordinating outfits, we didn't practice dancing. The

Sword just grunted at me in annoyance when I pestered him about it, and my heart beats ever faster as he leads me onto the black-veined marble floor.

One warm hand drops to my waist, his callouses rough and catching on the sheer fabric. I inhale.

He exhales, and we move.

My eyebrows rise in surprise.

"You are surprisingly graceful."

"You're shocked," he huffs, his dimple showing as he smiles down at me.

That's all it takes for heat and lust to replace the simmering anxiety. I tilt my head back and laugh as he twirls me, marking both the exits and where the King of Diamonds' guards are as we move.

Everything is as I expected; as I remembered, too.

The last time I was here, it was the dead of night and my own blood stained these floors.

"I am," I say as he pulls me back into him, the heat of his palm searing through me. "I am very surprised someone as big as you can move like this."

"Death's embrace, no matter how expected, always comes as a surprise."

I sigh, trying not to roll my eyes. "Do we have to talk about your religion right now? Can't we just enjoy this moment without your god getting between us?"

His dark eyes glimmer, a lock of his silver hair escaping the leather he's tied it back with. "He's closer than you think," he says.

I do roll my eyes this time. "That's so encouraging, thank you for that."

"Do you fear Death so much, Kyrie?" he asks, his tone different, deeper than usual.

The string quartet playing from the raised dais crescendos,

and the Sword turns me out, then tugs me into his body, my back against his chest.

"I am not afraid to die, but I want to live," I say easily.

"You're a liar, through and through," he says, and for some reason, the words are sad.

"I can want to live and not be afraid of death. I have things I need to do first," I say, my steps faltering slightly.

Maybe his frown is just my imagination, though, because a moment later, he's laughing, leading me into an elaborate pattern of steps that ends in a low dip. His mouth hovers over me, a whisper of a breath over the skin of my neck.

"What is it you so desperately want to do, Kyrie?"

I give him a smirk, glancing up and down his body suggestively. "I could show you."

His hand spasms against my lower back and I laugh loudly, causing more people to stare at us. I exaggerate my movements more, selling it.

I do love to put on a show when the occasion calls for it.

"Is he here?" he asks quietly.

"Oh, yes."

"Is he watching?" He spins me again and I float along the floor, my dress twirling around my legs as I survey the crowd.

Alaric, King of Diamonds and criminals, isn't just watching. He's staring at me with open hatred, a muscle in his jaw ticking.

Love it for me.

"Mission accomplished," I tell the Sword sweetly as I lean into him.

He picks me up by the waist, surprising me, but I lift my arms in a hopefully graceful approximation of whatever step this is, my anxiety over pulling off this heist turning to sheer confidence.

"Let's give him something to watch, then," the Sword says, and it's all I can do to keep up with him.

His body moves to the music with strength and ease belying his size and musculature. I've been so distracted with planning for this moment that I didn't notice how much bigger he's gotten since Cottleside.

I haven't been this close to him since the night we kissed.

The song ends and we stop, standing still in the middle of the dance floor. The other revelers are clapping, but the Sword stands there devouring me with his gaze while my chest heaves in a heady mix of exhilaration and anticipation.

A flash of green catches my eye and Caedia dips her head at me, a small smile playing at the corners of her mouth as Morrow leads her on the dance floor.

"That's our cue," I say breathlessly.

The Sword doesn't say anything.

Big surprise.

Instead, he grabs my wrist, pulling me behind him through the crowd of dancers and spectators. I laugh, a high-pitched, unnatural sound, and grab a flute of bubbling wine from an unexpecting servant. It goes down in one gulp, making my nostrils sting.

My feet follow behind the Sword as fast as they can, but I'm ninety percent sure he'd simply tow me along were I to fall.

Well, that's not true. He'd probably sling me over his shoulder and slap my ass, doing his trademark grunt for good measure.

The thought—or maybe the alcohol—has me laughing again, and I set the empty wine glass down on a small console table as he hurries me through a door out of the ballroom.

The sound immediately dampens, the music still floating on the air, but hushed the further we drift from the main party.

The marble turns to stone under my soft-soled slippers, unlikely cold seeping through, turning my toes to ice.

There's a faint hint of mist in the air too, and it makes my skin tingle, the hair standing up on the back of my neck.

The urge to turn around heightens, to leave and go back, to get away from whatever lies ahead as fast as possible.

"Warded," I say.

The Sword nods. "Just like you thought."

"How long would you say we have until someone shows up?"

Footsteps sound behind us, and his grip on my wrist tightens. "Not long at all, I'd wager."

Quick as thought, he pivots, pulling me in between his huge body and the oak-paneled wall. His elbows land on either side of my face, blocking me from direct view.

"What are you doing in here?" a voice barks.

I watch the Sword's expression apprehensively. My mouth's gone dry, my heart now slamming into my ribs.

"None of your gods damned business," the Sword responds.

Then his mouth's on mine, soft and warm and full of need.

My body responds automatically and I moan, my mouth opening, letting him in.

He pulls away, watching me warily, waiting while I gather my power.

"You should leave us alone," I tell the guard who's followed us, imbuing the words with as much power as I can. "Right now. Don't let anyone in here."

I peek out from under the Sword's arm, watching as my silver-tongued magic hits the guard full-force.

His face goes slack, his eyes wide and glassy.

I wince. I might have packed a bit too much into that order. The guard stumbles back down the hall.

"How much time do you think that bought us?" the Sword asks me, his fingers now playing in my hair.

"Ten minutes. Maybe a bit less." I hiss out a breath as his fingers slide up my neck, cradling the back of my head. "He'll fight to keep them out."

"How fast do you think I could make you come?" the Sword murmurs into my ear.

I get goosebumps for a completely different reason.

"What?" I choke out, his hot mouth on mine again in an instant.

"I wanted to fuck you as soon as I saw you. Then you danced with me, and I swear on my own life, Kyrie, if I don't watch you come right now, I'm going to lose my mind."

"This seems like the worst possible time," I gasp as his hand goes to the slit of my dress, calloused fingers gripping my inner thigh and crooking it around his waist.

He stills, fire in his gaze. "Are you telling me no?" The words grind out of him.

"No," I say, shaking my head. "No, gods help me, I'm not telling you no."

"Fuck, Kyrie," he says, and then his hand is there, in between my thighs, pushing my sex apart. "You are beautiful. So beautiful."

I make a wordless noise as his thick fingers find my clit.

"That's right, little liar. You can't lie about how good this feels, can you?"

My legs start shaking, and he looses a hoarse laugh. I grab his shoulders, hanging on for dear life as he teases it, teases me. He dips his head, his mouth clamping over the beadwork covering my nipple, and my head rolls back.

"If we had time, I would have you begging for it, Kyrie. I would have you on your knees, right here, asking me." He's rough, and my hips buck as he circles my clit aggressively. "You're so fucking wet. Tell me how good it feels."

"It feels... terrible," I lie, grinning up at him, nearly senseless, my body already climbing towards release.

He huffs a laugh. "You might be able to say the words, but your body speaks for you." He holds up his blunt finger and it shines with my slick wetness in the dim light. "This is all the proof I need."

I shudder as he draws the finger into his mouth, gaze hot on mine, as he tastes my most private self.

"Fuck," I moan.

He smiles at me in earnest and my knees go weak at that dimple. Pinning me against the wall, he kisses me hard, like he means it, and I taste myself on his tongue.

"Come for me while you have time, Kyrie," he whispers against my cheek. It's an odd phrase, and I wonder at it for a split second.

But his thumb works at my clit, his index finger dipping into my wet heat, making sloppy sounds that might be embarrassing were I not so impossibly turned on right now.

"So fucking tight. So perfect. Kyrie, you are mine, do you hear me? When this is over, you're mine. Mine," he continues on a growl, adding his middle finger, pumping in and out of me.

My shoulders scrape against wood paneling and I'm nodding in agreement, nearly senseless.

"Come for me, Kyrie, you'll only ever come for *me* again."

It's so possessive and ridiculous that it should do anything but make me come—but it's so him. It's so thoroughly the Sword, this impossible, swaggering Fae knight of death who's managed to go from driving me mad to driving me wild, pinned up against the wall.

I should tell him no. I should make him even wilder.

I don't, though.

"Please, yes, please, I want that."

He pulls back slightly, his eyes meeting mine.

I expect to see lust, I expect to see the same need in him he's wringing from me.

I don't expect to see sadness, so deep and ancient it washes over me like an icy wave.

His lips press against mine again, tenderly. I close my eyes and I let him take me where I want to go.

I gasp, clenching around him, my eyes flying wide open, coming hard.

"So beautiful," he murmurs. "So perfect, my Kyrie."

I rest my cheek against his chest, floating back into myself.

"What in the gods' names is going on?" an incensed male voice yells. The sound of a scuffle ensues, and the Sword kisses my collarbone, my cheek, as he sets my skirts to rights.

"We should hurry." My admonition is ruined by the soft smile on my face.

"I like that look," the Sword purrs at me.

"That's good, considering you gave it to me." I push off the wall, slightly dizzy, and head up the rest of the stairs. "Lara did well with the wards," I mutter to myself, glancing around.

The oak parlor isn't exactly how I remember it. For one, there are several barrels stamped with Dario's insignia in here, which isn't where they were supposed to be, but it will have to do. I shrug a shoulder, moving quickly around the room, the noise damped and strange here, like the air's heavy.

"The wards are still thick." The Sword's muscles strain and I lick my lips, unable to help myself.

"Too bad we don't have more time, or I would be the one making you beg." I run my fingers along the walls, searching for the access point. "Can you break the rest?"

It irks me that I still don't know everything he can do.

"I can't touch the wards around Sola's Crown," he says.

The sounds of a fight ring out, closer now, and I bite my lower lip.

"Maybe you should send up a prayer to your god for more time," I tell the Sword jokingly.

"Maybe," he says evasively.

I squint at him, but then my fingers find the knothole in the paneling.

"Open for me, Kyrie sworn to Sola," I whisper, infusing each word with a massive hit of power. I sway on my feet, the energy I expended to help convince the fucking lock to open leaving me drained.

Nothing happens.

"Fuck," I swear.

Then the door swings open and I clap my hands, rubbing my palms together.

Caedia emerges, slightly disheveled, but grinning like a weasel with a snake.

"I can't say I enjoyed that," she grumbles. "Of course, I did what you asked, and did it well."

"Sword, you know what to do, right?" I glance at him and he nods, his nostrils flaring.

"I have your back." He pulls his huge black-pommeled broadsword from where he hid it between his shoulder blades under his specially tailored jacket.

"And my front. You look good enough to eat," I tell him, winking obscenely. "I like your sword." I waggle my eyebrows at him, just in case he didn't get it.

He snorts a laugh, shaking his head.

"Stop flirting. Come on," Caedia says grumpily. "I didn't talk deadwood from Nivor Forest into granting me passage just to watch you two embarrass yourselves."

"I'm never embarrassed," I tell her truthfully, but she's not wrong.

I scurry into the secret opening, a strange tug at my center leaving me looking back at where the Sword stands in the room, his weapon out and ready to defend us.

The timing has to be just right.

Finding out Caedia retained her dryad magic was genuinely the key to this whole plan, but I try not to congratulate myself too soon. There are still too many pieces left for that.

"Gods, it's worse than I remember," I mutter, and Caedia makes a wordless sound of agreement from behind me.

The acrid taste of stale magic shivers through my senses and I cough, my lungs irritated, like the curse is somehow reacting to it.

"Are you ready?" I ask Caedia quietly, because I swear to the gods, if this doesn't go the way I have planned, I don't know what I'm going to do.

Well, that's not true.

I'll die if this doesn't go the way I have planned.

And I'm not giving Hrakan the satisfaction of taking me before I've done everything in my power to undo all of Sola's evils.

Finally, we reach the King of Diamonds' treasure room, lit up with dozens of smoking torches, light blazing off the jewels and gold, dazzling my eyes after the darkness of the stairway down.

There it is. My eyes stray to it immediately, a thin silver circlet set with iridescent opals.

I sigh in relief, making a great show of plucking it off the stone statue's brow and plopping it onto mine. A ring sits on a velvet pillow next to it, a dull, tarnished thing with one small onyx stone in the middle. I grab it, too, and tuck it into a hidden pocket in my skirt as I stroke the crown on my head.

"I bet it looks really lovely with my dress," I say loudly. Probably a touch too loudly, but overacting has always been my specialty.

"What a good little dryad," a familiar voice says. "Immediately came running to me, as though I needed help knowing exactly what you would do, you red-headed bitch."

It doesn't matter that I expected to run into him tonight. It doesn't matter that I told Caedia to do exactly this.

My blood runs cold all the same.

"That is such an unimaginative insult, Alaric," I tell him, sweat beading on my forehead despite the cool touch of the metal against my brow.

Alaric stands before me, blond and beautiful and slightly older than I remember, but all the more handsome for it, a scar along his throat that wasn't there the last time I saw him.

Mostly because it was a gaping wound. I grimace.

"Well, that healed nicely," I tell him, my hand still on the circlet in my curls.

Focus. *Focus.*

Steel on steel rings from above, and dust falls from the ceiling as something heavy smashes into the floor.

"Sounds like your lover is making some new friends," Alaric says, his ice-blue eyes stuck on the crown on my head, not noticing the empty spot the ring occupied.

My palms sweat. This is exactly what I wanted to happen.

Still—It *feels* real.

"He never has been big on conversation," I tell him very seriously. "He's much more interested in handling his sword."

Half of Alaric's mouth quirks up into a smile. "Too bad you never were very good at that."

My eyes widen in shock. "That's a lie. I am an expert sword handler."

"You would be," Caedia trills. I let my gaze slip to her, hurt and confusion on my face. A trio of barrels are behind where she stands.

Don't look at them.

"Why?" I ask her. "Why would you..." I trail off, letting the question hang in the air.

"Money." She shrugs in that easy way she has. "You paying me seemed likely, but Alaric paying me to turn you in... that's a guarantee. Plus, he has more to pay."

Alaric grins at her. "She's smart," he tells me, like I don't know that.

Self-satisfied little bitch. I seethe.

His smile widens, showing his lovely teeth.

"I knew you'd be back," he says, creeping closer, running his fingers along the statue I just stole the crown from, so damned sure of himself. "I knew it, and as soon as I saw you, I knew you wouldn't be able to resist coming down here. Of course, your little dryad running to me to tattle helped. Then it was just a matter of getting here before you."

"I like my currency in gold," Caedia tells him, clearly enjoying herself.

I exhale noisily, my stomach churning with nerves. Dark vines crack the mortar of the stones in the corners and I try not to notice them as they slowly, slowly slip along the floor like snakes.

"Give me the crown," Alaric says.

"No." Stubborn to the end.

"You think you can charm your way out of this?"

"That is sort of my whole... thing." I stumble over the word. Alaric's gaze darts to the space behind me and I realize how badly this could turn out in the blink of an eye.

He has guards in here, and they've outflanked me.

I swallow. I knew this could happen, I knew it was a possibility.

"You can't charm me." He holds up a coin, one from the Sisters of Sola themselves, those interfering assholes. "This is enchanted to protect against your power."

"Do your guards all have one?" I ask. "It would really be a shame if I used it on them, wouldn't it?" It's a bluff. I'm exhausted from the curse and from draining my power on the entrance to the treasury.

The ground above shakes twice. The signal the Sword and I decided on.

Alaric looks mildly bored.

"Give him the crown, or we'll take it off your severed head," one of the guards behind me intones. "Sola's sisters will pay handsomely for the return of your corpse along with the crown."

Caedia squeaks in terror and the vines keep pressing onward, towards where Alaric stands. I force myself to look away.

"Alaric, that's just gruesome." I wince. "I didn't mean to slice your neck, you know. You just... got in the way a little."

His fingers go to it, his eyes narrowed. "I think it adds to my charm."

"Very debonair," Caedia improvises.

We both stop and look at her.

She grins. The vines keep creeping towards Alaric.

"Give me the crown, Kyrie." Alaric's eyes narrow. "No, wait, don't—"

Something hard crashes into the side of my head, and the world goes black.

42

THE SWORD

I give the signal, and I stare down the trio of men trying their best to fight me.

Laughable.

Then Kyrie cries out, a sound so sharp and full of pain that it reverberates through my soul. Rage fills me up and I growl at the humans panting in front of me.

Our souls are already tethered.

My magic unspools, darkness feathering from my fingers in a torrent that turns the men who attempt to fight me pale with dread.

"Leave this place if you want to keep your souls," I rasp.

They flee.

A barrel behind me bursts open. Wine and bits of wood fly everywhere, and I stand my ground as another explodes, then another. Splinters lodge themselves in my arms and back, but I hardly feel it.

My magic continues to work, the corpses Dario and I

worked to shove into the casks reanimating, their eyes glowing black.

They kneel as one, each grasping a dagger formed from their own bones.

An ancient, foul spell, and one only I'm the master of.

"Rise, and do my bidding." My voice rumbles like thunder. The oak panels creak, the ancient life of the Nivor Forest responding to my magic.

Lara and Morrow run into the room holding hands, Dario on their heels.

"They hurt Kyrie."

Lara pales.

Morrow stares at the corpses behind me. "I imagined it, but... it's different to see it happen."

"You have seen nothing of Death yet, mortal," I rasp, turning for the narrow entrance to the treasury.

"That's encouraging," Dario quips.

Racing to where Kyrie, my Kyrie, is hurting.

"What in the hells?!" Caedia's indignant voice rises up through the stairwell to the King of Diamonds' treasury. "You didn't have to do that. She would have given you the crown."

"Are you a fool? That is the greatest thief of all time. She would not have given it to me," a resonant male voice says. "But the dryad is right, you didn't have to hurt her—"

Power ripples from my body in a sheet of pure, opaque black, and I hear more barrels exploding.

"By Sola's toenails, what in the fuck is happening?"

Dario laughs, a mirthless sound.

I storm on, down the stone steps, until the brilliant light of the treasury falters in the face of my darkness.

A lithe, limp figure in a white dress splays across an expensive rug on the floor.

Kyrie.

The guards swivel between the corpses holding their sharpened bones and me, trying to decide what's the bigger threat.

"Take them," I rage at the corpses.

"I didn't mean her any harm," Alaric says, his eyes wide but a fearless sort of expression on his face. Alaric glances down—too late. Fear drains the color from his face as he takes in Caedia's handiwork. "Fucking hells, Kyrie."

Caedia's vines finally grip his legs, climbing up his thighs, and the tiny dryad sighs in relief, her work done.

"Then who did this?" I thunder. "Who hurt her?"

Alaric's gaze flinches slightly right.

"Sola will reward me for the traitor's death," a guard hisses.

I spare a glance at him over my shoulder. I raise my hand, not even bothering with the sword, and the guard rises off his feet, his eyes rolling.

"Sword," Lara's voice whips out, a warning. "Remember. Remember her curse. Not like that."

The guard shakes as I set him back on his feet.

I step towards him, holding his gaze.

"Th-th-thank you," he stammers in Lara's direction.

I run him through.

Blood spills on the fine rugs of the King of Diamonds' treasury.

"There's no need for murder," Alaric says as I turn to him. "I wasn't going to kill Kyrie. Even if she did try to slit my throat and steal from me." It's a feral snarl, and I hear what he really means in it.

He would rather torture her, slowly, casually than end her so cleanly.

I tilt my head, knowing my power is shining through me, forbidden and dark.

Alaric swallows, but he doesn't back down. "Kyrie was my whole world. Then she took everything from me."

Caedia sniffs. "I think we should keep him here a little longer." The vines wrap around the King of Diamonds' waist.

Morrow, glowing red, steps between all of us. "This doesn't have to end in more bloodshed and death." He gives me a meaningful look.

He's seen my truth.

I stopped hiding it the minute I heard Kyrie scream.

"What is it you offer, King of Diamonds?" I ask him, stepping closer. My necromantic magic swirls and eddies around our ankles, turning the floor black as night. "What is it you offer for safe passage from your crime against Kyrie?"

"You could have bartered with me for the crown," Alaric says, opening his hands wide. "I am not an unreasonable man."

"This is the way things had to be done," Lara intones.

Alaric glances at her, uneasy. "Nakush?"

She nods.

I am barely keeping my rage in check, my need to hurt him for what happened to the woman lying on the ground. My woman.

He clears his throat, running his fingers around his collar, a lock of his gold-blond hair falling over one eye. "I don't have much to offer. Keep what she's taken. Or whatever else you want."

The magic of those words rings through me, and I hold back a sigh of relief.

"A new god will rise," Lara continues, stepping forward. "You will swear your allegiance."

Alaric blinks.

The reanimated corpses step closer to him, brandishing their bones.

He laughs nervously, holding up his hands. "Right. I will swear my allegiance to a new god. Apologies to my current master."

"She would cut off your tongue for sport," I tell him.

He raises his eyebrows, tilting his head. "That I believe. Tell Kyrie..."

I step closer. "I do not like her name in your mouth."

Alaric, King of Diamonds, raises his chin, defiant in the face of Death.

"Tell her I am sorry."

I don't answer. He doesn't deserve it.

Instead, I scoop Kyrie up from where she's crumpled on the floor, her shallow breaths breaking my heart.

Caedia chants under her breath, and Lara joins hands with her. Magic swells.

"Oh gods, you can just leave out the front door, you don't have to do that—" Alaric begins, but a look from me silences him.

The wall of the treasury explodes outward, revealing a snow-covered lawn.

Behind us, Alaric sighs. "Are you going to take your bodies with you?"

I wave a hand, and the corpses fall to the ground, the necromantic magic sustaining them withdrawn.

"Of course not," he mutters.

"Shut down the flesh trade and brothels or you'll find those corpses haunting you," I roar at him. The nearly full moon overhead shines silver on the snow, cold and sharp as a dagger's edge.

Caedia laughs, her hands fluttering over Kyrie's head. "Tricking him was fun. More fun than I thought it would be." The warmth of a spring day surges as she forces what little power she has left into Kyrie. "I think I'll let those vines hold him a little longer," she continues.

"We're running out of time," Lara says.

"I cannot change that," I tell her.

"I know." The pleading way she looks at me tells me differently, though.

Kyrie stirs in my arms and Caedia slumps, clearly spent.

Green eyes look into mine, and my heart skips a beat.

"What did I miss?" her words are slurred and slow, but she's awake. She's speaking.

She's alive.

43

KYRIE

My entire body hurts.

We've set up camp in Nivor Forest, or more accurately, everyone else set up camp while I sat on the ground, aching.

And coughing.

It's worse now. I hold the green cloak Lara gave me all those weeks ago over my mouth, coughing so hard I retch. At least the green will hide any... unfortunate excretions.

My pretty white velvet cloak was lost at Alaric's stupid palace, and I scowl at the thought that that asshole has something else of mine that I liked. Even though the green is much more sensible, I wouldn't mind having something frivolous and soft like that.

The others filled me in on what happened after the guard knocked me out.

"I still can't believe you just impaled a guy," I call out to the Sword.

"I was angry." He jams a tent pole into the ground.

A loud mew echoes from the massive trees around us. I try to look left, but only manage to make my headache worse.

"Fil?" I say into the night.

Sure enough, the huge direcat wanders into camp, purring loud enough to elicit looks of surprise from everyone.

"I still don't understand the cat," Dario says.

"And I don't understand why you are still with us," Caedia tells him, handing him a length of waxed canvas. "We don't need you."

"I think I should lie low after the stunt with the casks and corpses." Dario shrugs a shoulder. "Seems like going back to Nyzbern right now would be imprudent."

They told me about how the corpses barreled from the wine casks (heh), doing exactly what I wanted and providing the perfect diversion.

Sure, it didn't all go to plan, considering the massive bump on my head and the fact I feel like complete shit.

My fingers go to the ring in my pocket, the real Crown of Sola a boring piece of metal in the shape of an old-fashioned crown, with one ugly black stone set in the middle.

"I'm still disappointed that he just let us walk away," I say. "I really worked hard to make him think we were after the circlet. It should fetch a good price, though."

"He didn't just let us walk away," Dario huffs, but falls silent at a long look from Morrow.

I get the feeling they're not telling me something.

"What am I missing?" I make myself ask.

"Other than regard for the law or your personal safety?" Morrow asks. "Nothing, really. It went off better than we planned, except you getting hurt."

I want to smile, but moving my face makes my head hurt,

so I lean up against the direcat's deliciously warm fur and focus on breathing.

Lara turns from where she's building a fire.

Her eyes glow purple.

"Sola sends her regards."

"Fuck," Dario says, staring at her. "That is uncanny."

"Right?" I agree, annoyed. "Nakush, Lara, whoever's in there, can you be more specific?"

"What kind of regards?" Caedia asks.

The Sword stares at me, terror in his eyes.

Lara wilts, toppling forward, but Morrow is there to catch her before she lands face-first in the ice-dappled ground.

The Sword is moving, faster than I've ever seen, removing the stakes he just plunked into the ground.

"What is going on?" Gods, I am so tired.

"The Sisters of Sola," Lara chokes out, the purple still glittering in her eyes. "They are coming for you, Kyrie. They know you have it. They will end you."

"Them?" What the hells do they want with me now? "Haven't I spent enough time with them?"

My stomach hollows out, and for a moment, I want to throw up.

They will end me. End me. All the good I want to do, all the victims of Sola's tender fury who I want to help—all of it, wiped out.

"Them," the Sword agrees. "They will kill you all."

You all. I tilt my head, trying to make sense of that. Well, I suppose an immortal Fae isn't concerned about the Sisters of fucking Sola.

"We need to split up."

Everyone stares at me. I pat Fil and he nudges my hand, asking for more.

"Absolutely not, Kyrie, you need us there with you after the ritual," Lara says.

"Lara's right," Caedia agrees. "We need to be there. You're sick, and you're hurt, and you will need help. That's a big magic."

"We don't even know what the ritual is—"

"I do," the Sword says, and hatred fills the two words.

I flinch, confused and tired. My lungs burn, and a cough sputters from me, then more.

"We are running out of time, Kyrie," he says in quieter voice. "We have to move."

"They're approaching Nyzbern," Lara says darkly. "The sisters will find us. We need to lead them away. You and Kyrie need time to complete the ritual."

"We'll lead them away," Morrow confirms. "They'll be safe."

"How? How do they even know where we are?" *I'm missing something.* The curse is clouding my brain, the wound on my head making it worse. I'm so gods damned tired.

"The, uh... the magic we used—" Caedia falters, looking to the Sword for guidance.

"The necromantic magic I used for the corpses in the barrels was like lighting a signal fire," he finishes for her. "That's not a normal spell."

"So they are after *you*, not me." That makes sense, considering he murdered a whole bunch of my so-called sisters.

"They are after us both," he says shortly.

A cough rips through me, my lungs on fire. Then another, and another, until I'm gasping for air. Stars wink in front of my eyes.

"Give her this three times a day," Caedia says, though she sounds far off. "This will help her sleep. This one is for her head injury. You need to hurry—the curse, it shouldn't be progressing this fast."

"More time was never an option," the Sword says.

I blink, trying to scatter the dots swimming in my field of vision because I can't make sense of what he's saying.

"Here," Lara says, and I stand unsteadily while she helps me tug on my old faithful leather trousers.

"I don't want to leave the gown," I say plaintively. My teeth chatter, and I'm shivering as Caedia and Lara both work to get the white dress off and replace it with the soft chemise. "Please," I add.

"That's how I know you're feeling terrible," Lara tells me. I think she's smiling, but focusing doesn't feel great. I swallow against the bile rising from the effort. "You're being polite."

"Here." Caedia gently stuffs my head through a thick wool sweater, and I obediently put my arms through like a sullen toddler.

I close my eyes, and a memory floats to the surface: my little brothers giggling furiously when I tried to help my mother dress them for the day. The softness of their round cheeks, their chubby hands and wrists.

"They're gone," I say sadly, opening my eyes.

They'll never know what it's like to ride a horse through a snowstorm, or drunkenly laugh with their friends by a roaring fireplace.

"Or fall in love," I say out loud.

Lara's watching me through slitted eyes as she ties the green cloak she loaned me all those weeks ago.

"Caedia, can you do anything else for her head?"

"Did I ever tell you about my baby brothers?" I ask her.

Caedia's fingers flutter over my cheeks, luna moth light, green-tinged and every bit as delicate. I look at Lara, my heart in my throat.

"I miss them. They were just babies, and they had them killed. They killed them all."

"I know," Lara tells me, her voice thick. "I know they did, Kyrie. You're going to fix it. You're going to make sure that doesn't happen again. You will do it."

"I can't do it if I die. The curse," I am babbling, and I can't seem to stop. "The curse, I can feel it, Lara. It's worse now."

"You used too much magic tonight," Caedia tells me. "Stay with the Sword, let him take care of you."

Lara's putting my boots on, jamming my feet inside and lacing them up.

"I miss my family," I tell her. "I miss them, and I've never been allowed to. I wonder who I would have been if they'd lived. I wonder even more who they would be."

She holds my chin in hers, Caedia's fingers still tracing a delicate dance around my temples.

"We're your family now, Kyrie. You hear me? You've been like a sister to me since that day we met, and you will be long after this is all over, no matter what. Morrow can be the big brother you never wanted, Caedia's the wild little sister we're all slightly frightened by, and Dario is the annoying cousin you want to slap sometimes."

"Hey," Dario says. "I don't appreciate that."

"He's more like a second cousin from a branch of the family tree we don't talk about," I manage.

"There," Caedia says, her fingers stilling in my hair. "I think that helped set her to rights. Sword, take care of her. She's going to be delicate for a day or two."

Morrow lifts me partway up onto a horse and a big arm wraps around my waist, hoisting me the rest of the way up.

"We will see you again, Kyrie."

"Meet us in the Wastes in no more than three weeks' time. You'll know where to go," the Sword snaps at Lara.

"The Wastes," I repeat. "There's nothing there." Including Sola and her cursed followers. "Perfect."

"The Wastes in three weeks' time," Morrow says. "We'll lead the sisters away."

"Where will you go?" Caedia asks plaintively, gaze flitting between us.

"Somewhere you can't follow," the Sword answers.

Fil stares at me with luminous eyes from the snow-covered ground.

"Tell me it's going to be alright," I say to no one in particular.

The only answer is the pounding of the horse's hooves against the icy ground, and the plaintive sigh of the winter wind against in my ears.

44

THE SWORD

Kyrie falls limp against me in a matter of moments, her head lolling against my chest as the magic Caedia performed to speed her healing takes effect.

Were it not for her deep and even breathing, I would be frantic with worry for her. As it is, I am worried enough. Kyrie's mare and Mushroom the mule nimbly follow behind us, loaded down with our share of supplies.

Sola's Crown dangles on a chain around my neck, unassuming but strangely heavy where it rests between our bodies.

A tree limb rips at Kyrie's cloak, tearing a piece off, a stolen leaf against the moonlit snow.

Sola's minions would steal everything from her, from me, all over again.

I won't allow it.

Kyrie is mine.

In the distance, Kyrie's direcat roars a challenge, and I hear an echo of my thoughts in it.

I will do anything to keep her from them—but her fate has been sealed since her lips touched the chalice.

※

I've changed mounts twice by the time we stop, riding through the day and most of the night. The two horses and Mushroom are spent, blowing air and stumbling too much to press on.

I would run them to the ground were it not for Kyrie's soft heart and love for the creatures.

What I must do weighs heavily on me.

I won't waste Kyrie's good feelings towards me on hurting our mounts, not when I'm going to need every ounce of her trust to ensure what must happen comes to fruition.

Slowly, I dismount, hefting Kyrie's slight weight off the horse, who whickers in tired appreciation. The noise of the River Blanst is a fast rush in the near distance.

The direcat, Filarion, strides out from the scrubby underbrush. He flops down on the rocky shoreline, lapping at the water while managing to shoot me a look of pure disdain at the same time.

"Sorry, friend," I murmur. "Speed was the best option."

I do my best to lay Kyrie alongside the big cat, spreading one of the blankets out beneath her.

I'm stiff all over, but there's no time to rest. Not now, not when so little time remains.

The horses are spent, though, and I take my time relieving them of their tack and cleaning the worst of their lather off, massaging their sore muscles. They drink well from the river, and once they start in on the good-quality hay I bundled onto the pack mule in Nyzbern, I relax slightly.

The horses will survive.

The thought has me glancing to Kyrie, who twitches in her

sleep, her slim thieves' hands curling into Filarion's thick grey-brown fur.

She moans and I'm back at her side in an instant, Caedia's potions in my hands.

"Drink," I tell her, helping her sit up and forcing the bitter-smelling herbal blend down her throat.

"Sword." She opens her eyes, the green in them standing out against the stark greys and whites and blues of this branch of Chast river country. "Tell me your real name. Tell me your story."

My heart *hurts*. I clear my throat, smoothing a curl off her forehead, and she blinks sleepily up at me. "What do you want to know?" I ask, my voice hoarse from a day and half a night of riding and the fear that kept trying to claw itself out of me.

"Everything," she says simply.

I can't tell her everything.

I can't even tell her my real name.

Not yet.

"Soon," I murmur instead, still caressing her forehead, unable to keep my hands from her. "Soon, you will know everything. But for now, sleep."

"Hold me," she commands.

"I can do that," I tell her. "It's the least I can do."

Holding her will be a memory I treasure forever, even when she looks at me with disgust at the depths of my betrayal.

But I hold her and she sleeps, and I listen to the river rushing over rocks, knowing our fate will never be different.

45

KYRIE

My mouth feels like I ate dirt. I splutter, sitting up fast, too fast, if the splitting ache in my head is any indication of my poorly chosen speed.

"Shit," I mutter, my eyes widening as I take in my surroundings.

A river rushes and eddies in front of me, blocks of scuzzy ice on the quieter parts of the shoreline, all grey and white and deepest blue. I blink up at the sky, trying to figure out what time it is, but it's too cloudy to tell, the sun blotted out by them.

"We're at the River Blanst," the Sword says, jogging over to me.

The horses are eating, tails flicking behind them and breath clouding in front of their nostrils in the cold.

"Blanst," I echo, rubbing the back of my neck.

The Sword crouches next to me, fingers gently prodding behind my ear.

"Ouch," I say, swatting away his hand and glaring at him.

"The swelling's gone down." He closes his eyes slowly, relief relaxing the furrow in his brow. "It's better."

"What day is it?" That's not what I meant to ask. "How long—"

"You slept for a day and a half. I woke you to give you the potions Caedia made for you, and we rode here."

"And now we can do the ritual?" I ask.

Filarion, who apparently was acting as my pillow, stretches out long behind me, his tail twitching as he saunters off.

"We need to be in a certain place to do the ritual."

"A place? Now we have to be in a certain place? What's wrong with this place?" I hedge, looking around.

"There is a cavern, not far from here. It's sacred. The spell will be more powerful there. I don't want to risk—" he pauses, swallowing so hard his throat bobs. "We cannot risk it going wrong."

"How far?"

"Not far."

"Then let's go." I try to stand, but dizziness makes my knees weak. The Sword holds a hand out, steadying me.

"No," he says, shaking his head.

I scowl at him and he sighs. "Why?"

"You need your strength." He won't look at me. He's staring at the river.

"Fine. Give me some food and then we can go." I jut my chin out stubbornly.

"You could make me take you, you know? With your powers." The Sword finally meets my eyes. "Why don't you just do that?"

My scowl deepens.

He doesn't look away, just watches me carefully.

"I'm not going to use that on you."

"Why not, little liar?"

I huff.

He waits, his calloused palm finding my cheek, barely touching me there. My eyes sting with tears, and I try to swallow them.

"Because I care about you," I finally answer.

The truth of it, of my feelings for him, shines between us like a beacon, like it's something I could hold and shape with my hands.

Then the Sword is there, me in his hands instead. He holds me in his arms carefully, like I'm fragile, like I'm precious and breakable and he's scared he might break me.

"You can't, you know?" I pull away slightly, and our breath mingles together in white vapor.

"Can't what?"

"Break me." It's a whisper, a secret. "You won't break me, Sword. If I were capable of breaking, if I were something delicate—I would already be broken."

"Kyrie." My name sounds like an entreaty when he says it like that. "Kyrie," he repeats, and I close my hands over his cheeks, putting the tip of my nose against his. "I'm afraid."

It's so quietly said I almost miss it.

"Don't let your fear dictate your reality." I shake my head slightly, not wanting to move too suddenly, not wanting to scare him away. "I have been afraid my whole life. I am afraid right now. I am tired of that fear keeping me from *living*."

"I want you to *live*, Kyrie." A desperate ache colors the word.

I exhale in confusion. "Why would you assume I think otherwise?"

He just watches me, wordless, hardly breathing.

I smile up at him through my bewilderment, making up my mind in the span of an instant. "Then let's live. Let's live in this moment, this small space of peace we've stolen, and let's live for each other. Right now."

He surges against me, his mouth on mine in an answering promise.

His hands are in my hair, gentle, but there's no restraint, no sense that he's holding me back.

It hits me then, with a force that takes my breath away.

I trust him. I trust him not to hurt me, I trust him to treasure this as much as I will. As long as we've been at each other's throats the past weeks, this—this thing between us—has been there too, simmering, making every barb especially sharp, especially poisoned.

Because we knew we could hurt each other.

My heart sings to know he's choosing a new path for us.

That we're choosing it together.

His lips leave mine, pressing a trail of tenderness down the pulse in my neck, across my collarbone.

"I'm sorry," I tell him, trying and failing to catch my breath. "I'm sorry I have been afraid and cruel to you. I'm sorry I didn't see what we could have right away."

He stills momentarily. His dark gaze goes to mine, holding it, silent.

The Sword shakes his head subtly, and I know what he's thinking; I don't need to ask.

"Don't apologize for trying to protect yourself in a world that's made you afraid," he growls, the words reverberating all the way to my bones, like he's carving the sentiment into my marrow.

His hands rip at my clothes and we're crashing into each other, tearing at anything so foolish as to stand between us.

"Kyrie, I have wanted you like this, with me, for so long." Silver strands of hair caress our skin as he shakes his head, unable to finish the sentence.

"I know—"

"You don't know. You can't know."

My chest heaves and I'm completely naked in front of him, so much more vulnerable than ever before, more open and willing than the manticore's poison made me in the hot springs.

"Then show me," I murmur.

Something changes in his gaze, desolation and desire flickering through his dark brown eyes in equal measure.

When he unleashes himself, my entire being responds, like our magic, our souls, are calling to each other, like this is meant to be.

His mouth finds the tip of my breast and I rip at his pants with a moan on my lips, the noise of the river drowning out the rising sound.

He helps me, shoving his pants all the way off, and I push at him gently.

"I want to see you," I tell him. "Let me look."

There is no shyness in him as he pulls away, letting me look my fill. Everything about him is exquisite.

Broad shoulders and a chest sculpted by the gods themselves. Narrow hips and powerfully muscled legs, everything about him screams warrior, from his huge arms and calloused hands to the network of scars across his skin.

"What do you see, little liar?" he asks, tilting his head.

"I see a male who is worthy of being trusted." I pause, licking my lips. "A male worthy of love."

"Fuck, Kyrie." He dives back on top of me, pinning my wrists over my head as his mouth teases and bites one nipple, then the other.

I am powerless to do anything but cry out, to arch my back and beg for more.

I am powerless against him, and for the first time in my

life, gods, it feels good to stop fighting, to trust that he will give me pleasure, that he will keep me safe.

My leg goes around his hip, his cock nudging at my entrance.

He hisses out a breath, his teeth rough on the peak of my nipple, and I cry out, making the nearby horses stamp at the ground in concern.

"We have an audience," I tell him on a laugh.

The sound of my laugh abruptly cuts off as he thrusts my legs apart with his knees. A muscle jumps in his temple.

"I don't care," he tells me. "Do you care? Do you want to stop?"

I shudder, shaking my head. "No. No, please don't stop. I need this. I need you." I thrust my hips up and we both groan as the tip of his cock grazes my sensitive clit.

"Are you wet for me?" he asks, and I smile mischievously at that.

"You could find out," I say archly. "It *is* a large sword to sheathe."

He huffs a laugh, his big hands smoothing over my naked body until they're at my hips, holding me in place.

When his mouth dips between my thighs, I immediately buck at the hot warmth of his tongue. He swirls it around my clit slowly, tantalizing me, one hand palming my breast and pinching my nipple until I can hardly breathe.

Need rages through me and I'm babbling senseless words, begging for more.

"Still not wet enough," he growls, and then his fingers are inside me, stretching me, filling me.

When he sucks on my clit, forcefully, demanding—I scream as I come.

A flock of birds wing from the trees above, black specks against the grey winter sky.

"Now you're ready for me," he says, and despite the gruffness in his voice, there's tenderness there, too. "I want to watch you ride me, Kyrie."

He rolls us then and, chest panting, I do as he asks, needing more, wanting more from this male, this opposite of me, this creature who answers a question I didn't know I was even asking.

I take his cock in my hand, marveling at it, and the Sword groans, the muscles in his neck tight with his own need.

"You want me?" I ask him, grinning like a maniac.

"Kyrie," he says, a note of warning in his voice.

A bead of pearlescent fluid drips from his thick cock and I bend quickly, lapping at it, loving the way he doesn't push me for more, the way he lets me take my time with him.

"Do you like that?"

"I would like anything you do," he answers softly. I glance up at his face and the sweetness there sends a fresh wave of lust through me.

My plan to tease him dissolves and I readjust myself, ignoring the discomfort of the rocky ground beneath my knees. I position him at my entrance, rocking slowly back and forth on his length.

"So big." My voice comes out strangled.

"You can take it, Kyrie. You were made for me," he murmurs the words like they're the greatest truth he can give me.

I rock again, nudging him deeper. He settles one hand on the curve of my hip, the other reaching between our bodies, his gaze ravenous on me as he finds the bud of my pleasure again.

A gasp tears out of me and I lean forward, kissing him hard, kissing him like I mean it. Like it might be the last time.

I whip my hips down and he sucks in a breath as he sinks into me to the hilt.

We pause, panting, holding each other. His gaze is the fathomless dark of death—but there's inexplicable comfort in it, the warmth of a lover's embrace at midnight, of laughing with a friend when you should be crying.

There is joy, too.

"Kyrie," he grits out, and I start to move. He does too, and it doesn't take us long to find a soft, steady rhythm.

It takes even less time for it to turn wild as we both chase our pleasure.

"I can feel you getting closer," he says, sitting up, nibbling at my ear.

"So close," I tell him, my fingers tangled in his hair.

"You are beautiful. You are mine. Mine, Kyrie." He shifts again, and suddenly I'm the one on my back, hanging on for dear life as he slams into me. Our bodies make wet noises where they meet, his flesh in mine, both of us building to a crescendo that won't be denied.

"Yours," I say on a sob, so close I could scream, and he kisses me fiercely, his teeth marking my lips, his touch marking my soul.

When I come, he follows quickly, holding me tight against him, and it feels like the whole world has shifted underneath me.

46

THE SWORD

I will never be the same.
    The thought's chased off by a worse one.
    It will never be like this again.
Kyrie dozes in my arms, the blanket pulled over our bodies.

I am as much a thief as the woman in my arms, ravaged by a past she had no control over and a curse she unwittingly chose. I have stolen these moments with her, this joy, and I will pay for it for the rest of my eternal life.

The worst part is, I am past caring.

I will spend eternity hating myself for what fate and the gods have decreed will happen next in exchange for these stolen moments of joy and pleasure.

That is the worst part of the curse we both bear.

I tuck her in more gently, slowly moving away from her to dress.

Sex with Kyrie was selfish. It was unkind, and it was cruel

to her. Unnecessary to do what needs to be done, and thus out of character for me.

Still.

Still, I would not take it back, I would not trade it.

I still possess enough of my mortal soul to know that I am weak enough to do it again, should she let me.

"Where are you going?" she asks sleepily, her red-blonde lashes fluttering as she stares up at me.

"I was going to make a fire. You need to eat."

"Come back to me," she says, yawning and patting the blanket beside her. "Let's stay like this until morning."

I hesitate, knowing I should distance myself from her, that I am only making things harder for both of us.

Kyrie smiles at me, though, so soft and trusting, and all my defenses crumble.

I have done my best to hate her, to keep her away—but the truth is, it's only made me love her more.

I curl myself around her soft, mortal body and I breathe her in, holding her until we both fall asleep again.

❄

THE CLOUDS ARE DISPERSING by the time I wake again, whisps of white against a topaz winter sky. A lone scarlet cardinal hops from rock to rock, peering this way and that.

The direcat's waded into the river and I watch him for a long moment as he waits for an unsuspecting fish.

Kyrie stretches out next to me, making a quiet sleepy noise that tugs at my heart.

Tugs at it, and threatens to shatter it in the still of morning.

That's exactly what I'll do to her, after all.

I get up, making sure to tuck the blanket in tightly around her, and set about making a campfire. My own stomach growls and I'm sure the mortal woman who holds my soul in her small fingers is likewise hungry.

Between preparing a meal for us, I steal glances at her. The spill of her wild red curls across the grey blanket, the slash of peach lips against her freckled face.

Before long, she sits up, blinking at me and sniffing the air thoughtfully.

"Hi," she says, the shyest I've ever heard her.

As if I didn't spend the night lapping between her thighs. "Good morning, my Kyrie," I tell her.

The blush that colors her cheeks at the words splits my heart in two.

Sola's curse on that chalice was a clever one, her vengeance colder and more calculated than even I could be.

There is only one way forward, though, and the dies of fate have been cast.

47

KYRIE

Lazy beams of sun dance across the icy surface of the River Blanst. The wintery afternoon light is pale and too harsh all at once, amplified by the water and the lack of leaves on the trees all around.

I expected things to be different.

I feel different.

Where there was an itching hurt, now I look at the Fae male across the fire and feel something like hope kindling.

He's distant, though, distant and cold as the occasional snowflake drifting onto my cheek, unexpected and soft. It shouldn't hurt as much as it does, pain lancing into the soft place he made inside my heart.

The nearly empty potion bottle Caedia gave us twinkles in the light and I turn it over in my hands, knowing it's nearly gone, knowing time for me is likewise running out.

My head has healed, yes, but whatever damage the chalice's curse is doing now feels permanent.

I glance up and the Sword is watching me, his face that bland mask I thought I'd managed to cast away.

"Are you ready to do the ritual?" I finally make myself ask, unable to stand his silence any longer, unwilling to analyze what it might mean.

He told me not to be afraid, and not to apologize for the fear.

I let it shine in my eyes.

He glances away.

A nervous laugh bubbles out of me, dying into silence. A log on the fire pops and I startle.

That feeling, that nagging, persistent feeling that I can't seem to shake, crawls over my skin.

I've missed something.

I've missed something important.

It feels like the chance to figure it out has slipped by me, or that the damned curse is clouding my ability to see it.

Suddenly, I don't just want to do the ritual. I need it.

As soon as I think it, the nerves, the fog, melt away. It's time.

I might be a liar gifted with magic, with a silvered tongue, but the truth has always shone for me just as brightly.

"We are doing it now," I say in a clear voice. "I don't want to wait until I am too sick to pronounce the words."

He finally, *finally* gives me the grace of looking at me, though it seems his gaze slips right through me.

Where are you? I want to scream at him. *What happened?*

I don't.

I'm not sure I want the answer.

I do know I want the cure, though.

The Sword stands, offering his hand to me. I take it, curling my fingers into his.

Let me hold you near me, I try to say. *Let me have your comfort for a while.*

When our eyes meet again, I see him there, I see the piece of him he's trying to keep from me.

And it's full of fear. My throat goes dry and I try to swallow.

What are you afraid of, Sword?

He doesn't answer my unspoken question. I pull the green cloak—a link to Lara and our friendship—close around me, knowing somehow I'll need it—this memory of her, of all my friends—and that I'll need to remember what I want from this life.

We walk a long way from our small makeshift riverside camp, Filarion the direcat at my side, in stilted silence.

The river grows louder the longer we walk, raging against the rocks.

Still, I cling to the Sword's hand, letting him lead me.

Trusting him to guide me where I need to go, like this arcane ritual we're about to perform is the most natural thing in the world.

I don't really care if it's the most unnatural thing—I'm doing it.

I refuse to let some curse beat me.

I can't let Sola and her fellow gods win. I won't.

"Here," the Sword says and I blink, looking away from the white-water rapids of the River Blanst.

"Oh," I say softly. It's a cave, much like the one we went through all those days ago in Hiirek. "A barrow?"

"A sacred place." He squeezes my hand, looking so deep into my eyes that I feel it sear my soul—my soul, which wants to be near him, which wants to be seen.

"Sacred place," I repeat.

He pulls the Crown of Sola, the small, unassuming ring, from the chain around his neck.

I wondered where it went. My mouth is dry and I lick my lips, anxiety climbing.

"Here," he says. The silver chain flashes in the sunlight, the tarnished ring sliding off of it into my palm. "Wear it," he commands, and I slip it onto my fourth finger, unquestioning.

"What is going to happen?" I ask, my voice trembling slightly.

His warm, big hands cup my face and I bite my lip.

"Do you trust me?" he asks.

I nod. "I trust you." I trust him so much it hurts. So much it scares me.

"Then you enter this sacred place willingly, with me as your chosen partner to perform the ritual?"

Magic grasps at me, whipping tendrils of my hair around my face, and I know instinctively that this is part of whatever lies ahead for me, this is part of what's going to save me.

"I do." The pull of the magic intensifies, clawing at us, tugging us into the mouth of the river cave.

"Then come, and fulfill your destiny," the Sword intones.

I hold my head high, and I follow him into the dark.

I think I will always follow him into the dark.

❅

THE DIRECAT TREADS LIGHTLY beside me, paws soundless on the damp cave floors.

The Sword is just as silent and I keep one hand in his, letting him guide me, letting him hold my whole heart with the other.

We come to a stop and I sway into him, off-balance, as I cough.

Dripping water sounds and the Sword murmurs a foreign

word—Fae, probably—and the cave blazes with a fierce white light.

"That's handy."

The Sword deigns to give me a hint of a smile, though his scowl quickly replaces it. The light dazzles and I shield my brow with my hand, giving my eyes a moment to adjust.

We're standing in a large circular chamber, cold water lapping at my boots. Fil paces in the narrower entry behind us, tail twitching as he watches with great glowing eyes.

"It's okay," I murmur, and he bares his teeth. "Right."

The Sword is silent.

I take a step, water sloshing around my ankles, my eyes growing wide as I take in what's all around me.

"Are those..." my voice echoes weirdly the further I move into the chamber.

Life-sized statues of the gods ring it.

These are carved from marble, their features flawless and perfect, filled with emotion that makes it hurt to breathe.

Could be that's the curse, though.

"Nakush," I say to myself, staring into their open eyes like they might see me in front of them. Their hands are wide, palms up, a mage pose.

The next is Heska, the mother of the gods, the namesake of my country, and her face is carved in such loving detail that it hurts to look at.

It reminds me of my own mother.

My hand goes to my throat and I close my eyes.

"Why are they so... lifelike?" I ask. "Most religious statues and paintings... they don't have any—" I pause, fumbling over the words as my attention falls on Sola.

She's ageless in the stone rendition, a cruel smile on a plain face, a high ponytail hanging over her shoulder, carved as tenderly as the rest. A dagger in one hand slicing the palm of the other, a warning to all.

My swallow is too loud in my own ears.

"This is a sacred place," the Sword finally answers, the sound of his deep voice booming.

Or maybe it's something else, something magic, because the water around my feet seems to vibrate in response.

I shake my head, feeling fuzzy, trying to focus.

"Lojad," I mutter. The god of order and war stands beside Sola, face hidden by a helm, a shield and sword in hand.

There are two statues left, Dyrda, goddess of the wild places and life, and Hrakan, the god of death and time.

"Every god has two faces," I say. The next statue is male.

Hrakan, then; Dyrda must be the last in this strange circle.

I pause before him, studying the skull in one hand. The other's empty, though the stone fingers look like they once did hold something.

I step closer, inspecting the empty hand of Death, feeling the Sword come up behind me. His breath warms the top of my head.

My gaze climbs to the statue's face and my stomach plummets as I take it in.

As I recognize it.

"You," my voice cracks.

I turn slowly, my heart hammering as though it's trying to escape.

The Sword studies me, that sad, unfathomable expression suddenly all too familiar, suddenly too knowing, too much.

I step away rapidly, my back thudding into the statue of Death behind me. Cold water seeps into my leather leggings and I shiver, my eyes wide.

"I know who you are."

"It's funny how mortals always recognize me in the end,"

he answers, voice sad and ancient—the voice of the god of death.

Hrakan.

The Sword... the Sword is Hrakan.

"How?" I ask.

The room spins and the Sword—Hrakan—puts his arm around my waist.

"Are you still willing to partake in the ritual?" he intones, the air around us thick with latent, powerful magic. White vapor rises from the cold water on the floor and my teeth begin to chatter. "Are you willing to seal your fate, Kyrie Ilinus, Sola's sworn and silver tongue?"

I am afraid.

Don't let your fear dictate your reality, I told him, just last night. *He's still mine. I'm still his, at least in this moment.*

I am a liar, but I can tell the truth, too.

"Yes," I say, mustering a serenity I'm not sure I feel. "I am willing." I take a deep breath, speaking the greatest truth of all. "I trust you."

He takes my hand, kissing the Crown of Sola where it nestles on my fourth finger. My heart wrenches at the sadness in his eyes.

"Kyrie," he says, darkness beginning to eddy around my knees, blotting out the white. "The curse on the chalice. It bound you to me. Only one sworn to Sola, one with all her gifts, could drink from it."

"And now we're going to break the curse, right—" I pause, unable to bring myself to call him Hrakan. The god of death holds my hand. "Aren't we?"

Totally normal.

"The curse will be broken," he says slowly. "You made me swear an oath, remember? A mortal convincing a god to swear to her." He smiles at me, and it's so full of affection my heart slows, my racing pulse returning to normal. "I don't think that has ever been done before."

"Well," I drawl, raising an eyebrow. "You would know, oh great and terrible god of death and time."

The dimple I love flashes in his face before sorrow and trepidation wash it away once more. One hand sits at my waist, at the belt of daggers I foolishly brought with me, thinking I needed them when the god of death walked at my side.

"The curse wasn't just that you and I would be bound together," he continues. His jaw twitches and he twirls one of my red curls around his finger. "It was that to save you, I would have to do the unthinkable."

"Laugh at a joke?" I ask, uneasy again at the way he's staring at me. Watching me.

"That too, though that isn't part of the curse."

"So glad to have been a great influence on you." I make myself smile through my jangling nerves. The black mist creeping over my thighs isn't helping.

But this is the Sword.

I know him. I trust him.

I exhale my fear.

"The curse is that I would love you, Kyrie Silver Tongue. That the chalice would bring me the one mortal I should hate the most, one sworn to my greatest enemy, Sola, and that I would love her anyway."

"You love me?" My voice sounds higher than before, and emotion tightens my chest.

"I love you," he tells me fiercely, "more than all the stars in the night sky. More than the ocean with its bottomless depths could understand."

Intense.

"Lucky me," I say, falling back on old habits and winking

up at him, unable to keep from touching that silver-white hair, the dark stubble on his jaw.

"I love you, Kyrie, though I tried as hard as I could to resist it. To resist you, to resist this moment, to resist Sola's curse on us both."

"Why is it a curse?" I ask softly. He closes his eyes as I stroke his cheek. "Why is our love a curse?"

He pushes his forehead against mine tenderly—then kisses me, so hard it takes my breath away.

His hand leaves my hip, leaves the dagger belt at my side feeling lighter.

Too light.

Confused, I cock my head, then look down.

"Because the only way to save you, Kyrie, the only way to bind you to me forever as the god of death is to do this." He chokes on the words and still I stare at him, confused and trusting and foolish.

He drives my blade into my chest and I gasp at the wicked pain of it.

"Every god has two faces," he intones. "You prayed for time. You have received death."

I cough and droplets of blood spray across his beautiful, godly features.

The Sword holds me upright.

In Death's arms I die.

"Only your love and trust—earned wholly—and mine freely given, could bring this curse to completion." A tear streaks down his blood-spattered cheek and I blink, trying to draw breath, shock numbing the pain.

I glance down, the dagger's hilt all that's visible where it's pierced my chest.

"Sola is cruel in her vengeance. She didn't like that I took it upon myself to try to bring justice to her sisters. Your sisters.

Cottleside was a coward's way from her grip. My way to avoid seeing this prophecy fulfilled."

His voice is a whisper, but I hear everything he says as clearly as ever, even as that black mist rises and rises, a tangible thing, wrapping around Sola's Crown on my finger, climbing up my arm.

"This curse was her revenge on me, and on one who would have the audacity to accept her gifts and still turn away from her to another god. To me."

"Hrakan," I try, copper filling my mouth, running warm down my front.

"Because the only way to save you, Kyrie, the only way to bind you to me forever as the god of death is to do this." He chokes on the words, and still I stare at him, confused and trusting and foolish. "The only way to break the curse, and her hold over both of us, is to do this, my Kyrie, and then to raise you as my bride." His eyes are cold. Dark. They promise exactly what he's given me.

I cough again, indescribable pain shooting through my chest.

He betrayed me. He betrayed me, the bastard, and I trusted him.

I loved him.

The thought hurts more than the bleeding wound in my chest.

The tip of the dagger scrapes the statue behind me as I slide down its front, the living likeness of it watching me die a slow, painful death before him.

Sign up for my newsletter to be the first to hear about book two of Kyrie and the Sword's story, OF GODS & GOLD!

ACKNOWLEDGMENTS

This book would have suffered greatly, as would have I, were it not for many people who put up with either me blabbering on about plot points, magic systems, and external politics, and/or who reacted appropriately when sent many, many out of context snippets.

Massive thanks to Lauren Cox, for being a fantastic cheerleader, early reader, and my PR Queen.

I couldn't have done this without Tee Harlowe and Ashley Reisinger's enthusiasm and encouragement. Y'all helped me think through every plot point and laughed at all the right jokes.

Thanks to Hattie Jacks, Grace Reilly, and Steph Archer, who put up with a ton of random snippets and kept me excited to write.

Thanks to my husband and sons, who inspire me to work harder every day.

Lastly, thanks also to my readers, my incredible ARC team, and everyone else who has championed this book. It felt so good to write something different and know you would go along for the ride with me.

Also by January Bell

FANTASY TITLES:

A CONQUEROR'S KINGDOM

Of Sword & Silver

FATED BY STARLIGHT

Following Fate: Prequel Novella
Claimed By The Lion: Book One
Stolen By The Scorpio: Book Two
Taurus Untamed: Book Three

SCIENCE FICTION TITLES:

ACCIDENTAL ALIEN BRIDES

Wed To The Alien Warlord
Wed To The Alien Prince
Wed To The Alien Brute
Wed To The Alien Gladiator
Wed To The Alien Beast
Wed To The Alien Assassin
Wed To The Alien Rogue

BOUND BY FIRE

Alien On Fire

ALIEN DATING GAMES

Alien Tides

NEON RENEGADES

Stranded With The Cyborg: Prequel Novella

Rescued By Her Enemy

Hard Drive

About the Author

January Bell writes steamy fantasy and sci-fi romance with a guaranteed happily ever after. Combining pure escapism, a little adventure, and a whole lotta love makes for romance that's a world apart. January spends her days writing, herding kids and ducks, and spends the nights staring at the stars.

For the latest updates, sign up for my newsletter by visiting www.januarybellromance.com, or follow me on Instagram and TikTok.